how far will you go
to keep a promise?

a novel

Promise
Me This

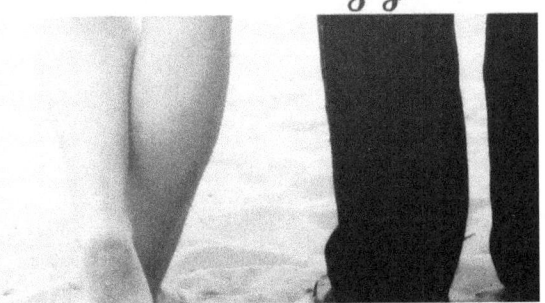

sarah ashley jones

Promise Me This

a novel

Sarah Ashley Jones

Table of Contents

Chapter	Page
One	1
Two	5
Three	18
Four	22
Five	31
Six	32
Seven	42
Eight	49
Nine	67
Ten	70
Eleven	78
Twelve	87
Thirteen	100
Fourteen	106
Fifteen	113
Sixteen	116
Seventeen	128
Eighteen	136
Nineteen	146
Twenty	154
Twenty-one	161
Twenty-two	164

Chapter	Page
Twenty-three	171
Twenty-four	179
Twenty-five	191
Twenty-six	98
Twenty-seven	212
Twenty-eight	222
Twenty-nine	233
Thirty	237
Thirty-one	241
Thirty-two	245
Thirty-three	247
Thirty-four	251
Thirty-five	254
Thirty-six	258
Playlist	266
Acknowledgements	269
About the Author	274

For my mom.

Without you, this book would still be a half-finished attempt at one of my crazy ideas. Thank you for believing in my dream and being by my side every step of the way.

ONE

Charlie

Deep breaths. Keep breathing. Keep moving. Deep breaths.

That was looped on repeat in my mind for two weeks. I was a walking zombie for two weeks, just going through the motions of real life and numb to the world. I hadn't even cried yet. I just kept moving forward. It was the only thing I knew how to do.

As I stepped out of the car that my parents arranged for me at the airport, my stomach began to twist into a knot. Anxiety flew around in my throat. I tried to remember my mantra: *Keep breathing. Keep moving. One foot in front of the other.*

"Uh, Miss? I think you're forgetting something." A deep voice snapped me out of my thoughts.

My eyebrows knit together in confusion as I turned around to see what the commotion was. The car I had just exited from was still parked and running behind me. The driver, a silver haired, middle-aged man who reeked of cigars and bad decisions, draped his arm over the passenger seat, as he looked me up and down. His fingers tapped on the headrest impatiently.

"I'm sorry. What?" He was still staring at me and as hard

as I tried, I couldn't place why. Did I suddenly grow a second head?

"Forty-two dollars. That's your total," he spat out, obviously in much more of a hurry than I was. Which was probably true, since I didn't really want to hurry up and face reality.

"Sorry. I'm not myself today." Or any day in the near future, I thought to myself, and handed him a fifty-dollar bill. "Keep the change." He mumbled something under his breath, but didn't care to keep the conversation going any further. I just shut the door, picked up my bags from the curb, and started to head up the stairs of the apartment in front of me. Those stairs shouldn't have felt foreign, but they did. I had walked them only a few months ago, but everything was different then.

"Race you, Charlie," he yelled, and made a mad dash towards the stairs.

"Not fair. You didn't help me with my bags and I don't even know my way around. I'm pretty much running blind here, Cameron!" I shouted after him, but I couldn't help but laugh. It was always this way. Nothing was ever serious when it came to the two of us.

"I am so sorry, my little damsel in distress. I just did not realize how frail and dainty you have become since I left!" he said, in what I could only assume was his best southern gentleman accent; but really, he sounded like a drunk southern belle. Within seconds he found me and scooped up my luggage - all five bags, since I wasn't sure what to expect - and made his way back up the steps.

I followed him up to his apartment and gave him a good once-over, noticing how much he changed since he left Tennessee. His blonde hair had grown out into shaggy golden locks that fell right above his eyebrows, and his skin was definitely kissed by the sun. I was envious, not because he looked different, but because it meant he escaped our small town.

"Welcome to your new home away from home. Well, at least 'til you either run back to Lame-ville, population fifty, or you finally move out here with me. And don't think I'm not counting down the days waiting for that to happen. But for now, mi casa es su casa."

I sighed and walked through the tiny front door to apartment 7B. I couldn't help but think about how that moment was so completely different from the one I was currently in. So many things changed in just a few short months. It was then, while throwing my bags down on the couch that it hit me - *he* hit me - or rather, it was everything that wasn't him anymore. I could still smell him, and that's all it took to open the floodgates. The tears came, and I saw no reason to stop them anymore. My back slammed against the closed door behind me as my knees betrayed me; giving in as my body folded in on itself with grief. My body shook with the sobs that refused to stop.

"Deep breaths. You can do this, Charlie. You can do this." Great. I was talking to myself. Might as well send me straight to the psych ward, I thought as I wiped my face with my jacket sleeve. Who was real lady-like now? Debutante school taught me *so* much.

Pushing myself up off the floor, I decided that it was as good a time as any to call home. I pulled my phone out of my pocket and called the house.

"Hey Sweetie! You made it to California okay? Was your

flight fine? Did they lose your bags?" My mom's thick southern drawl began to hound me with questions.

I simply shook my head. Cameron was gone, she sent me to do her dirty work, and she was worried about my bags being lost? "I'm fine, mom. Yes, I made it all right, and no - remember? I carried my bags on this time. I only had two when I left."

"Oh darling, you know me; always the forgetful one. How is the house?"

"Apartment. And it's the same as before, except there's no Cameron." My voice cracked. It shouldn't be doing that. "Mom, I can't believe he's really gone. It's like I can feel him here, but I know he's never coming home."

I should have known better than to try and confide in my mother. There was a long, deep sigh on the other end of the phone. I always questioned if she had any real emotions coursing through her body. You would think that with her being Miss Prim and Proper, she would know exactly what to say to me in a situation like this...in a situation like ours. This couldn't be good. "Baby, let me tell you something. Sometimes in life, you get thrown curve balls. Now, you just have to figure out if you're going to swing and strike out, or hit the ball way out into the stands for a home run."

"Mom, nothing good can come out of this. Why am I here? Why couldn't you just come and take care of it?" I was bitter, and the words came out like fire. But it was her response that burned me instead.

"Because no one knew your brother like you did, Charlotte."

TWO

Charlie

Bang. Bang. Bang.

I sat up straight, my head spinning from the sudden movement. I had fallen asleep on the couch, and was sharply reminded that the windows in the living room lacked any kind of curtains. As the light stung my eyes, I threw an arm up to shield my face; letting out an annoyed groan. I felt around blindly for my phone so I could check the time. From the glaring sun that streamed through the windows, I could tell that it must be morning, and a morning person I was *not*. Peeking out of one eye, I saw my phone lying on the floor beneath me. I leaned forward, trying my hardest to make my fingers grow just a few more inches.

Bang. Bang. Bang.

My heart jumped out of my chest and my body followed suit, rolling me off the couch with a loud thud. I shot an evil glare in the direction of the door. Seriously, who would be at the door this early in the morning and *not* use the doorbell? Finally reaching my phone, I flicked the screen to show the time. Ten o'clock in the morning. Not exactly the butt crack of dawn, but 'before noon' was a time I didn't see very often during the past few weeks.

I smoothed out the shirt I'd slept in with the hopes that it wouldn't be too noticeable and made my way to the door, rolling onto my tiptoes to peek through the peephole. A brown uniform and a big, goofy grin waited for me on the other side. Someone obviously already had their two cups of happy this morning.

Opening the door, I stood in the doorframe with a hand on my hip. "How can I help you on this fine, beautiful mornin'?" My voice dripped with sarcasm, which caused my accent to show up front and center. This only seemed to happen when my emotions ran wild.

The jolly brown giant smiled and shoved a clipboard into my hands. "Just sign right here and we'll bring them on up." The look on my face must have told him that I wasn't following his train of thought. "The boxes? We have an order for a fifty pack of moving boxes and supplies." My face remained blank. "Ma'am, are you Charlotte Jennings? It says here that this order was placed yesterday by a Rosalyn Jennings."

I saw red. My mom attempted to come to the rescue again. When did she even think to do this? Did she have no tact? Did she even think about how I would be handling this? Like I would really want to pack up Cameron's whole life the first day I got there.

"Ma'am? If you could just sign right –" I scribbled my name on the paper and tossed the clipboard back at him with a smile that normally would have been accompanied with some not-so-nice words.

"Just leave them in here." I pointed toward the living room and then turned back down the hall, not even looking at the man with boxes of what mom had thought was rescue. There really wasn't much to his apartment. There was a living room, a kitchen, a bathroom, and situated at the far end of the hall was his bedroom. I hadn't made it any further than the bathroom last night, and that was only because I had to go in there. The apartment didn't have many decorations, either. Only a few posters and picture frames. That was the way he liked it - after all, it was his bachelor pad. He tried to explain that to me the one time I insisted on buying curtains for the place. I guess when you come from a home where every nook and cranny was decorated with some kind of gaudy, expensive knick-knack, you tended to not win any awards for interior design once you moved out.

"Miss Jennings? We're all done now." He yelled through the apartment again. He was still here? Why didn't he just let himself out? I shook my head when I heard Cameron's voice in my head. "Charlie, you're not in Kansas anymore." As I walked to shut the door behind the moving men, something on the fridge caught my eye that I didn't noticed on my visit a few months ago. There were two pictures, side by side, held in place by none other than a Johnny Cash magnet; a token from home. Instantly I was drawn to the pictures. The door could wait. The boxes could wait. The pictures could not.

I grabbed the smaller of the pictures first and brought it right up next to my face, recognizing it almost instantly. There were two little kids, no older than five, sitting on big, white front porch steps and eating popsicles. You could almost feel the heat of the humid Tennessee summer by the way the popsicles were all over them and not in their mouths, which showed matching semi-toothless grins. They were almost identical. In fact, if you weren't paying attention to their clothes, you would have thought you were looking at two little boys. But what stood out the most were their piercing blue eyes. You couldn't see the little girl's well, because she was looking up at the slightly bigger boy, but you could feel the adoration in the sea of those sapphire eyes.

"Thank God mom had some fashion sense back then and actually put me in those ridiculous dresses, or else people would have thought I was a boy." Note to self: Stop talking to yourself. I slipped the picture back under the magnet and let my thoughts linger as I stood there smiling at the second photo on the fridge. It was us again, from the time when visited before school started back up from winter break. A stranger had snapped it of us as soon as Cam had taught me how to ride my first wave down at the beach. Surfing was something he always dreamed of learning to do, and he assured me that I would be a natural just like him. It wasn't shown in the picture, but the successful wave only came after attempting to catch it for three hours straight.

But our faces didn't tell that story. My long blonde hair curled slightly at the ends from the salt water, my freckles stuck out in the watercolor of red on my cheeks from the sun, and my wetsuit didn't fit in all the right places...but Cameron looked like a movie star, as he always did. He seemed like he belonged in San Diego, holding up his hand in victory while I held onto my board like it was an Oscar, giving him the same goofy grin I had all those years ago. He always pushed me to try something new, even when I didn't want to, because he believed I could do it.

The hole in my heart where Cameron fit shot me a painful

reminder to snap back into reality. I looked over the rest of the items on the fridge, most of them random and meaningless. A few concert tickets were stuck up in a fan arrangement. Social Distortion, Dropkick Murphys, Mumford and Sons, and some other bands I never knew he liked. Without thinking, I ripped them off the fridge, threw them into the drawer next to it and slammed it shut. I didn't like feeling as if maybe I hadn't really known my own brother as well as I thought. I stomped out of the kitchen; pitching a fit like a little kid.

My foot caught on something as I made my way into the hall. Before I could process what happened, I fell backwards and was flat on my back, staring up at the obnoxious white popcorn ceiling. "Really? Is this your idea of a joke?" I shouted into the silence of the apartment. No one could hear me, but I thought, maybe *he* could. He used to be able to practically read my thoughts, anyway.

I rolled over from my back and onto my knees. I was about to get up when a white paper napkin caught my eye. Or rather, it used to be white, before it was dragged through a dirty movie theater floor from the looks of it. Or maybe that was from the trip it had taken across the kitchen when I slipped on it? I started to toss it into the trashcan, but noticed that there was a note written across the back in gorgeous cursive handwriting.

Had a great time tonight. Sorry I had to leave this note...girlfriend emergency. Catch you next Riot Night. Love, the girl you'll dream about. Ginger

I flipped the napkin over in my hands. The Pointe, San Diego was stamped on the back. This was a classy napkin. 'The Pointe' didn't sound like a place that would host a Riot Night, and whoever this Ginger person was, she obviously wasn't *that* important since her name didn't ring a bell.

"I hope you showed her a good time, Cam," I told the note as I stuck it back onto the fridge. I couldn't throw it out now that I knew that he actually kept something from a girl. He never found anyone he considered to be a keeper to take home to mom and dad. He always said that none of the girls could 'tame the beast'. He wasn't the hopeless romantic type, but I was, so maybe this girl was special. He did keep a crusty napkin, so who was I to judge?

An unexpected shiver ran down my spine as a gust of wind crept through the house, and I remembered that the door was still wide open. I quickly closed the tiny gap between the door and I in a few steps and kicked it shut, the rumble from the slam causing the neat stack of boxes to sprawl across the floor. "I seriously can't catch a break, can I?" I shouted into the air again.

Picking up the tape Mr. Happy Moving Man brought me, I grabbed the first box to assemble it. Maybe mom was right. The faster I packed everything up, the faster I could go back home and return to normal.

Normal was not *here* for me. 'Normal' was going to school at Vanderbilt University. I was a junior, in the honors society, and planned to get my Bachelors in Fine Arts. Running away, or as Cameron liked to call it, 'exploring your options,' just wasn't in the cards for me. Cameron always tried to convince me to move to California with him. He talked about it since middle school when we flew to San Diego to watch Dad speak at one of his motivational speaking conventions. I never thought he was motivational. He was just a good bullshitter. But people simply ate his words up and no one ever knew the difference.

"You're really going to move away? Wasn't that just all talk from when we were little? I wanted to grow up and be on Sesame Street, but Cam, sometimes we just have to suck it up and deal with it. Life's not fair, and we can't always get what we want." I tried to put on my most persuasive front, but I knew that he could see through it. He picked up another rock and tossed it into the pond with a splash, not even acknowledging my words. "You're ignoring me. Don't shut me out, too."

Cameron turned to face me, crossing his feet underneath him on the dock. "Charlie, I know you still have dreams. You've always been a dreamer. But instead, you like to play it safe. It's one of your only downfalls." I chewed my lip, trying to think of a response, but none came. He was right and he knew it.

It wasn't quite summer yet, but it was warm enough for us to start spending our nights at the pond down the hill from our house. In a few weeks we would occupy the long, hot days and the even longer, humid nights around that place. It was a tradition for our friends for as long as I could remember.

"What about college? You know mom and dad said they wouldn't pay unless you go to school here. You can't afford out-of-state tuition on your own. They've got your trust fund on lockdown and-"

"They have us on lockdown, Charlie! Why do you think they don't want us to spread our wings? To explore the world? They've had the reins on us pulled tight since we were able to walk. It's always been their way, and I'm sick of it. I'm sick of pretending to be someone I'm not. I'm not the money, the parties, the suit and tie, nor do I have the prestigious stick up my ass like everyone else around here!" He waved his hands in the air, clearly showing me the stick and where it was shoved, in case I missed that one.

"Hey. I don't care about those things, either. And I don't have a stick up my ass. I'd rather just do it their way than fail on my own. I need to go to college, Cam. Four years is all I have to endure, and then I'll join you wherever those crazy wings of yours take you. Just stay and do that with me. Please?" My eyes pleaded with him, but his blue eyes reflected just as much pain as mine. I knew that he couldn't stay here. He was right; he wasn't that life.

"I can't, Charlie. Just think of it as exploring your options. You know that mom and dad will accept you back with open arms if you want to come back…you've always been the favorite. But once I leave, I'm never coming back. This isn't your life either, little sis." He looked up at the moon, one foot splashing in the water below us. I was envious, something I felt about Cameron often. He always seemed to have a plan worked out to get him out of that life, and he never let on that he was scared he might fail. I for one never doubted him, but I wondered if maybe this life was for me. If it wasn't, then I should have no problems disappearing just like him. Or would I?

It obviously wasn't the movers' first rodeo. They left packing paper, as well as a giant marker. Maybe I looked as lost as I felt, or maybe this was just their protocol. I never moved anything myself before, so it was a 50/50 chance as far as I was concerned. I inventoried the living room and the kitchen. I saw nothing major to pack, and the furniture I could sell. Or maybe not. Who was I kidding? I couldn't sell any of his things. Donating it seemed like the less heartbreaking option.

The most logical choice was to start in the bedroom. I said a silent prayer that I wouldn't find anything too disgusting as I pushed the door to his room open. He was my brother, after all, and I'd rather not dig through his sock drawer. Knowing him, it would probably be like opening Pandora's Box. I decided to start with his sheets - they had to go. His bed set ripped off easily, and I squished them into one of the newly erected boxes. If mom wanted his stuff, she was getting everything whether she liked it or not.

Next stop was his closet. I grabbed the bottom half of as many shirts as I could hold in my arms and yanked them towards me. Anxiety rose in my chest and I knew that I needed to get these things out of my sight. None of them would make him come back. I reached up to grab the next batch of clothes, but the sight of his black leather jacket stopped me mid-reach. I took it in without touching it, until I couldn't stand it anymore. I gingerly took it off of the hanger and wrapped it in my arms. The leather was cold and unwelcoming as it rested on my cheek, but it was his.

I ran my hands down the smooth black surface. I couldn't help but think how much better he looked in this than in the suit and tie they put him in for the funeral. 'Monkey suit' is what he would have called it. Dad always hated that jacket, and that fueled Cameron's fire to wear it to school every day his senior year. It became his second skin. He even wore it when he brought me to the airport to go home. It was the last thing I saw him in.

Shaking the memories away, I shoved it into the box with the rest of his clothes. *Just pack it all, Charlie. Just pack it all.*

5-1-5-0 by Dierks Bentley blared from my pocket, piercing the silence. A picture of my best friend smashed up against a window popped up on my phone as I pulled it into view. Her dark brown hair was long, straight and always in her face, but it never took away from her big brown eyes, or the smile that she wore permanently on her lips. She was the craziest person I knew - my complete opposite - and my soul friend.

"Hey Hannah," I answered. I decided to give up on packing anything else for the rest of the day, and sat down on the now bare bed.

"What's up girl? You don't sound as dead to the world as I thought you would. You've only been gone a day and you already found yourself a hot surfer boy, didn't you?" She was her typical blunt and high energy self. "Ah ha! Silence. Guilty as charged. Tell me everything about him. When is the wedding?"

"Good Lord, Hannah! Calm your britches. I haven't even left the house yet, and the only people of the opposite sex I've come in contact with was the moving box delivery man, and the cab driver that took me to the apartment from the airport. And believe me, neither one of them qualify as hot *or* surfer guy material." I laughed for the first time that I could remember since Cameron died. Hannah was good at making me do that, and I missed her. The last time we saw each other was before Cameron's accident. She couldn't make it to the funeral because she was stuck in New York, cramming for finals.

"Hold the phone and back it up. Moving box delivery man? What happened there? Didn't you just get there yesterday? Wait. Let me guess. Mrs. Rosalyn Jennings, at your service." She did the perfect impression of my mother's southern drawl. She knew me better than I knew myself; I always considered her the sister I never had. Ever since the day in Kindergarten when I spilled milk all over my lap and she stood up to the mean girls who teased me, we were inseparable. "I can't believe she did that to you. I guess she wants you out of there quick. She's scared that all of that California mojo will rub off on you and you'll be stuck there in a downward spiral of surfing, weed, and tattoos. Oh my! By the way, did you find any of the above in Cam's apartment? I know he had to be hiding some of the good stuff."

I should have been taken aback and hurt by Hannah's comments, but I knew that she wasn't trying to be insensitive. She was known for harboring a school girl crush on Cameron since the time they kissed during a game of spin the bottle during one of those summer parties down by the pond. I figured that was probably one of the reasons, besides finals, that she wasn't able to pull herself together and make it to the funeral. If she came, it would have made it too real for her, and she was never one to face reality head on.

"Nothing that would interest the likes of you, Miss Delinquent. I did find something interesting, though. There was a note from some girl stuck up on his fridge. It was a napkin from a place called 'The Pointe', saying she couldn't wait to see him at the next Riot Night. And she signed it, 'The girl you'll dream about.'"

"Weird. So maybe he didn't bat for the opposite team after all?" I scoffed at her remark, knowing it was made out of sheer bitterness. There was never any question about Cameron's sexuality, and she knew that firsthand. "So what's a Riot Night? Did he take you there when you visited?" Sherlock Holmes suddenly went into overdrive mode again.

"No, we didn't go to any bars or clubs. Only twenty, remember? I don't just stumble upon fake ID's like someone else I know," I countered.

"Oh, I stumbled upon plenty for the both of us. You just didn't have the balls to use 'em like me. Sucker!" Her enthusiasm was sickening, but she was right again. The thought of getting caught with a fake ID made me want to hurl. "Apparently, 'Riot Night' at The Pointe happens every other Thursday. It's some type of music night at the bar where everyone dresses like they stepped out of *The Outsiders*." Hannah sounded so excited that I was scared she might actually fly out on a plane and come to this thing.

"And how did you figure all this out?" I asked her, wondering if I even wanted to know the answer.

"Google, duh. Don't you do anything useful with that iPhone of yours? And guess what? It's an eighteen and up night, *and* the next one is this week. You're *so* going. I need you to find out who Miss-Dream-About-Me is." Oh yeah. She was jealous, even though it didn't really matter. No one had the chance to fight over Cameron anymore.

"Ginger. Her name is Ginger. And I'm not going. That's my final answer, Hannah." I should have hung up on her right then.

"Oh no, ma'am. Must I remind you of your New Year's Resolution? 'Try something new or spontaneous every month.' Check and check. You're going. At least find *Ginger* and let her know about Cameron." Hannah surprised me. She was actually being sincere.

Damn her and her sneaky reverse psychology. "Maybe I'll go," I thought out loud.

"That's my girl. You've got three days, Charlie. I expect a full report when you get home from this Riot Night. Maybe this is like Cameron's way of saying goodbye. He knew you never did like the unexpected." She didn't give me a chance to think about her last comment, and certainly no time to respond to it. "I love you, girl. Be brave."

I heard a click on the other end and she was gone. Sighing, I threw myself back onto the naked bed, watching the fan spin in circles on the ceiling. What did I just get myself into? I picked up my phone again and sent a text to my mother. I knew she wouldn't be able to figure out how to respond back, so it eliminated having to hear any immediate arguments from her.

Staying a few extra days. There's something I have to take care of. Love you.

I tossed the phone away from me onto the bed. I knew to expect at least a dozen return phone calls from her, but I didn't want to hear it. I just wanted to pretend that everything was normal.

THREE

Charlie

I spent the next few days tying up loose ends. I didn't have much left to do. I finished packing up the rest of Cameron's personal items, with all but thirty-five or so boxes to spare. Apparently, Cameron never inherited the hoarding gene from the Jennings legacy. The only things still left in the apartment were the couch, TV, some random kitchen items, and his bed. I was still sleeping on the couch; it didn't feel right to sleep in his bed.

A text from Hannah lit up my phone.

Don't forget. Riot Night is today. Wear a dress. I sent the directions. No excuses.

Her text actually made me laugh out loud. No excuses, huh? And a dress? Yeah, right! Jeans and a hoodie was more like it.

I sent her a text back.

No dress. I'm not going to a fancy party.

The directions didn't look hard to follow, but The Pointe was a good thirty-minute walk away. I'd have to take a taxi.

It's a party year round there. Not an excuse. Get the damn dress on.

"She's lucky I even packed a dress," I mumbled out loud,

as I finished the rest of my lunch and tossed the leftovers out. I had about four hours to get ready and be on my way. I couldn't believe I was actually going to go there. *This one's for you, Cameron.*

After degreasing myself in the shower and putting the finishing touches on my hair and makeup, I pulled the one and only dress I thought to pack out of my suitcase and held it up to my body. Looking down confirmed my suspicions. The dress looked miserable. There was no way it was going to work. What used to be a sassy red and white striped dress was now a hot wrinkly mess of cotton. Tossing it onto the floor, I went back to my suitcase and dug around until I found what I was looking for: my dark jeans, a yellow tank top, and a grey cardigan. It was just going to have to work.

I slipped on my new outfit, sans wrinkles, and looked in the mirror. That was the first time I got a chance to really looked at myself since the night we were told about Cameron's accident. I felt like I aged about ten years since then. I left my blonde hair loose and parted down the middle; its natural curl at the end hung just to my elbows. I didn't feel the need for much make-up, only a little blush and some chapstick. Fortunately, my eyelashes had a mind of their own and never required curling or mascara, and putting on any amount of eye shadow resulted in my already blue eyes to look even more intense than normal. My thoughts wandered to Cameron getting ready in the same mirror every day, and a smile crept into my lips. I could almost hear his voice echoing through my head. *'Atta girl. There's your beautiful smile.'*

Obnoxious honking snapped me out of the staring contest I was having with myself in the mirror. The taxi was actually late, making me wonder if maybe the honking was just a normal thing for them. Snatching up my purse and phone, I headed down the stairs and to the parking lot where the car idled nosily. I jumped in the front seat with as much enthusiasm as I could muster. The driver was caught off-guard and his gaze fell over my body, creating an unwelcoming smile on his lips. He gave me the willies.

"Um, to The Pointe, please?" I pulled out my phone, leaning in towards him reluctantly to show him the map.

"I don't need a map - everyone around here knows where The Pointe is. You don't look like *you* know where you're going, though. You're not from around here, are you?" He didn't wait for my answer as he took off down the street. If that was his sad attempt at small talk, the next fifteen minutes were going to be the longest of my life.

"I actually just, uh, moved here," I lied. I hated to do it, but it sounded so much better than, "I'm packing up my dead brother's apartment."

"Well, I can't imagine who recommended this place, then. Just make sure you keep your wits about you tonight. It's a whole different world in there." His comment shocked me as I scanned his face for help. He made it sound like I was being sentenced to life in prison. Surely, this place with its stamped condensation catchers would not be as bad as he made it seem.

Slowing down, he pulled up next to a tall building, complete with a multicolored lighthouse that looked like it had sprouted out of the top of the place. "Keep the change." I shoved a wad of cash into his hand.

Once out of the taxi I hastily assessed my surroundings. No one stood outside, but I could hear music that I recognized coming from the inside. *Folsom Prison Blues* by Johnny Cash. How appropriate.

I found my way to the entrance and pushed through the double doors, only to assume I should follow the stairs, since no one waited to greet me or check my ID. The bass of the music hummed through my body, growing more intense as I made my way up the musty stairwell; the music becoming louder with each step. When I rounded the corner at the top and stepped out onto the floor of The Pointe, nothing could have prepared me for what I saw. It wasn't just music - it was a live band - and this was no prison. This was the 1950's reincarnated.

FOUR

Charlie

Clearly I was in the wrong place. 'The Pointe' sounded
like it should have been dimly lit with lots of couches and
lounges where people in business suits drank away their
problems after five o'clock. I didn't know when it happened,
but it was as if I stepped into the scene from *Grease* when
everyone dances the Hand Jive at prom. There were just a few
tables in the back, a bar that looked like there was never a cold
seat, and the rest of the space was occupied by the giant stage,
which held a very unique looking band with a sea of couples
spinning their partners around.

I stood there for what seemed like hours as I watched a
new world unfold around me. A man jogged past me and
headed down the stairs, making me painfully aware that I
probably stood out like a sore thumb. I silently cursed Hannah
for being right. I should've worn the damn dress. I was the
only girl there wearing jeans, which from the looks of things, I
assumed was only acceptable for the guys. Most of them wore
their jeans with cuffs at the bottoms, and a t-shirt or some sort
of slacks with a button down shirt. The girls, on the other
hand, all looked like they enjoyed being thrown around by
their male counterpart as their dresses swirled up around

them. Watching the dancing couples was captivating, but it was the band on stage that I could not stop staring at.

Only four people stood on stage. There was a drummer, a man singing, someone playing what looked like a giant violin without a bow, and the guitarist. My eyes wandered over each guy, finally settling on the one to the far left. His eyes were closed while he made the guitar purr with a passion that seeped through his fingers to the strings. Watching him play was like being put in a trance. His black t-shirt sat just right over the upper half of his body, while his jeans matched the rest of the guys around him. His almost jet black hair was slicked back on the sides, with an Elvis-esque pompadour in the front. It was his arms, however, that drew me in. They were laced with tattoos that ran all the way from under his sleeves to his wrists. I was fascinated by them, so much in fact, that I didn't realize his eyes were glued to me as well. I was frozen, my instincts told me to run away, but my body didn't care to listen.

Finally tearing away from the eyes of the guitarist, I somehow managed to make it to the bar; my gaze never left the ground. I slid in front of the plastic-coated red barstool and leaned over the long wooden bar top, desperately searching for someone who seemed to live in my century. I caught the attention of the bartender as he slid down the inside of the bar to me. "What can I get you, pretty lady? You look like a rum and Coke kind of girl." He waited for my order with his palms resting on top of the bar.

"Oh, I'm not twenty-one so just a water will be fine." I evaluated him in my head as he turned to fill up my glass. He looked pretty normal to me. He wore slacks with suspenders that rested on top of a white button-down shirt, complete with a red bowtie just under his chin. He pushed the glass towards me, his eyes never leaving mine, making me shift in my seat uncomfortably.

"You're not stamped. Didn't someone check your ID at the door?" He tried to break up the uneasiness as he pointed to my hands.

"There was no one at the door when I walked in, so I just followed the music up here," I replied, looking down; trying to do anything to make him stop staring.

"Sorry, we're short-staffed lately. Here, let me check your ID." I nodded, and then reached into my purse and pulled out my wallet, ready to present him with my ID. He took it in his hands and flipped it over as he studied it for just another second too long. He was seriously starting to creep me out. Eventually, he set it on the counter and pushed it over the grainy wooden bar top towards me. "So, Charlotte Jennings...Tennessee, huh? That's a long ways from here. What brings you out to lovely San Diego? Hands, please." He made a gesture with his own that indicated I should give him mine. When I did, he stamped a drunken elephant onto each one. Coincidental since, being underage, I couldn't drink.

"My, uh, brother comes here a lot. And you can call me Charlie, everyone else does. I just wanted to check and make sure he wasn't hanging out at a crack house or something like that." I stumbled over my words, frantic that my awful poker face gave away my secret. "So what's *your* name, since now you know mine?" I tried my best to steer the conversation in a different direction, turning on my southern charm.

"It's Danny, Charlie from Tennessee. You know, we don't get many people from out of town come through here, especially with the last name Jennings. Can I ask you another question? You're not Cameron's sister, are you?"

My heart stopped. Danny felt like he was fifty feet away as my vision clouded and sheer panic took over. The color drained from my face; his shocked expression told me I had just confirmed his suspicions. My mind swam. This was such a stupid idea. Why was I there? Why couldn't I just listened to my mom and got the hell out of town as fast as I could? That was what I got for trying to do things that I thought sounded like a good idea. I looked around, formulating my escape route.

"Look, I'm sorry. I shouldn't have just come out and asked you that. You guys just look so much alike, and it really threw me for a loop, since well, you know, that accident happened and all." There was sorrow in his voice as he tried to calm me down. It distracted me long enough to realize that I was already out of my seat. He knew about the accident. How did he know? Who *was* this guy? "Um, are you okay? You don't look so good." His voice sounded like we were underwater. I tried to control the spinning feeling that was slowly overpowering my head.

Anger snapped me back into the moment and I let it take over my body. I had enough of being asked if I was okay. It was a question that I recently grew to hate. "Am I okay? You're *really* asking me if I'm okay? I guess it's pretty obvious that Cameron was my brother, and it's obvious that you know what happened to him, so do you really think I'm sitting here for my own health? I just wanted to feel close to him for one last time. I found this freaking place on a napkin that he left on his fridge, and somehow I got it into my mind that this would be a good idea. But boy, was I wrong coming to this

1950's flashback nightmare." My chest heaved up and down as I choked back the tears that threatened to spill onto my cheeks if I stayed a second longer. I turned my back on Danny and the bar. There was only one way out, and I was already headed that way.

"Charlie, I didn't mean it like that. It's just that-" Mr. Oh-So-Concerned shouted at me as I barreled for the stairs. I knew that I made a scene, and immediately regretted blowing up like that.

I flew down the steps at a frantic rate, only looking down to keep my feet in check in case I tripped. As I reached the bottom of the spiral staircase, I walked toward the double doors I entered only a little while earlier, flinging them both open. I took a few steps before my shoe caught on a split in the concrete and I knew I was going down - and fast. My hands thrust out in front of me to try and break my fall, but there was no helping myself at that point. I landed flat on my face, splattered across the sidewalk like a bug in shock.

I lay there for a while, wishing I could wake up from the nightmare I was living. There was no way this was real life. I squeezed my eyes shut hard and began to pray with everything I had to make myself wake up, when footsteps caught my attention. I barely opened my eyes, terrified to see the person who just witnessed one of the most embarrassing moments of my life. All that was visible were a pair of shiny black shoes, as they stood right in front of my face.

"Did you have a nice trip?" a voice from above me asked. I couldn't convince my body to move, but at least he didn't he ask me if I was okay. "Here, give me your hand and I'll help you up."

"I don't need your help. I'm fine!" I placed my hands on both sides of my body, pushing myself from the concrete up to my feet, only to end up inches away from a solid black shirt. My eyes focused in on the vibrant tattoos that decorated the arms of the guitar player from the bar. I sucked in a sharp breath as I wavered, my balance betraying me. He reached out and caught my elbow in an attempt to steady me on my feet. The sudden contact with him made my eyes dart up to his. I took him in, feeling the adrenaline rush through my veins as I breathed in what smelled like the outdoors on his skin. He stood a good bit taller than me, but at the moment his face was bent down close to mine, and it was hard to tell just how tall he really was. I was lost in his rustic brown eyes that stared straight into my soul. It was too intense; I had to look away.

"Look - I told you I'm fine." I finally broke the silence and backed away from him cautiously. I made a sweeping motion over my head and down my body to my toes, indicating that I was still in one piece. "See, not even a scratch." His forehead creased in confusion, as if he couldn't believe I was still standing there. In fact, I couldn't believe I was still standing there. "I have to go." Turning on my heels, I took off in the direction that I thought was the direction back to Cam's apartment. A breeze whisked past me, sending a chill down my spine. I hugged my gray cardigan closer to my body and picked up the pace.

I could feel him staring a hole in my back. After walking a few more steps forward, the feeling of being watched overwhelmed me. "WHAT?" I whirled around to face him, ready to strike. Seriously, what was this guy's problem?

He leaned up against the brick wall that led into a small

alley; I hoped he wouldn't pull me down it and disappear with me forever. With one leg crossed in front of the other, he tilted his head and gave me a quirky smile that lit up his whole face. "Oh, by all means, keep going," he teased.

"Fine, I will." I didn't have to put up with that from a guy I didn't even know. Why did Cameron ever hang out with these people? None of them had any manners.

Slow footsteps interrupted my internal rant. "But if you're going to walk the wrong way, at least let me follow you in case the Goblin King decides to come out and take you back to his Labyrinth." He chuckled, obviously amused with his not-so-witty sense of humor.

"I'm pretty sure I'm going the right way. I think I would know how to get back to my own house." I stepped forward again, refusing to give into his childish games.

"Your house? Don't you mean Cameron's? Or did you finally grow some balls of your own and move out here?"

My mouth fell open, his comment stopping me dead in my tracks. Where in the hell did this guy get off talking to me like that? I turned around a final time, marched right up to him, and pushed my finger into his chest as I spoke. "Look, you listen here…." I paused, realizing that I didn't even know his name.

"Jhett," was all he needed to say to put a name to the face that drove me ridiculously insane after knowing him for only ten minutes. He stood completely relaxed, staring at me with a pompous smile, his thumbs looped in the back pockets of his jeans.

"Alright, *Jhett*. You don't know anything about me. I've never met you before in my life, and I highly doubt that

Cameron would ever be caught dead around the likes of *you*."
I fingered the cell phone in my purse, just in case I had to
make a quick 911 call. Playing with fire like that wasn't always
a safe thing to do, but my temper rose faster than I could
control it.

"Well little do you know, Charlotte Jennings, that I *do*
know you, although we've never had the pleasure of being
introduced. I actually know a lot about you. But most
importantly, I know you're going the wrong way home. I
figured that your crazy twin senses would've kicked in by
now." He stood there, watching me with his curious brown
eyes, making my heart flutter in my chest again. Sucking
down a few cold, dewy breaths of air, I silently convinced my
heart to stop betraying me.

"How did you….?"

He cut me off before I could even finish. "Know that you
were twins? You didn't think Cameron went all this time
down here without a best friend, did you? Well he didn't, and
you're looking at him. Now come on, let me take you home.
You can't walk around here all by yourself when you
obviously have no sense of direction. And besides, Cameron
would kick my ass from his grave if I let his sister walk
around the streets on her own."

His tone changed fairly quickly as his face softened,
making me want to reach out and touch him. He looked at me
with the same pain I felt since Cameron died. I knew that you
couldn't fake that kind of hurt. It wasn't *completely* unknown
to me that Cameron had friends down here, but I didn't get a
chance to meet them when I visited. He always said they were
busy. Why would he never mention his supposed best friend?

I realized I was at a fork in the road and I needed to make a decision. Go with the guy who I barely knew, who strangely knew me, or keep walking without any directions to follow. I figured there was nothing to lose at that point. "Fine. And it's Charlie – not Charlotte...Let's go," I brushed past him on the sidewalk, and headed back in the direction we came from.

It took a few minutes before Jhett and I fell in sync with each other's steps, quickly making it back to the entrance of The Pointe. "Wait here. I'm going to go get my bike." He motioned with his hands for me to stay put as he took off behind the building. My insides churned at the mere mention of a bike, and I started formulating another exit route. Jhett looked exactly like the type of guy who would wear a leather jacket and drive a motorcycle. He probably smoked cigarettes and spent all his money on his tattoos, too. There was no way he could possibly be my brother's best friend.

Jhett appeared from the darkness, walking his bike up to where I stood. Stopping in front of me, he let the kickstand out. He looked my way briefly, his expression so serious, it was practically daring me to laugh. But I couldn't help it - the giggles just kept coming.

FIVE

Jhett

I watched her as she stood in front of me, her tiny body shaking from her fit of laughter. She brought her hand up to cover her mouth, making me wonder if it was out of habit or self-consciousness. Either way, I knew that I wanted to find out more about her. I thought it was odd to feel like I already knew her, but I was a stranger, and that didn't sit well with me now that I finally got to meet her. Cameron was smart when he decided to keep me away from her.

"Were you expecting something else?" I asked.

Charlie lost it again, her giggles high pitched and soft, all at the same time. It was then that I knew I would do anything it took to keep hearing that sweet sound.

SIX

Charlie

I couldn't control the laughter that was erupting from my throat as I took in the scene that unfolded around me. Mr. Tattoos rode a baby blue beach cruiser? This had to be some kind of joke. "Yeah, something with a motor, perhaps? Where am I supposed to sit? On your shoulders?"

He paused and pursed his lips together as he thought up an answer, which made me instantly regret my last comment. "As much as I like the sound of that, I think we'll save that for another day. You, my dear, get to ride on the handlebars."

"You've got to be kidding me. You know we're actually living in the twenty-first century now, right? People drive cars. I'll just call a taxi again," I explained. I reached into my purse and grabbed my phone, attempting to pull up the number for the cab.

"No, I'm not joking. And what makes you think I don't have a car? This is just more fun to get around town with, and besides, it's eco-friendly. Aren't you girls into that *go green* stuff?" I had to give it to him; he really was giving it his best shot at trying to convince me to jump on the bike.

"Well, yeah, but I just figured a car would be easier…and honestly, I've never actually ridden a bike, and definitely never ridden on the handlebars. Wanna help a girl out?" I smirked, and decided to give in to his mind games. If he wanted to play cat and mouse, I could do that. It's not like we would ever have to see each other again. I walked around to the front end of the bicycle and began to inspect it. I looked at it from a few different angles, trying to figure out how I was going to manage hopping up on the handlebars.

"You're telling me that you never learned how to ride a bike? Ever? No summers spent riding around with your friends until the streetlights came on?" Jhett stood with his mouth hanging open so wide that I was scared a bird would set up shop in it. Clearly, riding a bike was a staple in childhood that I missed out on. I couldn't help but wonder what the big deal was.

"Did I stutter? No, I've never been on a bike. We had horses," I replied dryly.

"Horses...?" A laugh escaped under his breath as he shook his head in disbelief. "Well are you ready? Just plant yourself in front of Lucy here, and jump. I'll make sure that you land safely." I bit the inside of my cheek to stop my laughter from coming again. *He named his bike? This was going to be interesting.*

Jhett got into position behind me. Throwing one leg over the seat, he watched as it landed on the other side. I took a deep breath, embracing my new attitude the best I could, as I turned around again and squeezed my eyes shut. I counted to three in my head and jumped up, falling into place on the handlebars with only a little guidance from Jhett.

"Hold on, cowgirl! You're in for a wild ride," Jhett spoke in my ear. He pushed off, propelling us forward. My grip on the handlebars tightened as we picked up speed. "Relax...."

His voice crept into my ear again.

I attempted to take Jhett's advice and I focused on the buildings flashing past us. The sidewalk was dimly lit by the random streetlights; the natural glow of the moon illuminated the way instead. My feet dangled freely in front of me, and my hair whipped around my face as Jhett guided us in and around the few people who still meandered on the sleepy streets. I closed my eyes and enjoyed the way my mind cleared as I finally gave in and relaxed. Leaning back absentmindedly, I rested my shoulders against the warmth of his chest behind me.

"We're here, Charlie." Jhett's voice swam around in my head again. It was stoic and unemotional as it startled myself out of the dream-like state I found myself in just minutes before. I felt him pull away from me as he stopped the bike; my relaxation just a fleeting thought in the past. He waited for me to jump down before he got off, and then propped the bike up on the kickstand. As I looked around us, confusion set in. Jhett said that he knew how to get me back to the apartment, but this certainly wasn't it. This was the boardwalk on the beach.

"Hey Jhett - sorry to burst your bubble here, but the apartment isn't this close to the beach. It's still a few blocks down. I thought you said-"

"Shhhh," he cut me off, startling me. I glanced sideways at him, irritated with his sudden indifferent attitude, and tried to figure out what changed during the bike ride here. I watched him as he took his shoes off and placed them on the cement barrier just before the sand. Without looking back in my direction, he walked out towards the ocean like I didn't even exist.

My arms crossed over my body, feeling like I was exposed and alone, and impatiently waited for him to say something. Instead, he kept walking until the salty water lapped at his toes. I did not want to go out there. The last time I was at the beach was with Cameron, and even though those were happy memories, the fresh wounds of losing him still stung.

After waiting a few minutes, I came to the realization that Jhett wasn't going to come back anytime soon. I began to weigh my options. It was only a few minutes walk to the apartment, but walking alone at night probably wasn't the best idea, seeing as that was how I got myself into this mess in the first place. Staying with Jhett was now the safer option, which wasn't a good sign.

Giving in, I threw off my shoes and tossed them to the side, stepping out onto the beach; my bare feet not used to the grainy feel of the sand between my toes. I made sure to follow the fresh footprints Jhett left behind, leading me next to him as I stood ankle deep in the freezing water. The ocean seemed as if it went on forever, and the reflection of the moon lit up Jhett's face; giving him an ethereal look as he stood with his eyes closed facing the water. The sight caused another giggle to escape from my lips.

"Shhhh," he silenced me again. That was enough. His attitude was out of hand.

"Jhett, I really just want to go home now," I whined, not taking my eyes off him from where I stood at his side.

"You can't hear that?" His own eyes remained closed as his toes wiggled their way into the wet sand.

I looked around and tried to see down to each end of the

beach. "Hear what?" I couldn't understand what it was we were listening for. We were the only people out there.

"The music..." he stated with zero emotion.

"I can't hear a single thing except the ocean." The salt-stained wind whipped at my exposed skin, stinging with the cool air of the night.

"Exactly. I'm going to tell you something that someone once told me. The voice of the sea sings to the soul. I heard that when I first started coming down to the beach. I met someone who acted as if the salt water could wash away all your worries, and it wasn't until recently that I discovered that what he told me was true."

I couldn't bear to look at him. I knew who he was talking about right away; there was no mistaking it. Cameron was convinced that the beach was a way of life, not just someplace you visited on vacation. My heart couldn't decide if I should feel comforted or completely scared out of my mind.

"I know that you've got to have a lot of questions about me and how I knew Cameron, and I wish I could explain it all to you." I could feel his gaze move down in my direction. We were standing so close that our arms were almost touching. I pretended not to notice, and instead looked off into the distance; trying not to feel the gaping hole growing in my heart again. "How much stuff do you have left to do here? What else do you have to take care of? I mean that's why you're here, isn't it?"

The sudden shift in conversation made me uneasy. One minute he was shushing me and the next he was concerned about what I was doing? "I'm only here to take my brother's things back to my parents. I have to pick up my rental car in a few days."

"You know what he used to tell me? All his stories from when you guys were little. He seemed to always mention how he was the reckless one and you were the one who played it safe. I guess some things didn't change..." His words trailed off. I couldn't comprehend where the conversation came from, which left me at a loss for words. "What are you going to do when you go back home?" he asked.

"I have to go back to school in the fall." It was the truth - but I wasn't planning to tell him that I had no other plans for the summer.

"I have a proposition for you, Charlie."

I snapped my head up in his direction. I didn't have the slightest idea what was on his mind. "What's that, *Jhett?*"

His eyes met mine again, and the look he gave me made my heart stop beating. I expected them to be dancing, playing the same flirty games he started after I threw my fit earlier. Instead, his eyes were daring me to take a chance at life.

"Stay a little longer. If it's one thing Cameron didn't stop talking about, it was how he wished that you came out here with him. Do you know he actually had plans to keep you out here this summer and show you what you were missing? Well you still have the chance to find out. I can help," He pleaded with me. A stranger I didn't even know for two hours was fighting for me to stay in California. My mind swirled with so many thoughts; I couldn't even begin to sort them all out.

"Let me get this straight. You want me to move out here for the summer so you can act out Cameron's last wish? That's just crazy talk, Jhett! I've known you for what - sixty-seven minutes - and you just want me to board this crazy train? Did you think that using my dead twin brother was going to make me jump in the sack with you? Is that what this is? A ploy to get me to sleep with you? Because if that was your plan, Jhett, you are a total asshole." My pulsed raced beneath my skin.

"It's not like that. Cameron was like family. He had a great heart and he became like a brother to me. I'm not asking you to do this for me. I'm only trying to tell you what your brother wanted. He wanted you to figure out the person you really were, *away* from that town of yours - that's what he told me. We made some promises to each other that I didn't think I would ever get the chance to keep. Are you really going to make me break a promise to your brother?"

I gave him a hard look, staring directly into those deep eyes, and tried to search out an ounce of truth in his words. My heart knew my brother, and it sounded just like him. My mind told me to run...run from this stranger and this strange place. Don't stay a second longer. Go back home.

When I didn't respond, Jhett turned his back on me and began to walk back to our shoes on the boardwalk. "Guess Cameron was wrong when he said you were always secretly seeking an adventure. We can walk the rest of the way to the apartment." He never turned around to face me as he spoke into the wind.

Images of Cameron and I when we were little flew through my mind. We got lost in the woods when we were six, and I was terrified. He kept telling me that I should put my hat on backwards, because then it would turn into an explorer's hat and explorers always knew the way home. We picked apples when we were eight, and I tried to climb the highest tree but I was too scared. He lied and told our parents I did anyway, just so they would be proud of me. We were thirteen and I was too scared to jump off the cliff into the lake. He told me to trust him, that it was an *adventure*. And we jumped off together; Cam held my hand until we reached the surface of the water, because he was always the one to take care of me.

I thought about the question Jhett asked me. It felt like I was jumping off the same cliff, but instead of breaking through the water, I was drowning.

"Fine. I'll stay." My eyes lingered on the waves that kissed the sand for a few more moments, my mind trying to process what I agreed to. I wasn't ready to face Jhett just yet.

Eventually, the chilling wind sweeping off the water was more than I could take. Turning away from the ocean, I began the trip back to our shoes while the cold sand squished between my toes. The walk back was even harder than before, but I managed to somewhat-gracefully make it to the boardwalk where Jhett had already begun to slip his shoes back on. He made a point to avoid my eyes, which filled my thoughts with worry.

I became so absorbed in finding the shoes that I tossed without thinking that I didn't notice Jhett was walking away, back down the boardwalk. I slipped the last part of my shoe around my heel and sprinted after him; terrified he was going to leave me to walk home alone. "Hey. Earth to Jhett! Did you hear me? I said I'd stay." I caught up to him and waved my hands around in his face.

"Loud and clear," he answered sarcastically, glancing sideways to meet my gaze.

His eyes were dark and intense with hurt and anger; making me uncomfortable. I couldn't stand to see him like that. I decided that my feet were the safest place to look. I focused on each step forward instead of searching out the reasons behind Jhett's sad eyes. The fact that he went from hot to cold on the emotions meter so quickly made me really nervous.

"Are you just going to leave your bike back there?" I asked. It was my desperate attempt to ease the suffocating tension. "I mean, what if some bum comes in off the street and steals it? How are you going to save all the girls who run out of that bar, then? I'm not a betting gal, but I'd say that I'm not the first girl to make a quick exit."

"I'm sure the bike will be fine. I do have a car, remember. But don't flatter yourself, you hardly needed saving. Some good sense knocked into you, maybe, but definitely not saving." Softness came creeping back into his voice as he spoke, which only minimally calmed my nerves.

"You really know how to flatter a girl," I said coldly. I recognized the bright buildings around me; the two story apartments, which looked more like beach bungalows, lined the streets next to the beach. "Well, I guess you weren't lying when you said you knew how to make it back." I slowed down once we reached the bottom of the stairs to Cameron's apartment.

I mentally prepared myself for an awkward goodbye. This was always the part where things got weird fast in movies, and I wasn't the type to put up with any funny business. Spinning around on my heels, I turned to face Jhett. "So, um, this is me. Thanks for making sure I made it. Are you positive you don't need a ride back to your bike? Or to your place? I can call you a cab or something."

He chuckled and reached up to smooth the sides of his

hair back against his head, his hand lingering at the nape of his neck. "I think I can handle it. Have a good summer, Charlie." He gave me one last sullen smile before he began to walk back in the direction we had come from.

My mouth fell open in shock. "That's it? Have a good summer? Really? After all that talk about hopes and dreams? I honestly expected a little more than that." I called after him before my mind could even process what I said out loud. I had to remember to work on not spouting out everything that just popped into my head.

He stopped walking and glanced over his shoulder. I could see the smirk that was becoming all too familiar start to form on his lips. "Are you really going to question everything I do?" When I didn't answer, he rotated himself to face me again. "Yes - have a good summer. You won't be seeing me again. That is, unless you want to?"

His last statement came out as a question I was *not* ready to answer. "I guess we'll just have to wait and see. Goodnight, Jhett." I bit my lip, swaying a little as I spoke. I gave him no time to answer before I ran up the stairs. I slammed the door shut behind me and reality hit me hard. What the hell just happened?

SEVEN

Charlie

Trying to wrap my head around what exactly happened two nights ago was not an easy task. Each time I ran the night through my mind, the more come up. I knew what I needed to do. Fixing myself a cup of hot tea, I made my way out on the deck that overlooked the parking lot and busy streets. There was no furniture, so I settled for throwing a blanket down on the concrete slab. I relaxed against the stucco wall and stretched my legs out in front of me as I tried one last time to dissect the whole Jhett situation.

It was mid-afternoon by the time I hunkered down to call Hannah. I was done trying to figure this out on my own. I needed my best friend.

"WHAT IN GOD'S GREEN EARTH WERE YOU THINKING, CHARLIE?" Hannah's thick southern accent that matched mine screeched into my ear, as I finished explaining the details of The Pointe, Jhett, and his proposition for me.

"What was I SUPPOSED to do? Between your pep talk about trying new things and Jhett's speech about Cameron…I don't know. It was a moment of weakness." I tried to convince her that it all made sense, but it was me who really needed the convincing.

"That's your excuse, Charlie? A moment of weakness? Maybe if this weakness wasn't tall, dark and handsome and also happened to be covered in tattoos," she scoffed. Honestly, I expected her to be all over this idea. She was the free spirit, after all, and I was just trying to follow in her footsteps.

"It wasn't like that. Nothing even happened on the walk home. Don't you think if it *were* like that, he would have tried to pull *something*? He didn't even give me a hug. Not even a handshake." For some weird reason I felt compelled to defend Jhett's honor, even though I barely knew him.

"Yeah, yeah, yeah. I've heard it all before. I'm all for you doing this, Charlie, I really am. You know I think you deserve a good adventure, and if it gets you out of this hell hole we call home, even for a little bit, I can't tell you no. But how are you going to make this work?" she asked. She was genuinely concerned. I couldn't blame her.

"Before I flew out here, mom told me that Cameron paid his rent in chunks. That gives me a while to figure out how to come up with the rent after that. I can try to find a job, or I may even look at colleges while I'm here. I hear SDSU is really nice…" I trailed off into fantasy land when something on the sidewalk caught my eye. "Hey, Hannah. I have to go." I hit end, cutting her off mid-conversation, and deposited my phone into the pocket of my hoodie. Squinting to get a closer look, I stood up and bent over the deck railing.

Right there in front of me, rounding the corner of the stacked apartments that I could now call home, rolled a baby pink beach cruiser being pushed down the sidewalk by none other than Tattoos himself. My blood boiled with the realization of what a stupid idea it was to agree to his proposal.

I raced through the sliding glass door into the apartment and out the front door. I hurried down the steps, each one causing my blood pressure to rise even higher. It was a good thing I looked up when I reached the platform at the bottom of the steps. If I hadn't, I would've endured round two of falling on my face in front of Jhett.

My bare feet hit the sidewalk just as he made it to the front of my building. He paused when he saw me, and put the kickstand into place on the bike.

"What the hell is that?" I flung my hands in his direction, but I already knew the answer. The bike was mine. He got me a bike I couldn't even ride.

"Well, I know pink isn't exactly my color, but you don't have to be so rude about it." A smile crept up the side of his mouth. Clearly, he enjoyed my misery.

I wasn't in the mood for his snarky attitude. "Look, I know I agreed to stay, but I'm pretty sure you said that I wouldn't have to see you again if I didn't want to. So please, explain to me why you're here in front of my apartment with this ridiculous bike?" The words came out like fire on my tongue.

"Correction, you told me to 'wait and see'. Well, I waited, and now - as you can see - I'm here. How did you think you were going to manage getting around town without some mode of transportation? I'm just helping a friend out." He spoke to me as he carried the bike up the stairs with little effort. Leaning it against the railing, he waltzed right through the front door as if he lived there.

"Hey! Where are you going? That was not an invitation to stay, you know." Running up the stairs behind him, I went into panic mode over Jhett being in the apartment. It was one thing to walk next to him, but it was another thing entirely to be alone in the same room with him.

I reached the doorway and grabbed onto the frame with one hand as I swung inside the living room. Jhett's back was turned to me as he stood in front of the fridge. I walked slowly to him, my heart beating loudly in my chest, as he held one of the last pieces I owned of Cameron in his hands.

"You look like a little boy." He looked up at me, laughter lightly caressing his words.

"I do not. I'm wearing a dress. Not that it concerns *you* any," I said, snatching the picture out of his hand and placing it back up on the fridge where it belonged. My eyes found his when I turned around to face him. "I think you should go."

"I'm not going anywhere. I got you a gift, and you haven't even said thank you. That's no way to treat your new friend." He found his way to the couch, flopped down and laced his hands behind his head as he made himself at home.

A flush crept into my cheeks at the mention of us being friends. I began to make a numbered list with my hands. "Okay, first - we're not friends. I just met you. And second - thanks for the gift and all, but if you don't remember, I can't ride it."

"Okay first - I'm the only friend you've got in this town." He mocked me, right down to the hand motions. "And second - you'll learn, since you'll have the right motivation. Think of the bike as my 'welcome to the neighborhood' gift." As he finished his sentence, he stood up and made his way towards me, closing the gap across the room between us.

"Welcome to the neighborhood? What's *that* supposed to

mean?" I asked, matching his forward steps with backward ones of my own, until I ran out of room to move. My back collided with the living room wall. There was no place else for me to go as I tried to melt into the white walls; my last attempt to avoid getting any closer to the most irritating guy I'd ever met.

Jhett was now mere inches from me, saying nothing to answer my question. Instead, his eyes answered with a predatory stare that made my mind scream. Squeezing my eyes shut, I braced myself for whatever plans he had up his sleeve.

"Meet your new neighbor," he whispered next to my ear. My hand was enveloped in his and he shook it like we were meeting for the first time. My eyes popped open at his sudden, intimate body contact. Just as quickly as he came in close to me, he moved away and opened the door to leave.

I didn't move as my mind tried to comprehend what he just said to me. "You're joking, right?" I asked him, and peeled myself off of the wall to follow him out the door. He bounded down the stairs with ease and was halfway to the sidewalk before he turned to look back up at me.

"Guess you'll have to find out. You do have a phone, don't you? You're not Amish or anything like that, right?" His eyebrows wrinkled as if he was concerned that the latter part of his question might actually be true.

"Yes, I have a phone and no, I'm not Amish," I countered, crossing my arms and leaning over the railing at the top of the stairs.

"Think fast, then!" Jhett shouted, leaving me no time to figure out what he meant. My eyes focused on the sleek black phone that he sent catapulting through the air, headed straight for my face. There was no way I was coordinated enough to catch it, even if I tried. I cradled my hands in front of me and prayed for the best. Thankfully, the phone dropped right into my grasp. I stared at it with disbelief.

"Put your number in there and keep your phone handy around, let's say five o'clock? I've got plans for us. Now toss it back down," he said, holding out his hands the same as I did before.

I quickly punched in my number and hit 'save'. I didn't get a creepy vibe from him - bipolar maybe - but not creepy. I figured having him around couldn't hurt too much. Looking once more to make sure he was ready, I closed my eyes and flung my hand back behind my head, ready to launch Jhett's phone down the stairs. My silent countdown was interrupted by the sound of feet barreling up the stairs.

"On second thought, maybe I'll just take it from here." He hovered close to me, easily reaching my hand that was still in the ready-to-pitch position, and slipped his phone out from between my fingers.

Jhett's woodsy smell was picked up by the wind; the same smell I remembered from the other night. It piqued my curiosity as to how someone who lived so close to the beach could smell so much like the outdoors back home. It was strangely familiar and drew me in. "Good idea," I said, attempting to pop the tension bubble that had formed around us.

"Yeah, well, you look like you throw like a girl," he said, winking at me, and then he once again boyishly ran down the stairs. He made it to the front corner of my apartment building before he turned around again. "Don't forget: Five o'clock. And if I were you, I'd start practicing your biking skills ASAP, because you don't want to make me come and get you. That wouldn't end well for either of us."

He was out of sight before I could speak. Before heading back inside, I took one more look at the pink bike that stared at me. One way or another, he was going to be the death of me.

I spent the rest of the afternoon failing miserably at learning to ride my bike. There was just no easy way to keep my balance and pedal at the same time, and I had the scuffed knees and elbows to prove it. After humiliating myself in front of countless strangers, I gave up. I was just going to have to walk everywhere. Screw the bike.

Sitting down on the couch, I flung my legs up and over the armrest furthest from me. Taking a deep breath, I let my body relax into the welcoming softness of the couch. I had a few hours to kill before Jhett's mysterious text was supposed to come through. I closed my eyes, but my thoughts lingered on him. He was everything that I was told to stay away from. He was hot and cold with his emotions, he had tattoos, and an overwhelming feeling of uncertainty oozed from his pores. He refused to give me any straightforward answers about Cameron. I determined that would be my goal for the night: To get answers one way or another.

My mind flooded with memories of Cameron, and I felt myself slip into the blackness of sleep.

EIGHT

Charlie

My phone vibrated on the counter that separated the kitchen and living room, startling me awake. I sleepily dragged myself to my phone, frantically checking the time. Five o'clock on the dot, and there was already a text from Jhett.

Good evening, Charlie. Your first task is to get your ass on that bike and go out your apartment to the corner of the street. Go down to the next light and wait for further instructions.

I rolled my eyes and shoved my phone into the pocket of my denim shorts. What did he think this was? His very own episode of Charlie's Angels? I slipped into the bathroom and gave myself a good once-over, deciding to ditch the hoodie and switch my shirt. I opted for my favorite pastel tie dyed t-shirt, the same denim shorts with lace on the ends, and my white flats. I used my fingers to tame my wild blonde waves, quickly throwing together a French braid from one side to the other, and secured the ends in a messy side bun.

I took one last look at myself in the mirror before dashing out of the bathroom. I grabbed my purse, slung it over my shoulder and across my chest, then headed out the door. The pink bike caught my eye, and a guilty feeling crept into my chest. Jhett told me to ride it, but I just couldn't figure it out. I checked my phone again, looked at the directions, and decided I to push it there instead. I mean, *he* did it, so why couldn't *I*?

Following his directions, I walked down the sidewalk with my bike in tow. I was two blocks in from the beach, but people still meandered around with surfboards and swimsuits, something I would never get used to seeing. I crossed the street and came upon the light where I was instructed to wait. Without missing a beat, my phone buzzed. Seriously, how did he expect me to read a text and ride a bike at the same time? He didn't know that I decided to push it instead. He was reckless.

Once you get to the light, make a right. Find the house with the white fence.

I sighed, only slightly freaked out by the perfect timing of his texts. I turned the corner anyway, but couldn't keep going. Before me was an entire street of tiny houses, all with yards and white fences. I tired to give Jhett the benefit of the doubt, but irritation set in quick. This had to be a joke, and it wasn't funny.

Immediately I called Jhett. No answer. I was done playing his games. Maybe I was wrong about him. I turned my bike around and began to walk back to the corner to go home.

"I thought I told you to ride your bike? I don't remember saying to push it." Jhett's voice came from behind me. I whipped around to face him and sure enough, there he was, standing outside of the very first house with a white fence.

"Apparently it's not like riding a horse. I think I'll just stick to things with four legs or four wheels," I said crossly, my nerves still on edge.

"That's a shame." He smirked again as he opened the gate of the front yard behind him. "After you." He guided me past him with a sweep of his arm.

"You weren't kidding when you said you were my neighbor. You live what, like five minutes away? That's really not creepy at all." I walked past him and rolled my bike with me into the front yard. My eyes widened in awe.

Jhett's house looked as if it was out of the movies. It was definitely not someplace I imagined he would live. The front yard was simple, surrounded by the same white fence as everyone else on his street, with a few trees framing the yellow one story bungalow. There was a concrete walkway lined with beautiful tropical-looking flowers in riotous shades, all leading up to the front stops of a small porch. I noticed Jhett's blue bike sitting at the end of it. I carried mine up the steps and left it to stand next to his. When I got to the front door, painted a deep maroon, I paused, not sure if I should open it and walk in, or wait for Jhett, who still lingered at the gate.

"So just go in?" I asked, motioning to the door.

"Oh, yeah, sorry." He leapt forward down the walkway and met me at the door. He turned the handle and with one big push, the door flung wide open. He gently placed his hand on the middle of my back, ushering me forward and into what felt like Alice's rabbit hole.

The inside of his house was even more magnificent than the outside. The kitchen and living room were completely open to each other; in fact, the whole house seemed to flow right into one big room. The walls were full of color; some painted a bright blue and others painted teal, with wall-to-wall wood floors. There was an island in the center of the kitchen painted a bright orange with four bar stools lined around it, each a different funky color.

I blinked, hunting for something that looked like it belonged to Jhett. I just knew were in the wrong house. As if reading my mind, Jhett began to explain. "Is it that bad? An old hippie lady owned it before me, but I fell in love with it the second I saw it and knew that I had to buy it." He walked past the grey couches in the living room - about the only *normal* colored thing in the house - and over to the fridge.

"You own this place? Seriously, where do you hide your stuff? You've got to have some skulls or zombies or pin-up girls or *something* in here!" I said, as I followed him to the kitchen and perched myself on a pink barstool. Taking off my purse, I set it on the counter and leaned in on my elbows, watching him travel from the fridge to the stove and back again.

"I didn't take you as a girl to judge a book by its cover." He banged around in the cabinets as he spoke, pulling out pots and pans.

I thought about his comment while I watched him prep what was obviously going to be dinner. I enjoyed the fact that there were no awkward silences with him, no pauses as he figured out what to say next. I was envious of the ease in which he carried himself, because when I was around him my stomach did flip-flops.

He wore cuffed jeans like the ones I saw him in at The Pointe, and just a white tank top this time, giving me the opportunity to actually look at his tattoos. They started right at the spot a t-shirt would sit on his neck, and spread down his shoulders, across each arm, and down his back. There were still a few spots that lacked the colorful ink, but each one of them was beautiful. I wanted to run my hands over them, find out their story, and see them up close for myself.

"Is that okay, Charlie?" Jhett stared at me, holding a pack of steaks in his hand.

"I'm sorry, what?" I felt the pink creep into my cheeks, realizing that he just caught me checking him out.

"I asked if burritos were okay. I was going to make carne asada," he replied. He placed the pack of meat on the island I sat at, along with a cutting board and some other items that looked to prove useful for cooking.

I bit my lip. "I've never heard of this 'car-knee-a-saw-uh', but if it's meat, then uh…I'm a vegetarian." I looked up into his eyes, trying not to give away my secret.

Instantly, he scrambled around the kitchen and to the fridge, his nerves obviously making him uneasy. He didn't expect me to say that. "Well, um, I have lots of vegetables, too. I've got onions, carrots, bell peppers, and well, lots of different stuff. I just didn't know…I should have thought about it…" He trailed off, his head stuck deep into the fridge.

I couldn't hold myself together anymore. "Just kidding!" I shouted, as I moved to stand right behind him, my laughter giving me away. "So what can I do to help, Top Chef?" I asked, picking up a knife and grabbing an onion out of his hands as he closed the fridge with his foot.

"You think you have jokes, now? You know, that wasn't very funny," he said, raising an eyebrow at me and sliding a cutting board my way. "Chop that up and put it in the bowl." He pointed to the onion in my hand and then to the bowls that were stacked in the center of the counter.

"Oh, it was plenty funny. You should've seen yourself running around like a chicken with its head cut off. 'Oh no! What do I do now?' I'm dying to know what you would have done if I was serious?" I asked, starting my task of chopping the onions.

"I probably would've prayed to the vegetarian gods to have mercy on me for not thinking that possibility through." He paused, his eyes falling to the cutting board in front of me. "Have you ever prepped vegetables before?" He continued to stare at me, evaluating the spastic manner in which I wielded the knife around, causing chunks of onion to fly out in different directions.

Sighing with relief, I slammed the knife onto the counter. "No! I was wondering how long you were going to make me suffer through that before I actually had ask you for help. I didn't expect you to make me chop things up like that right away."

His mouth fell open in disbelief. "You're telling me you're...twenty, right? And you've never chopped vegetables before?" he asked, trying to mask the humor in his voice as he shook his head. "Here, let me show you." He slid behind me with ease; his chest pressed against my back as his arms reached around me, placing his hands on top of mine. He grabbed the onion with one hand and took the hand with the knife in the other. He began to lightly slice the onion in smooth, fluid movements.

I watched him do the work for me, praying that he truly knew what he was doing, because I lost all control and feeling in my limbs. Jhett's chin rested just over my shoulder, sending a sudden rush of butterflies through my body as he took shallow breaths behind me.

Before I could relax against him, he moved back to his spot beside me and took the rest of the ingredients over to the stove with him; leaving me with an empty feeling where he had been.

"Could you bring those over to me when you're done, please?" Jhett's voice no longer held the playful tone to it from earlier. I was seriously beginning to wonder if it had something to do with me or if he really did have some type of schizophrenia. I collected the vegetables in the bowl and brought them over to Jhett, who was busy flipping the carne asada on a cast iron griddle. I decided that any question besides 'Why did you just run away from my touch?' would have been acceptable at the moment, in a heartfelt attempt to suck the awkwardness that lingered in the air.

I hopped up onto the counter next to the stove and watched him work his magic. "So - you know a lot about me, but I know next to nothing about you. How old are you?" I asked him, crossing my ankles in front of me.

"Is this like a game of twenty-one questions?" he retorted, never looking up from the stove.

"Yeah, except that I'm asking the questions and you just answer them. And no answering a question with a question. So, like I said, how old are you?" I leaned towards him, enthralled with his culinary skills.

"Old enough," he snapped back.

I playfully punched him in the shoulder. He shot me a look that told me to just give it up. "Come on. This isn't going to be any fun unless you play along. Lighten up and humor me." Placing my hands on both sides of my legs, I swung by feet back and forth, waiting for his sour attitude to disappear.

He sighed, finally giving in to my game. "I just turned twenty-five a few weeks ago. Hand me that plate."

I reached over and grabbed the plate. He started to warm up the tortillas in one pan while sautéing the vegetables in another. "So how do you even afford this place?" I blurted out, cringing when my mind caught up to what I just said. I *meant* to ask 'What do you do for a living?' but apparently I came down with a serious case of word vomit.

Jhett laughed - I mean really and truly, genuinely laughed. "I didn't rob a bank or anything, so you can stop looking at me like I did. I was actually in a band for a few years. We got signed onto a record label when I was eighteen; we toured and put out albums up until a few years ago. After that, I only played music on the side and went to culinary school instead. That's how I ended up here in San Diego. I learned how to invest wisely from a young age, and was able to buy this house from the sweet hippie I mentioned earlier. I'm also pursuing my options of being a chef at a little restaurant in town. You know, putting my schooling to good use," he said, the conversation feeling natural and comfortable again.

"A musician-turned-chef. Interesting combination." Amusement soaked my voice. "But I saw you playing guitar at The Pointe. So you still play, obviously?"

Jhett moved from the stove to the island, setting up our plates and the food in a buffet-style line. "So you did notice me? What was it about me that drew you in? My amazing hair? My killer guitar skills? Or was it love at first sight and you just couldn't take your eyes off me?" he joked, handing me a plate. My body was frozen, making me nervous to think that my eyes might really bulge out of my head. "Relax, I was only kidding. What, you can dish it out, but you can't take it back?" He shook his head and gathered up pieces of meat on his plate, taking a seat on one of the barstools at the counter.

I joined him back on my pink barstool. "Ha ha ha," I pretended to laugh. "Keep dreaming, lover boy. This girl doesn't believe in love at first sight. But I'll throw you a bone. It was your tattoos. I've never seen so many on someone before." I stopped and began to shovel the most delicious homemade Mexican food I ever tasted into my mouth. "Mmmm. This. Is. Amazing. I guess you weren't lying about the chef part," I said through very unladylike chewing.

Out of the corner of my eye, I noticed Jhett stared at me with disbelief. "I'm beginning to wonder if you lived under a rock or in a convent or something. I've known you less than a week and already you've ridden your first bike, chopped your first vegetables, and you're just now seeing someone with sleeves. What other 'firsts' can we make happen?" A new twinkle formed in his eyes.

His comment replayed in my head over and over as we finished our meal without talking. I tried to avoid having to respond to him, because it made me realize just how much of the 'real world' I had yet to see. I felt like a child in his presence, inexperienced and naïve. "That carne-whatever was seriously tasty. This was so much better than the take-out I've been living off of," I said, getting up and dropping my plate in the sink.

Jhett followed behind me and started to rinse off the dishes that created a nice pile in the sink. "If you're seriously going to stay, you've got to at least buy some groceries. Or you're more than welcome to come over here and let me cook for you. It's never any fun cooking just for one." His voice wavered, only a little, making me wonder if it was sarcasm or sincerity.

"I'm sure you have plenty of girls lining up at your door for you to cook for and serenade them with your sweet, sweet, music. 'Oh, Jhett! *Please* play me a song! *Please* cook for me!" I used the best southern accent I had, and then jumped back up onto the counter.

He spun around quickly, a towel rolled in his hands as he playfully snapped it at my feet. "Oh, yeah. That's what they all sound like until they hear me sing. Then they're running for the hills. Why don't you hop down and meet me on the couch?" he told me before disappearing into one of the back rooms.

I sighed, not wanting to bounce right up and listen to him like a lost puppy dog, but there was no other option. I took my time making it to the oversized couches. Finding a spot in the corner, I pulled my feet up underneath me and enjoyed the feel of the cushions sucking me in. I felt relaxation wash over me as I closed my eyes and rested my head against a pillow behind me.

The couch shifted unexpectedly with the addition of its new occupant. Directly across from me sat Jhett with a guitar slung over his front, resting on his knees. He looked up at me with eyes that danced with enthusiasm. Only a dash of hesitation peeked through. "This is your last warning - your last chance to run out the door," he said, and waited for my response.

All I could do was shake my head, eagerness keeping me silent where I sat.

He began to effortlessly strum the strings of his guitar, closing his eyes; fully immersing himself in the music. It was when he began to sing that I couldn't catch my breath.

All of my dreams
Seem to fall by the side
Like a discarded thought
Or the day's fading light
But I know that if I could just
See you tonight
Forever

At times we may fall,
Like we all tend to do
But I'll reach out and find
That I've run into you
your strength is the power
That carried me through
Forever

Your kindness for weakness
I never mistook
I worried you often,
Yet you understood
That life is so fleeting,
These troubles won't last
Forever

Inspired me truly
You did from the start
To not be afraid
And to follow my heart

There's a piece of you with me
They can't tear apart
Forever

My chest tightened as the words enveloped me, forbidding any breath to escape as my heartbeat to pounded in my ears. I could feel it happening. I choked back the emotion that I buried deep inside my heart in that spot that was reserved for Cameron. I squeezed my eyes shut tightly as hot tears threatened to spill from them; pleading with myself to keep it together

"Charlie, are you okay? I warned you about my singing." He set his guitar down and leaned it against the couch as he pushed himself forward, closer to me in my hole of self-pity, but only my silence answered him. "Hey, Charlie, look at me. Open your eyes. I'm sorry; I thought you would see the beauty in that song. Please, just open your eyes for me," Jhett begged, his hand resting on my knee.

My emotions swirled with sorrow, confusion, hate, love, and so many other feelings that I couldn't process. It was as if I'd been taken back to the day my mom told me that Cameron died. Finally, anger won.

"How dare you." I spoke slowly, pronouncing every word as it came out. My eyes stung with the fresh tears that stained my face, as they finally met Jhett's. He searched mine for answers I didn't have. "You think you know what I'm feeling? You think you can waltz into my life and claim you knew my brother, and say that he was like family to you? I don't know you, and you know nothing about me *or* my brother. You didn't grow up with him. He wasn't the one who made sure you were safe and okay when no one else was around. I don't have him anymore. He's gone - just like that. So no matter what you or anyone else says, he's never coming back. He left me all alone when he promised he wouldn't. He promised." I screamed. I was a ticking time bomb ever since the day he left and I finally reached my breaking point. Somehow, I rose to my feet in the middle of my verbal attack.

Jhett looked up at me and tried to diffuse my emotion with his soft voice. "I'm so sorry, Charlie. I've lost people close to me too, and that song, it just-"

I was fed up. "Tell me everything, Jhett. Tell me everything right now, or I swear I'll walk out that door and get on a plane back to Tennessee. Fuck your 'promises' and your 'proposition'!" I clenched my fists tightly by my side.

"If you would just sit down, I'll tell you. But you can't interrupt me. You have to listen to the whole thing before you go running out that door," he said. His hand slipped into mine and pulled me back on to my spot on the couch. I tried to ignore the feeling that his touch sent through my body, setting all my nerve endings on fire. Finally he let go, took a deep breath like he was preparing for battle, and began his story.

"I haven't always lived in San Diego. I bought this house a few years ago, but I grew up further north of here, with my mom and my older sister. My mom passed away right after I turned eighteen, and my dad left the picture long ago. My sister, Gracie, was already here to go to college, so when I finally wanted to settle down, I chose San Diego so I could be closer to her. After moving into the house, I found myself drawn to the beach at night. When it's dark, it is like no other place I've been to. It's quiet and serene, unlike the hustle and bustle of the crowds during the day. I spent most of the time working or going to school, but about a year ago I met Cameron. He was lying on the beach just after the sun went down and I thought he was asleep, so I went over to wake him up. The cops can be kind of crazy about the 'No-one-on-the-beach-after-sunset' rule on that part of the beach.

"After that, we seemed to run into each other a lot, always around the same time of night. Apparently he liked to stay out on the shore after he finished surfing, and I liked the company. We talked a lot. My only guess is that both of us needed a friend. I eventually convinced him to check out Riot Night and listen to the band I play in now. It wasn't really his scene, but he had fun, especially after he met my sister. They hit it off right away, but were never really committed or anything.

"I went on a small tour with the band over the winter, which is why we didn't get to meet when you came to visit - even though Cameron threatened to never let that happen anyway. He claimed you were a real heartbreaker. You're the one thing he could go on and on about, Charlie. He really loved you, and always regretted not staying back in Tennessee with you.

"What happened with Cameron hit me really hard. He borrowed Gracie's car the night he got hit by the drunk driver. No one could believe it happened to him. He didn't just leave you behind he left Gracie, too. It shouldn't have been him, Charlie..." Jhett's words ended in a whisper, leaving me with an uneasy feeling that there was more to the story than he let on.

I was left staring at him. I planned on getting my

questions answered, but I never expected myself to lose control and not be able to gain it back. Trying to formulate my thoughts was difficult; I still had so many more questions to ask. All I could get to come out were sobs. As I looked at Jhett, I could see pain visible in his eyes, too, except there seemed to be traces of guilt as well.

Before my body could react, I was enveloped into Jhett's strong arms. I couldn't fight it. I just continued to cry, letting out all the emotions that I held up inside me for so long flow out of my body; nestling myself into a comfortable spot on his chest. He was no longer the irritating man who chased me down outside the bar. He was now the only person I ever cried in front of that wasn't family.

"You're okay, Charlie. Shhhh. It's okay." He repeared the same soothing words into my ear, and lightly held me against his chest. He didn't know it, but he kept me from shattering into a million little pieces all over his wacky-colored house.

I finally regained my composure and took a deep breath, only quivers of emotion left in my throat. I pulled away from him, strangely self-conscious of the emotional breakdown he just witnessed. I tried to wipe away the stains of tears that were left on my face, but I knew there was no use fixing that now. Shaking my hair out of its bun, I let the long waves fall over my shoulders, unruly and untamed as I buried my face in my hands. The silence that overtook the room hit me dead on, and I looked up to meet Jhett's concerned face. "I'm sorry. I'm not normally like that...I just...I can't...." My words refused to come out as I planned.

"Shhh. Stop. You're fine. You don't have to say sorry." Jhett reached over and let his fingers rake through my hair, pushing some rogue strands behind my ears. His gentle touch caused my eyelids to flutter. "I can drive you home, if you want," he offered.

I swallowed. The thought of being alone scared me. "Can I stay? I mean, just for a little bit? I really don't want to go home and be alone right now...." I shifted my eyes downward, suddenly interested in anything that would distract me from his mesmerizing deep brown eyes.

"You're welcome here as long as you want to stay. We can watch a movie." Jhett jumped off the couch, his excitement pushing away some of the sadness that still lingered. He began to rifle through the stacks of movies that sat in the entertainment center. "I don't have many chick movies, but...I can find something." Jhett was really trying, and I had to admit, I enjoyed it. It wasn't often that I had someone to fret over me like he did.

"Do you have any *Indiana Jones*?" I asked sheepishly, unsure of what Jhett's reaction would be.

"Ah...a girl after my own heart. Should we start with *Raiders of the Lost Ark* and work our way through them?" That boyish grin appeared on his face again. I didn't know when it happened, but I had a much different opinion of Jhett now. He was actually being genuinely thoughtful.

"Whatever you want," I replied, but he already started to set up the movie. No more than a few seconds later, he was back by my side on the couch. The movie started while I desperately tried to get situated, but my mind was still going a mile a minute.

"Here," he said, and placed a pillow from behind him on his lap. "Just get comfortable. I don't bite. I promise to keep my hands to myself." He held his hands up in the air, showing me both of them as if cops pursued him.

I paused, trying to think of what to make of the invitation. "Fine. Just don't get squirrely, Tattoos," I said, and my head found a spot on the pillow. Jhett held his breath, fighting with himself to stay true to his word and find a place for his hand. He sought out the safest spot, resting his arm right next to my head. I curled on my side, looking at the TV but not really watching it. I focused on the gentle up and down rhythm of his breaths, and tried to mirror mine to his. "Can I ask you something?" Thinking about it, I wasn't satisfied with his story. I needed more answers.

"Sure, shoot - as long as you keep tears out of those pretty blue eyes of yours," he responded.

I rolled towards the TV a little more, attempting to create a veil of hair over my face to hide my nervousness. "Who's Ginger?" I needed to piece together the puzzle I still wasn't even sure fit together.

"That's my sister Gracie's nickname. She goes by that because of her red hair and fiery personality. Why?" I could feel him looking down on me, searching my hidden face for clues.

"I found it on a napkin in Cameron's apartment. I didn't know he was dating anyone, but I kind of hoped he wasn't two-timing your sister after the story you told me. They were happy, right?" I turned my head to finally look up at Jhett.

He nodded. "I think they were. They tried to act like they weren't a couple for a long time, but everyone saw through it. I spent a lot of time over at her place after Cameron died. She is really struggling with him being gone and regrets not being serious with him when she had the chance. He really loved her - he told me he did. But that doesn't make her feel any better." Jhett didn't stay true to his promise. His fingers found their way back into my hair, tracing the waves that fell against my face. I didn't mind. I could feel the tenderness in his touch, and I needed to feel something other than sadness.

"Can I meet her?" I asked.

"I think she'd like that," he replied, slowly nodding his approval, and flashed another genuine smile down at me.

I turned again, Jhett's fingers still flowing through my hair. I felt a jolt of hope run through my veins. "Good. I don't want to have to live with regrets like that. I want to start living for me, the way I should have been doing all along. No more trying to please everyone." I yawned, the sorrow slowly starting to creep out of my heart. I was nowhere close to healing the hole where Cameron would always remain, but I could tell the stitches were starting to knit it together. I was comfortable here, and even though I didn't know too much about what `here` was, I wanted to see what it held for me.

NINE

Jhett

When Charlie rested her head in my lap, I couldn't help myself. I needed to touch her. It was torture to be so close to her, breathing in her sweet scent, a mixture of cotton candy and strawberries. It had been a while since I actually had to think about my actions around a woman. I promised her that I would keep my hands to myself, but she made it impossible. I settled with running my fingers over her smooth skin, right where her hair fell, and running down the strands that flowed over her shoulders and down her back.

I couldn't get a grip on myself when she was around. It was like she made me turn into two completely different people. I put my walls up when I was with her – I had to. She was Cameron's sister and she was off limits. I just wanted to make sure was okay when she ran out of The Pointe, but somehow, I managed to jack that one up, too. All because I couldn't stay away from her.

Every smile, every tear, every laugh drew me in. Cameron talked about her countless times; I knew everything about her, including stories from their past, about how everyone fell in love with her the moment they met her. How she could light up a room just by being in it, and could cut you down to ribbons when she was angry. She wore her emotions on her sleeve. I didn't believe it until I met her. She was everything that was good in life, and I couldn't compete with that. I told her what she wanted to know, but I couldn't tell her everything about what happened the night of Cameron's accident. One day, maybe, but not tonight. Not after seeing her like that and just started to open up to me.

We stayed like that for a while, watching the movie together and not speaking. When she mentioned that she was going to start living her life for herself, I needed to tell her how badly I wanted that for her, too. It was an odd feeling to care so much for a person you just met. I couldn't figure out if it was the regret I felt about Cameron, the responsibility I felt for his accident, or the fact that she was the only girl who seemed worth my time since I moved to San Diego. She was stubborn and untrusting as hell, a welcomed change of pace from the girls who basically threw themselves at me, although I never complained before.

The credits appeared on the screen in front of us. Untangling my hand from her hair, I whispered for her to wake up. "Charlie, the movie's over." My hands ran over her shoulder when she didn't reply. Instead, the soft sound of her steady breathing answered. She fell asleep.

Great, I thought to myself. I assumed that the time difference had finally caught up to her, but I also knew from experience with Gracie that so much crying could drain a girl. I lifted the pillow from my lap gently and shimmied out from underneath her resting body. Grabbing a blanket out from the closet, I laid it out and draped it over her curled-up form.

"Goodnight, Charlie." I leaned over to push the hair that

framed in her face away when that sweet smell hit me again, causing my gut to clench. Without a second thought I kissed her forehead, startling myself with my own boldness. Attempting to stay a gentleman, I planted myself in the recliner across from her on the couch. My eyes closed and I said a silent prayer that when morning came, she wouldn't freak out too bad. I just didn't have the heart to wake her up, or even make her leave, for that matter.

TEN

Charlie

Sunlight danced over my eyelids. The no-curtain-thing was killing me. Groaning, I rolled over to shield my eyes, but for some reason I couldn't get away from the light that seemed to flood the room, and opening them just caused more confusion. I blinked a few times in an effort to clear the fog from my head. It looked like I was still at…Jhett's house? Another groan escaped my throat, frustration building up in my body as I remembered my freak out last night. The only thing I didn't remember was falling asleep.

Sitting up, I looked around the brightly lit room. Jhett was stretched out on the recliner with his hands behind his head; snoring so loud that I'm surprised it didn't wake me up sooner. Panic crept up my spine. I had to get out of there.

I moved from the couch, trying to make as little noise as possible, my eyes fixed on Jhett for the smallest signs of movement, when a buzzing noise from the kitchen caught my attention. My phone was vibrating itself across the countertop. Ditching all attempts at stealth mode, I snatched my phone and rocketed through the back door into Jhett's backyard.

"Mom?" I asked into the phone.

"Why do you sound so tired, Charlotte? It's nine in the

morning over there. You should be up and getting ready." My mom's perky demeanor had no end. I was about to ask her what was so important, but it hit me like a ton of bricks. Today was the day I was supposed to leave to go back home, and I still hadn't told her I was going to stay. I hadn't even thought about what my excuse was going to be. She ignored my silence and continued to talk. "Well, just remember that the reservation for the car is under our name and-" I cut her off.

"Mom, I'm going to be staying out here until school starts." There it was again - the word vomit that came out as I told her my decision to stay for the whole summer. I wasn't able to hold it back anymore, and it just kept coming without a thought of the severity of the repercussions. "And before you even start to try and tell me otherwise, I'm going to save you the trouble and tell you that I won't need the lecture. I'm staying and I'm going to actually enjoy myself." The lump in my throat disappeared as I caught my breath and swallowed. I knew I couldn't just talk forever; eventually I would be forced to hear what she had to say.

"Charlotte, call this my motherly instincts, but I was afraid this would happen. So I already took care of any loop holes that you may think you had." Her voice was smooth, calm and collected, like we were talking about what to eat for dinner. But I knew that on the inside, my mother was screaming at me.

Without warning, a different person emerged from my body, taking over my mind and letting the words roll off my tongue. "I know that you're upset with me, and I know you're hurting like I am from losing Cameron. But mom, if you really loved both of us like you say you do, please let me do this. Let me do what I have to do." Whoever this new person in me was, she stood up to my mom, which was something that I never had the guts to do before.

"Oh, sweet girl. You think you're a grown up? What are you going to do next week when you can no longer hide away in Cameron's apartment? I have eyes and ears everywhere, Charlotte, and you cannot stay there any longer. There's a little thing called 'void on death clauses', so no matter what you think you understand, child, you don't. The apartment will be rented out as soon as possible to its new tenant. Now, I expect you to be in a car and on your way home in no less than two hours. Do I make myself clear?" She placed her bets and expected me to fold.

Basically she just told me, `You're homeless and need to run back home to mommy`. "Mother, maybe you don't know your daughter as well as you think you do. I have my own resources that I will be using to take care of myself. I'll be back at the end of the summer." There was no need to explain myself any further.

"Charlotte Caroline Jennings! You have responsibilities back here in Tennessee. There's absolutely nothing for you in California, and I will *not* have you gallivanting around the beach all summer! Mine and your father's deal is revocable. If you stay, don't expect to have Vanderbilt waiting for you when you get back." That was her sucker punch, my carrot on a string.

My throat tightened again, only this time, I was afraid it wasn't just word vomit. I hoped that either someone would come and knock me out, or the brave new girl would find her way back to me. When neither happened, I sighed. "Tell Daddy I'm sorry. I love you." I hit end, feeling defeated.

I tried my best to keep from passing out as the reality of the situation came barreling down on me. Not only did I basically told my mom to shove it where the sun don't shine, but I also had only a week to figure out my living situation. A knock on the kitchen window directly in front of me jolted me from my thoughts. Jhett watched with a worried expression, and then motioned for me with frantic arms to come inside. As if the last five-minute phone conversation wasn't bad enough, now I had to face Jhett.

My feet dragged reluctantly as I walked back into the house and the smell of pancakes overwhelmed my senses. Despite the worried sick feeling that lingered in my stomach, I couldn't fight the smile I felt on my lips, even when there were bigger things to think about than breakfast. But I did love me some pancakes.

"You're making breakfast? What did I do to deserve this?" I asked Jhett, as I made my way to where he stood at the familiar spot in front of the stove. He was already lost in his cooking.

"Why do you sound so surprised? It's just a box mix, nothing fancy. But from the looks of that phone call, it seemed to me like you needed something to eat. Arguments always make me hungry." He avoided my eyes, instead keeping his focus on the fluffy circles that he flipped in front of him.

"You were watching me?" My hostility was directed at him, but only to hide the fact that I enjoyed knowing he was curious enough about me to be nosey. "So you know what happened?"

"Well, I could only catch parts, because you were breathing fire out there. But I'm smart enough to figure out that you were probably telling your mom that you weren't coming home like she planned. I'm pretty sure I had that same look when I told my mom I was going on tour instead of graduating high school. I just wish you could have seen yourself. You looked like your head could've started spinning around at any moment!"

My eyes followed Jhett as he lifted two plates of pancakes over to the same spot we ate dinner at the night before. I imagined him calling the shots in a busy kitchen, and it made me wonder if he was as cool and collected under pressure as he was with me. Joining him at the counter, I hopped up onto my pink chair and took a seat. "Yeah, well, I'm surprised it didn't. By the way, know of any places for rent?" I asked. Half of me was hoping to get a rise out of him, and the other half was genuinely curious.

"You're moving?" His voice filled with worry. "I mean, you can't stay at Cameron's anymore?"

"My mom said something about some death clause in the lease. So it looks like I have a week to find someplace new." Anxiety crept back over me as I thought about what moving would really mean. It meant no more being close to the beach, no more being close to the last pieces of Cameron, and no more being close to Jhett – who, despite what I originally thought of him, wasn't turning out to be such a bad guy.

"Charlie, moving is expensive and-" I cut him off. I didn't need to hear his lecture, too.

"Look, I'm not worried about the money. Cameron and I both secretly set up savings accounts when we turned eighteen that our parents don't know about. I have money and I'm not afraid to work, either. I don't need to hear it from you too, when really this whole situation is your fault." His eyes locked with mine while he seemed to search for the right words to say.

"You're right. Maybe you should go home, Charlie. I can't sit here and think about everything you're going to give up just because I wanted to get to know you." He never looked away from me.

The flush in his cheeks told me that he had said something that he never planned to let slip out. "You...wanted to get to know me? That's why you want me to stay? But, your whole speech about Cameron and figuring out who I am..."

"I meant every one of those things. I can't explain it all to you right now. I remember the way Cameron talked about your parents and their crazy rules. He said he felt like he was drowning out who he was, just to make them happy. And that night I met you, I saw it in you, too - but I also saw flashes of him. It's like you have some eternal battle of wills going on inside you: what you *should* do and what you *want* to do. If you need to know one thing about me, Charlie, it's that I'll always be myself, no matter what others might want me to be." He turned his body on the chair to face me, placing his hands on both sides of my legs.

I studied Jhett's face. It was like he knew exactly how to get under my skin and find his way into my deepest thoughts. I wondered just how much Cameron told him about me, or if he really could just pick that up from being around me for one night. He was right, though; my mind was always in a constant battle with itself. I wanted to please everyone, and sometimes that meant losing parts of myself...the parts that were really me. The parts that wanted to throw away any reservations and paint for a living, the parts that let my parents influence my decisions, and the parts that wanted to come to San Diego with Cameron when I had the chance. Maybe if I'd done that, I wouldn't have lost him.

"Well, then here's one thing you should know about me. Going home wouldn't make *me* happy." It was my turn to break eye contact as I looked down at my lap. Jhett's dark brown hair fell across his forehead; much different than the way it looked a few nights ago when he slicked back and plastered it full of grease. Right now he looked like a normal guy, minus the hundred or so tattoos on his body - give or take.

"So enlighten me. What *would* make you happy?" He grabbed my knee closest to the counter and spun me around so that I was face-to-face with him, making me painfully aware of his legs so close to mine, as they found their way between my own like the teeth of a zipper.

A muffled giggle escaped my lips; an extremely annoying nervous habit of mine that I couldn't stand. When I looked up at Jhett through my eyelashes, I could think of a million different things that would make me happy, none of which seemed like the ideal situation as of right now, if I really did plan on staying. I couldn't risk scaring off the only person I knew here by throwing myself at him, even if he was seducing me with his eyes.

"Knowing I wasn't going to be homeless in less than a week," I spoke honestly. I was a planner at heart, and not having a plan at the moment was killing me.

"You could always move in with me." Jhett didn't miss a beat with his answer, which took me completely by surprise.

"I, uh…I don't think that's a good idea. I mean, you're a really nice guy and all, but we just met and…" I was trying to backpedal my way out of what was quickly becoming an excruciatingly awkward conversation. Well so much for not trying to get me in the sack.

"Geez! It's sincerely starting to hurt my feelings that you have me pegged as some kind of sexual predator. I didn't mean move in-*in* with me. I meant as a roommate. Despite its small appearance, there is actually more than one bedroom in this place," Jhett said, his charm caught me off guard; giving me only a second to feel bad about taking his invitation the wrong way.

"I really appreciate it, but, I just think that maybe I should try for a studio apartment or something small like that. They have those here, don't they?" As much as the thought of living in Jhett's house was intriguing, it just wasn't sensible.

"Yeah, I guess they do." He pulled away from me, picked up both our empty plates and made his way over to the sink.

I couldn't help but watch him as he cleaned up from breakfast. Jhett wasn't like the guys you saw on the covers of romance novels; they had muscles that could contend with a body builder, and were always close to being naked. Jhett was tall and lean, but his back was broad and you could see a hint of muscle in all the right places. It blew my mind that he could look so attractive in his previously slept-in clothes.

He stole a glance over his shoulder, only long enough to make eye contact and flash one of his thousand watt smiles.

I knew I was caught, but tried to play it off like I was taking in the rest of the house. Everything about this place was unique, just like Jhett. Each corner held endless possibilities of treasures, new and old alike. It almost made me regret turning his offer down, but I already accepted one offer from him. I wasn't about to get too crazy.

ELEVEN

Charlie

Over the next few days, I really started to become accustomed to having Jhett around. He was quick to take the reins in the search for a new place for me to live, and I happily accepted the help. It was either ride around on the pink bike, which I still couldn't quite figure out, or let Jhett drive us around in his beater of a truck, although he insisted it was just vintage. Either way, he was my only shot at getting around this town in a timely manner, and he knew how to get where we needed to go and fast.

I enjoyed his company when I was with him. He was easy to talk to, even when he wasn't very agreeable. We saw at least twenty different places and none of them were up to Jhett's high standards, but each one had some type of quirk that I fell in love with. I couldn't understand his reasoning behind disliking them all, except for one that he was not shy about expressing. They were all too far away from him.

My phone went off, lighting up with a text message.

Finished with work early. Dinner? You pick the place.

He only dropped me off a few hours ago from our latest apartment hunt failure. It amazed me that a few sentences could pick up my mood so quickly. I looked forward to any messages from Jhett.

Sorry. Going for a run tonight. Finally learned my way around the beach. Tomorrow?

I felt bad turning him down, but I actually put my phone to good use and downloaded a running app with pre-mapped out running courses using the GPS. It was perfect and just what I needed. I picked up a pair of running shoes while we were at the mall recently, and went on a few short runs during the day. Tonight I could feel the urge for a long run pulsing through my body, singing to me to get into that zone, begging me to clear my mind.

I guess I can wait until tomorrow to see you again. Run, Forrest, Run.

I plugged my headphones into my phone as I giggled and put on my Pandora running station. I always ran to the 'Hip hop and Rap Workout' station. Normally I couldn't stand that kind of music, but when you got into the running mindset, after three miles, you needed that tempo to keep you moving. I cranked out my stretches to some Nicki Minaj.

Bounding out the door, I made my way down the stairs and started a brisk walk covering the few blocks to the beach from the apartment. Once I hit the boardwalk, I picked up my pace to a jog. The bass thumped in my ears and I racked up mileage. The sun threatened to set soon, making the beach absolutely breathtaking; it was golden hour. After my phone alerted me that I hit three miles, I decided to turn back and head home. I wasn't paying much attention to the faces that I passed by, but I noticed that there seemed to be no particular person that enjoyed the beach; people of all ages and backgrounds were there.

Feeling recharged and rejuvenated, I made it back to the spot where I needed to turn to go back to the apartment, but the sunset captivated me. I stopped, facing out towards the water, just before the concrete barrier. I went through my cool down stretches, engrossed in the watercolors the sky painted above the horizon.

Goosebumps quickly crept over my body, causing the hair on my arms and neck to stand up as the feeling of unwelcomed eyes washed came over me. I popped my headphones out of my ears and looked around. Nothing seemed out of the ordinary; it was just the same busy boardwalk with people shuffling by. I continued to stretch, ignoring my gut feeling that something was off, and searched the corners of my vision for something unknown.

After five extra minutes of cool down stretches, I decided that whatever gave me the weird feeling was gone. I found no van without windows parked on the street, and no one who looked particularly questionable wandering in the shadows. I took it slow and walked home without my music playing, just in case.

I made it about a block away from the apartment, when quick footsteps coming from behind me made my entire body stiffen with fear. My breath quickened as I picked up my pace. Panic struck me when the realization hit that someone may really following me. I saw the Lifetime movies about girls being stolen and never found again. I suddenly found a new reason to run.

My jog stayed slow at first. I knew that if I needed to, I could probably outrun my follower, but I also knew that if I ran back home, I could lead the person back to my apartment. Taking a quick glance over my shoulder, I could have sworn I saw the outline of a man.

That was all I needed to set me off; fear toook over and I sprinted forward, adrenaline pumping through my veins. My only thoughts were about what I would do if he caught me. How would I fight him? Who would even notice I was gone? Would Jhett come looking for me?

Jhett! That's when I saw the little white picket fence only a few yards ahead of me. Rounding the corner and bounding into the front yard, I took one more glance behind me, but couldn't find anything but the shadows. When I reached the bright door, my fist beat against it as if my life depended on it, and for all I know, it really did.

Feeling the door give way beneath me, I shoved it open and blew past Jhett who stood in shock. "Shut it. Shut the door, now!" Panic rose out of my chest as tears stained my face. I couldn't catch my breath, much less concentrate on what just happened. My throat was tight and dry, refusing to let me swallow. All I could do was look at Jhett's bewildered face still standing by the door.

"Jhett! Someone was following me. I was done with my run and I started walking home and I could hear them behind me. I swear I saw someone. I just didn't know what to do and I panicked!" I panted, using my unsteady hands to tell the story.

My mind couldn't focus as Jhett's arms pulled me into his

chest, his chin resting on top of my head. Once again, those beautiful tattooed and muscular arms were holding me together. My hands found their way around his waist, gripping his shirt, willing my body to stop its violent shaking. I didn't realized just how terrified I was.

"Hey, you're safe now. No one is going to get you here. All the doors are locked." Jhett's raspy voice soothed my jumbled mind as he spoke. My eyes shut, reveling in the emotions I felt, as I rode out my dwindling adrenaline rush. He placed his rough hands on both sides of my face, guiding my eyes to look up into his. "I won't let anything happen to you, Charlie. I promise." He didn't have to say anything else because it was then that I knew he wasn't lying. He was my protector. It was like his soul had found it's way into mine with only his touch, and all I could do was bury my head back into his chest. I wasn't ready to let go.

"That was quite an entrance. I heard that you knew how to make grand exits, but *that* was talented. " A delicate, female voice came from the couches next to us, making me disturbingly aware that we were not alone. As I stood there in my tank top and running shorts, my skin still slick with sweat, my heart began to race again uncontrollably.

Reluctantly, I peeled myself away from Jhett, who stayed close to my side, his arm resting loosely around my waist. My mind tried to wander into thoughts of what would have happened if we were alone, but I unwillingly pushed them away. For all I knew, he really was just a friend, someone who needed to protect his best friend's sister.

The thought of another woman in Jhett's house slammed into me unexpectedly. I was shockingly irritated, and maybe even a little bit jealous. Jhett and I spent every day together recently, but it seemed as if I was reading everything wrong. Something deep down wanted to believe that maybe this connection wasn't one sided. It was stupid to believe that something could actually happen. I mean, we barely hugged, and now there was another woman in his living room.

Once she came into view, all my irrational thoughts slipped away. I recognized her based on her looks alone; there was no need for introductions. She sat on the shorter couch, wearing a baby pink button-down blouse with denim high-waisted shorts, but it was her hair that gave her away. A mane of fiery auburn hair fell past her shoulders and draped around her porcelain skin. She looked as if she were painted; she was that flawless.

"I'm, uh…sorry about barging in like that. I didn't know Jhett was having people over." Even though she obviously knew who I was and I knew who she was, I felt about three inches tall. Not making a good first impression was something I loathed.

"Well, I'm just glad that I finally get to meet you. I was beginning to think he was hiding you from me." She sauntered over to where Jhett and I stood in the entryway and threw her arms around my neck before I could protest. I was totally and completely taken aback by such a forward gesture.

After what felt like the longest ten second hug from a stranger in my life, she released me. "Just call me Ginger. Everyone else does." She had the same warm brown eyes as Jhett, but I recognized something in them that I had only seen in my own before. It was pain from the loss of someone who you loved as much as you loved yourself. You could try and push the sadness away, but a little always seeped through the cracks.

"I'm Charlie," I replied, mentally cursing the fact that I was never good in awkward situations. What was I supposed to say? Your brother told me that you had a thing for my brother and I'm sorry he died? Yeah, better just stick with the basics.

"Jhett's told me a lot about you. In fact, he hasn't shut up about you since you got here." She shot him a sideways glance that caused him to look down at his feet, which made him look so guilty, he couldn't try and argue it even if he wanted to.

"Hopefully he wasn't just complaining about me the whole time. I've been dragging him around trying to find a new place to move in to, but he hasn't been much help. Nothing is up to his exacting 'standards'." I used my best Jhett-voice to mock him.

"What can you expect coming from the guy who's the mayor of this hippie wonderland? Obviously nothing is going to strike his fancy unless it looks like it came out of a coloring book." Ginger rolled her eyes and motioned around Jhett's house with her hands. I wanted to tell her that this place was amazing, but decided to save that conversation for another day.

I loved everything about this house, hippie or not. "What's not to love about these colors? They're fun and warm." Throwing my hands on my hips, I tried to defend Jhett. He found his way back to my side. It was the longest we held body contact since he let me lay on his lap, and it was utterly distracting.

"Okay *girls,* this is tons of fun, but Charlie and I have someplace to be as of right now." Jhett looked at the clock on the wall.

I turned towards him and wondered what the heck he was talking about. I wasn't going anywhere in my sweaty running clothes. "We do?" I asked.

"We've got to go get your stuff from the apartment." His tone of voice was one I normally wouldn't try and argue with. He sounded as if we made these plans years ago and I was the forgetful one. But I still had no idea what he was trying to get at.

"Why? You can just drop me off there and we'll do something tomorrow." My eyes narrowed as I looked up at him, trying to figure out his game.

"We can get the big things tomorrow. For now, just grab your clothes and small stuff." He busied himself, searching for his keys among the clutter of items on the kitchen counter.

"Um, excuse me? Why exactly? You're speaking in code here, Jhett. I don't understand what are you're trying to say." Following him into the kitchen, I decided that I wasn't letting him off the hook that easily. Who the hell did he think he was?

He whirled around, only inches away from me. "You're moving in here like you should have done a week ago. You're not going to be staying in that apartment alone when someone just tried to follow you home. I'm not letting that happen. I refuse to put you in danger like that." His voice was a low growl, and his stare could have turned me to stone, it was so cold. His brown eyes had been replaced with a cold amber hue.

"Hey guys, I think both of you are getting ahead of yourselves, and I feel like if I don't stop this now, I'll have to turn into a referee while you guys duke it out." Ginger pushed her way in between us since neither one of us planned to back down from the other. I completely forgot she was still there.

Jhett seemed to elicit the most passionate responses from me, taking me from zero to twenty in five seconds, regardless of what emotion it was. "Charlie, why don't I take you home to get some stuff? Jhett's right, you shouldn't be alone tonight. You're still shaking." She placed an uncharacteristically gentle hand on my arm. Looking down, I realized that she was right. My hands were still trembling, but I couldn't be sure if it was from my earlier fear or from the urge to slap Jhett across the face for thinking he could just decide things for me.

"I've got it covered, *Gracie*." Jhett took his eyes off me for the first time since he tried to play alpha dog with me. The look he gave Ginger wasn't any nicer than the daggers he bore into me.

"It's fine, *Jhett*. I don't mind. That is, as long as Charlie's okay with it." She gave me the slyest wink that was meant only for me. She still had her hand on me, but this time she slipped her arm under mine, practically linking us together.

An irritated nod was all I could manage. Something was off. "That's okay with me." I couldn't stand to see the look on Jhett's face. I knew that he was furious, and as much as I hated being the cause, the new Charlie stood up for herself. Besides, he was the one who told me to do that.

Ginger didn't say another word as she started propelling me towards the door, only stopping to grab her keys from the couch. We paused for just a minute, long enough for her to turn around and look back to where Jhett stood. I watched her mouth 'not cool, bro' to Jhett, either not knowing or not caring that I could read lips. She was right, though. That wasn't cool of him.

TWELVE

Charlie

We sat in silence inside Ginger's apple red VW beetle. The tiny car still held that new car smell, making me wince just a little, realizing what that meant. Cameron's accident had totaled her car and this was her new one, the one Cameron would never see. Taking a deep breath, I tried to clear my mind, but my moment of meditation was short lived when we pulled up to the apartment. As we walked up the steps, I felt the fury come back in full force.

"I mean, who does he think he is? My dad? He gets to decide what I do now? He's lost his mind if he thinks I'm moving in. I can't go back there. I'm not the crazy one, here." I threw my hands in the air, storming through the front door and flinging myself onto the couch.

Ginger saved me from letting my true southern girl come out on him, because I was ready to light a fire under his ass. She made her way into the living room in a dream-like state, glancing at things, lingering longer on some items than others. When it finally hit me, I felt like the worst person to ever walk the Earth. Ginger hadn't been to Cameron's since he died. My stomach was heavy with guilt. Here I was whining about someone who wanted to care about me, and she lost the person who cared about her. I wanted to say something, but everything I came up with wasn't as profound as I wished.

She broke the silence first. "I can't apologize for the way that Jhett's acting. I know he seems like he flew off his rocker, but it's all he knows. He's a protector and even though he's my little brother, he kept me safe growing up, and he still tries to now." Her face softened, and only traces of a smile were left as sadness clouded her eyes. "I'm sure you can understand that."

I swallowed, forcing a lump down my throat. I knew what she was talking about; Cameron was the same way, but it still didn't make what Jhett did right. "I'm sorry about Cameron. Jhett told me how much he meant to you."

She shifted from one foot to the other, still acting unsure as to where she was supposed to stand in the room. "Thanks. I've never had that kind of love before. Although, I'm sure you don't want to hear all the nitty gritty details. He loved you, too, you know." She flashed me a lopsided smile, one that I knew all too well. It said 'I'm only smiling to keep from showing you how I really feel'. "So go pack your bag, at least." She motioned to my suitcase; the shift in her tone let me know that she was done talking about Cameron.

"I, uh…didn't we talk about this? I said I wasn't going back." I shook my head back and forth, trying not to get too worked up again.

"Well, here's the deal, Charlie. My brother is never going to let me live it down if I don't bring you back there tonight, and between you and me, he's already up my ass about enough things. I'm not telling you that you have to move in, but think about your options for a minute. You've got what, two days left until you're supposed to be out of here? And how many places have called you back?" She paused, as if waiting for me to answer. All I gave her was a hard, cold stare.

"None. I'm the queen of games, girl, so don't try and play this one with me. Jhett wouldn't hurt a fly. Sure he *looks* like a badass, but he's anything but. He lets his passionate side take over sometimes, which believe me, isn't a bad thing to let happen. You need people on your side every once in a while." She had made her way into the kitchen, her hair falling in her face as she pulled the napkin she'd given to Cameron off the fridge. "I can't believe he kept this…" Her voice was hushed and low, but I could still hear her from my place on the couch.

She got lost in the memories of Cameron while I, on the other hand, couldn't stop myself from thinking about how much Jhett actually told Ginger about me. It was clear she wasn't a stranger to my situation. "I'm all for passion and having someone in my corner, but not someone who's going to command around me like I'm some sort of lost child. He of *all* people should know better than to do that." I was teetering on the border of an endless rant zone again.

"To be perfectly frank, he's probably sitting back at the house praying that he didn't scare you off. Just go back and sleep on the couch again, or something. Even I don't want you alone after seeing you trample into Jhett's place like that, all shaky and crying. That was no joke." She was still rubbing the napkin between her fingers, glancing at it every few seconds as if to check and see if it was still there.

"Fine. I'll go back for the night. But I'm not moving in." I pointed my finger at her, as if to prove a point, and threw the rest of my stuff into the bag in front of me. I didn't have much to begin with, so it was only packed with bare essentials I would need for the night. Finishing, I tossed the tiny duffel bag over my shoulder. Ginger lingered where she was, lost in her own world again. "Hey, why don't you keep that? Cameron would've wanted you to have it." I placed my hand on top of her snow-white arm, just like she had done to me back at Jhett's. It was hard to place the connection I felt with Ginger. She was closed off from me, except for small windows where she acted like she cared.

Her honey-colored eyes were suddenly bright again. "Thanks." She shoved the napkin into her pocket and snapped back into her sassy self. "You ready?" she asked, looking around uneasily.

I shrugged, hoping that I made the right decision. "Yeah, let's get this show on the road."

As Ginger's beetle pulled back up in front of Jhett's house, she barely missed taking out the mailbox. I contemplated what I was about to walk into once I stepped through the door. I knew just one more crack, one more chip, and I wouldn't be able to hold it together anymore. *Something* was going to happen, and I wasn't sure if the pending explosion would be good or bad.

"So are we going to sit here all night and contemplate life? Or are you going to get in there and do that weird hugging thing you guys did earlier?" My head jerked towards Ginger in the driver's seat and I caught her wrinkling her nose at me, repulsed by her own thoughts.

"We don't do weird hugging things. I was just…scared," I snorted back defensively, leaving out the part where I thoroughly enjoyed being in those arms. I shook my head in an attempt to rid myself of those warm and fuzzy thoughts.

"Just go!" She reached for my arm and practically shoved me out the door. There was no denying that they were siblings with their matching pushy attitudes.

I slung my bag over my shoulder and made a last minute decision to confront him about his actions. I wasn't going to let him or anyone else tell me what to do. I was a new Charlie, and he of all people should know it by now. Before I could even reach the last step that led to his door, Jhett appeared in the doorway, just a broad shadow in the light behind him; his hand absentmindedly going to that spot on the back of his neck that he rubbed when he was nervous.

"You came back," he stated, his breath hitching on each word as confusion tried to surface on his face.

Keeping my word, I brushed past him and tossed my bag off my shoulder and onto the couch as soon as I made it through the entryway. "I almost didn't come back, Jhett. You shouldn't just spout off demands like that to people. It's arrogant, not to mention RUDE. What did you think I was going to do? Throw myself at you and thank you for saving me?" I whipped around to face him as he stood near the now closed door. I felt empowered; I was all *'Woman! Hear me roar!'*

He shook his head, that one-sided half smile dancing on his lips again. It was the one that always seemed to shoot down any hopes of logical thinking after I caught a glimpse of it. "I'm not sure how many times I have to tell you, but you don't need saving. That being said, I owe you an apology. I'm sorry for coming off too harsh and acting like that. I don't think I've ever seen someone so panicked before and, since we're being honest, it scared me. I've felt so helpless lately, and I just felt like I couldn't be there to protect you if you moved. And I know you don't need protecting, but I want to be there for you, Charlie. I want to be your friend." He closed the gap between us while he spoke, my legs pushed as far as they could go against the back of the couch. He was close enough so that if I reached out, I could touch him, but I still had room to take a step forward if I wanted.

"My friend?" I questioned, looking up at him through the veil of waves that fell across my face; uncertainty stained my voice. I wasn't sure why his last sentence caught me off guard. I knew that we were friends - he proved that to me and I knew I could depend on him. But I also knew that I wasn't the only one who needed to push away the what-if thoughts, or, at least I thought I wasn't the only one.

"Yeah. Friends." Jhett's voice sunk to that low tone that that made me fight against the gravity in the room that threatened to take me down at the knees. With each word he crept forward, putting even less space between us than before. His eyes never left mine; easily making it so I couldn't look away. I was stuck where I stood, with no room and no desire to move.

Time moved slower than I ever experienced. Jhett's scent was all around me, the perfect mixture of the woods during a storm, causing my eyes to close just a few seconds longer than I expected. A tingling heat was suddenly radiating on to my cheeks, making me open my eyes again. Jhett's hands found their way to my face, resting right along my jaw, as his thumbs softly explored the freckles that littered across my cheeks.

His eyes burned desire. I should have told him to stop; friends don't look at each other like that. It was almost as if he knew my thoughts when his lips found mine, placing only the slightest pressure against them, but the spark that ignited inside me could rival fireworks on the Fourth of July. His lips fit perfectly with mine. They were made to kiss me, and my body was meant to be in his arms. My hands grabbed on to to his beautifully inked wrists, holding them for balance as my body swayed closer to him.

Before I could satisfy myself with more of him, Jhett pulled away, his breath shallow as he attempted to regain his composure. His eyes remained shut as he brought our foreheads together. I tried to memorize every detail of his face, every piece of him that I may overlooked, because I was about to make one of the hardest decisions of my life.

"Jhett, I...I can't. Friends don't..." I was equally as breathless, my words coming from somewhere that my body couldn't comprehend as he dropped his away hands from my face. I was left with an empty feeling on my skin where they just touched me with so much need. I didn't know what I meant - I didn't *want* to say those things.

I stood up straight and absently realized just how much taller he was than me, or maybe I was feeling particularly small for stopping the one single kiss that ever elicited that kind of feeling through my body. The heat in his eyes disappeared, and instead, regret was written all over his face. He thought that he hurt *me,* when in reality, it was me who hurt *him.*

"I'm sorry. I don't know why I did that. I shouldn't have done that. I'm just...I've got to go...." Jhett came apart at the seams, trying to avoid any contact with me and rubbing his forehead with the same hands that I didn't want to be anywhere but back on my skin. He turned his body toward the door. He was going to walk away.

"Hey!" I shouted after him, grabbing his hand as he turned away from me. I knew I made the wrong decision earlier as a new sensation fell over me, starting from the inside out. I didn't just want Jhett; I needed to feel what he made me feel only moments ago. I needed that to be real. Placing his hand on my hip, I only had a few seconds to take in his surprised expression before I reached up and brought his face down to mine, mimicking his actions just minutes earlier.

I knew my answer. Jhett wanted me just as much as I wanted him. The way his lips came crashing down onto mine proved it. There was no soft, gentle touch this time around. He devoured me, his tongue dancing with mine, passion emanating from him and I wanted more; desire burned in my belly. I felt the unfamiliar roughness of his facial hair against my forearm as my arm circled around his neck, my fingers lacing through his hair, grabbing and pulling handfuls ever so slowly.

The deep, throaty groan that came from Jhett was enough to put me over the edge right there, causing a tiny squeak of pleasure to escape through my parted lips. He responded to my body by picking me up as if I weighed nothing. My legs wrapped around his waist and he walked both of us towards the kitchen counter.

Every chance I got I pulled him closer to me. There was no way I could get enough of him. I wanted every touch and every kiss to last forever. Jhett never broke contact with me as he set me down on the counter, finding a spot perfectly between my legs. His lips moved from mine, trailing greedy kisses down my jaw, stopping right below my ear on my neck. With one swift movement he brushed my hair away and wrapped one arm around my back, making sure I wasn't going to go anywhere.

My head fell to the side, exposing as much skin as possible for Jhett to explore. I wanted him to taste every part of me. My fingers danced over his tattoos on the arm that steadied us on the counter top. My eyes closed briefly as Jhett took what he wanted and nibbled at my flesh. I almost got lost in the colors and details in the ink that spread up to his shoulders, had I not felt the sudden lack of body contact between us.

Jhett panted heavily, both his arms placed on either side of me on the counter. Mine found their way around his shoulders, twirling the hair I could grasp in between my fingers as I kissed my way from the collar of his plain white signature tee up his neck and to his swollen lips.

"Charlie, are you sure you're okay with this? We can stop. We can go back to how things were going to be." He leaned back just out of my reach, putting the brakes on my trails of kisses. My heart sank when I saw the conflicted look on his face.

I pulled his hand from beside me and placed it on my chest, my heart beating so fast, I knew he wouldn't be able to deny what I was about to say. "Do you feel that? No one has ever made my heart race like that before." My hand stayed on top of his. "So don't tell me we can go back to how things were before. I don't want to. I want whatever we are now, right in this moment." My words surprised not only Jhett, but myself as well. I was never one to jump into things with both feet. I always held back in the past, but right now, I would hate myself forever if I let him walk away and think that I didn't want this too. That I didn't *need* this.

Jhett's free hand swept the tangled hairs that fell in my face and pushed them behind my ear. He leaned forward with ease and placed his warm lips against my forehead. Such a single, tender action only added fuel to the fire inside of me.

Pushing off from the counter and landing on my now mysteriously bare feet, I took off in slow strides across the hardwood floor toward Jhett's bedroom at the end of the hall. I never went in it, but I knew it was there. He always left his door open and the bathroom was down the same hallway.

Reaching the doorway, I paused and glanced back over my shoulder. My eyes trailed from the floor up to Jhett, who still stood next to the counter of the island, seemingly undressing me with his eyes. My pulse rushed in my ears as I stole one more look in his direction and then stepped into Jhett's bedroom.

The room I stood in was nothing like the glimpse you could see from the doorway, and definitely not like the rest of the house. The walls were painted obsidian black, which stood out from the harsh contrast of the light hardwood floors. One wall was made up entirely of ceiling-to-floor red curtains, while the opposite wall had the entrance to the bathroom and another smaller room. His bed was much larger than anything I ever saw before; it was made up of dark cherry wood and covered in gray and white sheets that looked like heaven. Above the bed were a few lights, along with a long, abstract painting of the beach.

I was speechless as I let myself get caught up in the essence of Jhett that filled his room. It was dark and sultry, just the way that he was with me. Running my hands over the matching dark wood dresser, my thoughts drifted to how many girls had been in the same position as me, captivated by him and the manner in which he knew how to make a girl go weak.

"It's amazing how good you look in my room." Jhett's voice startled me, my neck snapping to look at him as he leaned against the closed door, his arms crossed over his chest. Seeing him like that reminded me of the night he chased me down in the street, except that this time, instead of his arrogant remarks irritating me, it made my desire for him burn that much more. Something released between us with that kiss, or maybe I finally let go of my inhibitions. "You know, you're the first girl to actually be in here." He made his way over to me and snaked his arms around my waist, exploring the flesh that was exposed on my back as I wrapped my arms around his neck. He nuzzled his face against me, leaving wet kisses on the most sensitive spots.

"Somehow, I find that hard to believe, being a musician and all..." I tried hard not to succumb to the tingling sensation that was burning through my body again. A short little nip on my collarbone made me yelp.

"Don't forget master chef, too. And it was always their place, never mine." His blunt honesty was forgiven once he found his way to my mouth and intertwined his tongue with mine yet again.

Jhett stepped away, but I followed after him, matching each step, as I continued to get lost in the sweet taste of his tongue. Something else came over me while I fumbled with the hem of his t-shirt and pulled it up and over his head. When he reached the bed, he laid on his back onto the sea of fluffy covers. It was the first time that I really got to take in all of the art that covered Jhett's body. My eyes explored every inch of uncovered flesh, scanning up his arms and admiring his chest, adorned with just as much colorful work. My eyes were pulled down his stomach and to his hips, where only small bits and pieces of colors were visible from under the waistband of his jeans.

I was never assertive when it came to men. In fact, there was one other guy in my life who saw me in anything less than a bathing suit, and that was when I lost my virginity in the back of my high school boyfriend's truck my senior year. After that, it was just a handful of letdowns and pointless hook-ups that I never wanted to speak about again. But seeing Jhett lying on his bed, his hands tucked behind his head, I couldn't help myself.

I climbed on top of him and straddled his body, my legs landing on either side of his hips. Jhett's hand reached up, running the back of his fingertips over my hot cheeks and down my shoulders and arms, sending an electric shiver through my body. He finally rested his hands on my hips and pulled me into him as he sat up, catching my mouth with his once more. Passion crashed over us again; our lips only parting to catch our breaths.

Jhett's fingers slid under my tank top, now the only thing between him and my skin after changing back at the apartment. It was thick enough that I could go sans bra, and for once, I was thankful for that. My body screamed for more contact. Tracing his fingernails up and down my spine, my back arched and I pushed my body even closer to him.

Without hesitation, Jhett lifted my hands above my head and threaded my shirt up along with them, tossing it to the floor. I got lost in the look he gave me after that. It was one of pure hunger; it was a hunger just for me.

Jhett scooped me up with one arm and flipped me over

onto my back. I watched with disappointment as he climbed off the bed, but soon heat fired back into my core. Jhett dropped the rest of his clothes onto the scattered pile on the floor, and then climbed back on top of me, taking my last article of clothing with him.

I sucked in my breath; Jhett's warm skin was like fire as his lips trailed from my stomach back to their familiar spot on mine. He reached down and laced his fingers with mine, only to bring them above my head, capturing both of my hands in one of his. He held them in his grasp as he explored the rest of my body with his own, filling all the right spots. If this were how things were going to be, I would die a happy girl. My body craved Jhett's and begged for release. I didn't have to ask. Jhett's body answered for him, giving me just what I needed, and a feeling of euphoria swirled in my head. Nobody could take this moment of pure bliss away from me as I relaxed in Jhett's arms, right where I belonged.

THIRTEEN

Jhett

The smell of sweet candy filled my nose, my body recognizing the scent before my mind could. My eyes were greeted with the unfamiliar sight of the soft curves that outlined Charlie's body. Her back faced me; my tattoos a harsh contrast to her milky white skin as I held her close to me. Even though it was morning, the blackout curtains did their job by keeping the sunlight out of my room. My hands ran down the curve of Charlie's back, her body reacting with a small shiver. I waited for her breath to change, to show some sign that she was waking up, but she continued her calm up and down motions as she inhaled and exhaled.

When I was content that she was going to remain asleep, I carefully eased my body from hers and backed off the bed, placing my bare feet on the chilly wood floor. I took one last minute to admire the gorgeous view of her in my bed as the pang of reality hit me that she could wake up at any moment and regret what happened last night. I could replay her words to me over and over in my head, but ultimately it was her decision if she stayed or went, since I just made her life that much more complicated.

There wasn't much I could do while she still slept, so a

shower was the next best idea rather than waking her up to hear her answer. I was still in the buff from the previous night when I stepped into the bathroom. A double sink, vanity and the door that partitioned off the toilet took up only a small portion of the room. The other half of the room held a claw foot tub and an all-glass shower.

I let the water run at a much hotter than normal temperature from the showerhead. The room was already steaming up by the time I entered the glass box. The water relaxed my body, but did nothing to put my mind at ease. I tilted my head back and let the practically scalding water run through my hair and down my back. My thoughts drifted back to Charlie, remembering the way she moved, and the way she felt as she took what she wanted from me. She was a different person last night, confident and aggressive, leaving me with a desire for more of that side of her.

I only wanted to convince her to move in as a roommate. I planned to make her room someplace she wanted to be, not to kiss her and leave her to feel even more confused. I would be lying if I said the thought never crossed my mind. I really tried though; I tried to give her the chance to say no and she almost did. I should have walked away and just let her live the life she deserved, instead of getting wrapped up in my complicated mess. But the way she grabbed me - I knew then that she was my endgame.

Flashes of Cameron entered into my mind as I thought of one of the conversations we had a few months before he died.

"You know that she's my sister, so I'm obligated to tell you that if you hurt her, I'll kick your ass straight into next year. No more of your funny business. I know she's a tough pill to swallow

sometimes, but you treat her right." We sat across from each other in my living room, a guitar resting on both of our knees. I taught him to play on one of my older acoustics, but his true talent was singing.

"Yeah, I can't blame you. I'm the same way with Charlie, but I think I lucked out with her. She either doesn't see all the guys who chase after her, or she's just super picky. Either way, I don't really have to worry about her too much in the guy department." Cameron repetitively played the same few chords I taught him.

"So when's she coming out here? You said this summer, right?" I slicked back the hair on the side of my head.

"Yeah, I want to show her the colleges out here. I can't let her waste away back home. She's so much more than what our family thinks about her. She's an amazing artist, but our parents don't see that as an acceptable career. Hell, the only reason they let her choose it was because she was the one who agreed to stay in Tennessee." He set his guitar down next to him. He gave his shaggy blonde head a shake, and leaned against the back of the couch with a sigh. "And don't get any ideas. I'm still contemplating even letting you meet her. I've seen you with the girls around here, and there's no way I'm letting you put your 'I'm-a-musician' moves on her. She's special."

"And what do you think Gracie is? She's pretty special to me, too. I still let you meet her, and look what happened, southern Romeo," I teased. I knew that Gracie was happy with Cameron, and honestly, I couldn't have picked a better guy for her, except for the fact that he was terrified of commitment.

"Yeah ,yeah. Well just promise me that when you meet her, you'll keep your distance unless she wants otherwise. But I fully expect you to watch her back when I'm not there, too, even if it's from a distance. I trust you to look out for her like I would. She's not always the best at telling people what she really wants," he said, making my mind wander to the image I created of his twin sister in my head.

"You know you don't have to ask me twice. We all take care of each other around here. She'll be safe with me, I promise." I picked up my guitar again, and strummed the hard strings in a steady motion. There was no time to react when a pillow sailed my way and hit me square in the face. I held up my hands in a 'what-the-hell?' motion.

"I appreciate the gesture, but...can you just try to sound a little less creepy about it? Seriously, don't pull that shit with her. She's not going to fall for the knight in shining armor bit, so don't even try." He raised his eyebrows in an expression that said he meant business.

I felt as if I might be letting Cameron down. I didn't plan on ever meeting Charlie after his accident, but she just showed up; her ice blue eyes broken and unsure. Watching her run out of The Pointe, I knew I couldn't let her walk around the streets alone. But it wasn't just for Cameron; it was for me, too. She made something new stir inside of me that I struggled to suppress.

I prayed that things wouldn't change between us and instead would continue to evolve. Whatever decision Charlie made when she woke up, I would respect it. Whether she wanted me or she didn't, I would still keep my word to Cameron. The desire to protect her wouldn't go away, but it would be so much more intense if she actually wanted me like I wanted her.

The water ran cold, causing the rest of my shower to be rushed as I soaped down and rinsed off. I grabbed a black towel off the rack on the wall, rubbed my body dry, and wrapped it low on my waist. The steam filtered into the room around me as I opened the shower door and stepped out onto the mat, shaking my head side to side like a dog in order to rid my hair of the excess water that it tried held onto. I didn't even bother looking in the fogged over mirror as I passed through the bathroom and back into my bedroom.

Charlie still slept soundly, surrounded by white cotton and down blankets. She rolled over while I was gone and was now laying in what used to be my spot, with thick threads of hair falling into her face. I hated to see her gorgeous face covered. I pushed the stray stands behind her ear gently and reached down to press my lips to her forehead, which caused Charlie's eyes to flutter, just a little, but not open. She could sleep through bombs going off, I was sure of it.

Still in my towel, I headed off to the closest place I could think of to clear my head: my studio. Careful to be as quiet as possible, I cracked open the opaque glass door and entered the tiny room. The space used to be an office, but I knew when I first saw it that it would become my studio. I spent months getting it together, soundproofing the walls and installing all the equipment I wanted. It may have been small, but it was a mighty setup.

The far wall housed all my guitars. I guess I was known as somewhat of a guitar hoarder with my friends, because I had yet to get rid of any of them. Even my very first crappy acoustic was still there on the wall amongst newer and pricier ones. Picking up my favorite Taylor, I sat down in the chair closest to the computer and fiddled with a few programs before getting things set up to my liking.

It didn't take long to get lost in the music. I loved to play, and when I did, I drifted off into a whole different world; lost in the rhythm and feel of the various notes that ran through the air. There was no thinking when I played, especially when

I got into it enough to sing, and that was something I really needed right now.

FOURTEEN

Charlie

Searching for my clothes was pointless. They were scattered all over Jhett's room like in the movies. The only article of clothing that I could find was Jhett's white shirt. This will have to do, I thought to myself as I slipped it on over my head. It was big, reaching right above my knees, but it was comfortable; Jhett's scent still lingered on it.

The dulled sound of a guitar caught my attention and stopped me dead in my tracks. I was headed to explore the bathroom, but the music coming from the door that I wondered about last night was too much to walk away from. I'd heard Jhett play twice now, but this time was different. It sounded like someone else in there singing with him.

My curiosity got the best of me. I stopped in front of the clouded glass door and pressed my ear against it, listening intently. I was right, there *was* someone else singing.

Pressing myself closer against the glass, hoping to find a better spot to listen, the door went flying open beneath me, creating yet another unexpected grand entrance from me. It took a few seconds to catch my balance, especially considering that it was hard for me to be graceful in a normal situation, much less one where you got busted snooping on the guy you just spent the night with.

Jhett spun around in time to witness most of the fall, immediately jabbing buttons on the computer to stop whatever music played over the speakers. I barely noticed what else was going on, when I looked up to see Jhett still sitting there with only a towel wrapped around his waist and a guitar over his knee. He stared at me with a flustered expression.

"Eavesdropping?" Jhett's eyebrow rose as he called me out before I got a chance to formulate an excuse.

"I wasn't…I mean…well, I was listening…but…I…" None of the right words came out. I was still dumbstruck by the fact that I stood in the center of a studio with an almost-naked Jhett while only a thin t-shirt covered me.

"You do know it's not polite, right?" he asked with a condescending tone filtering back into his voice.

I sighed. I honestly didn't know how to take this side of Jhett after last night when he was so different. So…*loving*. "It just sounded like someone else was in here with you. I was curious."

"Curious….or jealous?" He grinned. I was used to his teasing now.

"What's it to you if I *was* jealous?" I ran a finger through my thick waves, and popped a hip out to one side.

A familiar flicker of passion appeared in Jhett's eyes as I moved. "You wouldn't be the first girl to get jealous," he spat.

Now he was back to irritating me and it was no longer funny. This was war. "And probably not the last, I assume. I'll just go check out my room, I guess. Oh and by the way, here's your shirt back, *roomie*." Slipping his shirt off over my head, I flung it back in his direction and turned to walk out of the room wearing nothing but my birthday suit. I took a deep breath, hoping that he would know I didn't mean it. I didn't *want* it to be that way. But if he was going to be a nonchalant jerk, I could be a tease.

"Good God, woman. Are you trying to kill me?" Jhett called from the doorway of his studio. I turned around and waited for some other indication of what he was thinking. Instead, his shirt smacked me in the face, falling into my hands. "Please put that back on before I do something crazy."

I sighed and slipped the shirt back over my head. "Better?" I asked, my head bouncing with attitude. What? Now he can't even look at me? This is going to work out real well. Way to go, Charlie.

"At least now I can think straight without all *that* distracting me." He motioned with his hands up and down, following my form from head to toe in the air.

"Really? You know, I don't know why I thought this was going to be any different. I trusted you…I thought you were special." I whispered the last part, suddenly feeling vulnerable and exposed.

Jhett move quickly before, but this time he made it to me in record time; his hand slipping into my hair, his lips eagerly upon mine, searching out my tongue. My arms wrapped around his neck as my body found its familiar spot pressed up against him. I didn't see that one coming.

"Charlie…" Jhett said in between breaths. I didn't want to hear it - not yet, anyway - so I covered his mouth with mine and refused to let any more words escape from his lips. His hands wrapped around the hair at the base of my neck, causing a gasp to escape from somewhere deep inside me as he exposed my neck and kissed the soft spot behind my ear. "Tell me you want me." His voice was husky and raw as he whispered in my ear, making my heart beat faster than it ever did before.

"I want you." The words slipped off my lips like honey; I never uttered truer words. In reality, he didn't *have* to ask me to say it. I knew those words would come out on their own eventually.

He refused to tear away from me, like kissing me was the last thing he was ever going to do. Finally he brought his hands to my face and forced me to open my eyes and look directly into his. "This is okay, right? You and me?" he asked; his eyes darting back and forth from mine, eagerly awaiting an answer.

"Nothing has ever felt so right." My hands still around his neck, I ran my fingers over the spot where his hair stopped and his neck began. "I told you last night…" I started to say, but Jhett cut me off, putting a finger up to my lip.

"I know what you told me last night. Believe me, I've replayed it more times than necessary in my head. I just wanted to be sure." His eyes shone with sincerity. Pulling me closer to him, I let my head rest on his chest while wrapped his arms around my waist. It was simple and sweet, and just what I wanted.

I sat in the practically empty apartment and leaned up against the living room wall. My arms were wrapped around my knees, holding me together in a tight human ball. I spent most of the morning making arrangements with a company to pick up all of the items of Cameron's I decided to donate. As much as I wanted to keep all of his things, some of them I knew I just couldn't; mainly the furniture, like his couch and bed, had to go. It wouldn't do me any good to hold onto those things, and someone who needed them could definitely use them.

The few remaining brown boxes lined the opposite wall. They contained the other small things of Cameron's that I just couldn't get rid of - little trinkets, books, his leather jacket and pictures. The bag that I brought from Tennessee sat closest to the door. It was swiftly becoming a reality that the small suitcase held the only things that were mine. I didn't feel sad looking at it. Truthfully, I was terrified that I made some wrong choices somewhere down the line. I was moving in with Jhett, but where would I even stay? In his room? In "my" room? I wanted this so bad, but what if it didn't work out? Things went from normal to complicated in the span of twenty-four hours.

Silently, I said goodbye to the apartment that Cameron called home for almost two years. I wished he could have been there with me. I barely knew what I was doing anymore. There was the 'me' that I've always known, and then there was the 'me' that wanted nothing more than to break free. I couldn't decide which one I was anymore, but I had a sneaking suspicion that Cameron would tell me to find a happy medium.

I checked the time on my phone and saw that it was past three o'clock. Jhett was already a half hour late, and he hadn't even bothered to call or text me to let me know what was going on. He'd told me that he had to run into work this morning to take care of some things, but that he would be back before 2:30 to pick me and the rest of my things up. When I attempted to call him, I was immediately greeted with a woman's voice expressing how sorry she was that my phone had been disconnected. *Seriously? Disconnected? Thanks again, mom.*

I tossed my phone away from me in frustration. I had no phone, no car, and now Jhett was nowhere to be found. I made myself a promise that I was going to start depending on myself, but here I was sitting in Cameron's bare apartment waiting on someone to help me. I decided that this would stop NOW.

I pushed myself up off the floor, grabbed my purse and made my way out the door. There was no reason to leave a note. Jhett was smart; he'd figure something out eventually. I was speed walking, no thanks to my seriously miffed mood. I knew exactly where I was going, and there was no stopping a woman with a plan.

It took me about fifteen minutes to get there, and maybe twenty minutes inside the shop before I was done. Walking out the door, I turned my new cell phone over in my hands and ran my fingers over the touch screen to test it out. I was holding a clean slate in my hands. This was something I did on my own and without any help. To some people it may have seemed silly to be that excited over having their own cell phone plan. But for me, it was huge.

The guilt of running out of the apartment without leaving a note weighed heavily on my mind, as the euphoria of signing my cell phone contract started to fade away. I stood in the middle of the sidewalk, trying to remember Jhett's phone number, but drew a blank. Numbers were never my strong suit.

I bit my bottom lip in frustration while shoving my phone into my back pocket and marched to the corner of the street. I pushed the crosswalk button repeatedly and scanned the opposite side of the street for the countdown lights.

Then I saw it, sitting on the lot across the street. The rapturous feeling of independence and adventure surged back through my body. Jhett was going to have to wait a little bit longer.

FIFTEEN

Jhett

Minutes blurred together as my mind raced with anxiety. Finding Charlie's cell phone thrown on the floor of the fully packed and empty apartment made me sick. She wasn't there, and there was no way to get a hold of her. The worst possible scenarios rapidly flew through my mind, with all of them leaving only one conclusion: It was my fault. I ran late at the restaurant and when I tried to call her, it wouldn't go through. It wasn't the first time my phone gave me trouble, so I figured she'd understand. I was definitely not expecting to show up to the apartment and have her not be in it.

I sat at the top of the stairs outside the apartment and rested my head in the palm of my hand, while I went through the contacts on my phone. My right leg bounced, a nervous habit I was never able to control, as I called Gracie. No answer.

My phone dropped back in my lap, both my hands resting in my hair right above my forehead. There was one small sliver of hope, stemming from the fact that her suitcase was still there. It meant that she wasn't running away from me. I couldn't handle that; I wasn't ready for her not to be there anymore. She planned on coming back. I tried to keep telling myself that to stay calm. Anger was building in my chest, and I had to stop it before it became too much. I wasn't angry with Charlie - I was only angry with myself.

The high-pitched sound of an old car horn blared from the parking lot at the bottom of the steps, pulling me out of the black rain cloud in my mind. I looked up and scanned the lot from my elevated view, but there was no one down there.

The same horn shrieked again, but this time I knew exactly where it came from. Pulling into the parking spot just in front of the stairs was a bright yellow Jeep Wrangler, soft-top removed. My mouth fell open when I saw who was in the driver's seat.

"What do you think?" Charlie pulled herself up, shouting to me as she rested her hands on the top of the windshield. Her eyebrows were raised, waiting for my response, but I didn't have one. All I could think of was that she was the most frustrating woman I ever met. Here I was, panicking that she was kidnapped and being held hostage somewhere for the past few hours, and she was out buying a Jeep. And a banana-boat-yellow Jeep, at that.

"You better have stolen it while escaping from your kidnappers who've been holding you up for the past two hours." Half-heartedly, I jogged down the steps to her. My eyes roamed over her body as she stood, the light breeze whipping her hair around her face. She wore a dress that hugged her body until it reached her hips, and then fell loosely to her knees. A teal bikini peeked out from under the top of it, making me realize that if I didn't know any better, I would have thought that she grew up here.

"Oh, hush. It was *not* two hours, and you were late

anyway. I needed a car, and I knew the moment I saw her that she would be mine. And I got this, too." She flashed me her new iPhone, sitting snug in a matching yellow case.

My arm reached up and leaned against the doorframe as I rested a foot on the floor of the Jeep. There weren't even any doors on this thing. It screamed rebellion, and made me dislike it that much more. It was nothing like the car I would have bought for her if she asked. I smirked at my own thoughts. I knew better than to try that; Miss Independent would bite my head off.

"In that case, please remind me to never be late again." The light in Charlie's eyes dimmed. I didn't want to be a killjoy, but I hated that I wasn't there to help her. They could have easily ripped her off and sold her a piece of junk for way more than it was worth. Charlie looked away from me as her smile disappeared. The look on her face made me feel even more terrible, because it was one that a child would wear while their parent scolded them. I reached under her chin and brought her eyes back to mine. "Hey, at least let me look under 'her' hood. I'm sure you did great. I'm proud of you." My lips met hers, and the familiar feeling of butterflies formed in my gut. I was never one for romance or deep feelings, so I didn't know what to make of us, yet. But it felt amazing, which in my case, was never a good thing.

SIXTEEN

Charlie

Jhett stood with his back towards me, his head ducked down underneath the hood of my brand new Jeep. I was still riding my wave of independence as I sat on the curb, waiting for him to finish giving the Jeep one final inspection. He didn't admit it, but I knew he wasn't thrilled that I went off and bought a car without telling him. But honestly, why did I have to? It was my money, and like he said, I needed to do what I wanted. And my heart wanted that gorgeous yellow machine the moment I laid eyes on it.

I couldn't help but think of Hannah and how she would flip out if she knew what I just did. She still thought of me as the girl who played it safe and would do anything to blend into the crowd – but not anymore. I changed, and that meant my vehicle should represent that. I couldn't wait until she could visit and see for herself.

I checked the time again. There was nothing wrong with anything under the hood, but Jhett seemed to have some control issues that I wasn't about to argue with. Pushing up off the warm concrete, I made my way behind Jhett and pressed my body against his back, causing his back to stiffen at my unexpected touch. My finger traced along the collar of his shirt and then down his neck as I tried to shift his focus to me.

I decided on my drive back that I wasn't going to worry about labels or over-think things between us. There was no point. I wanted to live in the moment, and that's what I was going to do. We already slept together, so there was no turning back now.

"Can't you just admit she's perfect?" I teased, as he slammed the hood down and spun around to face me. He leaned his back against the front of the Jeep and pulled my hips into his before giving me a quick peck on the cheek. I giggled, feeling like we were teenagers that were about to get caught by our parents.

"So if it's a she, what's her name?" he asked, his fingers lacing into mine as I brought our hands up in front of us.

I pursed my lips, pausing for a moment as I thought. "I think she looks like a Mable," I answered matter-of-factly, nodding as I spoke.

"That sounds like she should be sitting in a rocking chair in front of a fire, knitting socks."

"She can't knit. She has wheels, not hands. Duh," I answered with sass, pushing off of him and taking a few steps back. Keeping one hand in his, I led him up the stairs into the completely empty apartment. When I got to the doorway, I stopped, hesitating to go in any further.

Jhett's hands found their way around my waist, and he rested his chin on my head. His actions gave me the comfort and strength I needed from him. I didn't have to do a final walk through. I packed all the boxes into Jhett's truck myself, and I knew that there was nothing left of either Cameron or I inside those walls anymore. I swallowed in an attempted to choke back the pending tears. It was a complete shock on my system to go from such pure happiness to the sudden feeling of emptiness.

I must have stood there in silence for longer than I thought. Jhett trailed sweet kisses down my cheek and neck. They weren't like any other kisses I ever experienced from him; the tenderness of his lips attempted to kiss my pain away. I turned in his arms, pulling mine in towards chest as he pressed me closer to him. I managed to hold back most of my sobs, but a few shaky tears fell from my eyes, staining his shirt with drops of wetness.

Once again, Jhett was there to hold me together. "It's okay. Everything is going to be okay, Charlie." He told me those words a million times already, but it didn't matter how many times he said it, nothing was going to make that empty feeling go away completely.

"It's like I'm erasing him somehow. This was all that was left of him, and now it's just another empty apartment. I'm scared that no one will remember him anymore - that he'll just disappear from everyone's memory when there's nothing left to look at." I held onto Jhett's shirt with white knuckles, scared I may not be able to support myself if I let go. My head fit perfectly, as always, right under his chin, next to his neck. He held me there and lightly rubbed his hands over my back.

"You're not erasing him. He will always live on in here." Taking my hand, he gently placed it over my heart with his own resting on top of mine. "He's always with Gracie, too, and his words of wisdom play on repeat in my head. You know he's looking down at you and he's so proud of you, especially today. In fact, he's probably laughing about how he couldn't have picked a more perfect car for you."

"I guess you're right," I finally spoke, and lifted away from his chest. My fingers swiped underneath both my eyes, hoping to catch any makeup that may have found its way down there during my mini-breakdown. I straightened myself up and ran my hands down my dress to make sure everything was still in place. "I think I'm ready now." I peered up, only looking at Jhett, before I walked straight down the stairs without a backwards glance. I heard the apartment door shut, and then Jhett's footsteps as he followed me.

"You're okay to drive, right?" Jhett walked up next to the Jeep as I hopped in and turned the key in the ignition.

"Yeah. I'm fine. Back to the house?" I asked, faking a smile. I knew I was going to be okay, but it was painful knowing that all that was left of Cameron were a few boxes.

The short drive back to Jhett's house gave me enough time to pull myself together. I parked on the street and entered through the white gate into the front yard. Jhett was ahead of me and already started unloading my boxes. "Are we bringing them into…my room?" I struggled to find the right words. Even though I told myself that things weren't going to get awkward, I think I knew they *had* to be just a little bit, at least until we figured out what exactly we were doing.

"Uh…yeah," Jhett replied, just as uneasily. Picking up a box, I walked through the house and into what was supposed to be my bedroom. Setting the box on the bed, I was surprised to find that the room looked like someone tried to decorate it. The bed was made of white wood, and draped on top of the mattress was a yellow and teal chevron comforter, complete with matching pillows. Along the wall sat a tall dresser and a vanity that didn't match completely, but still gave off the same vintage feel.

Jhett came in unannounced and set his box on the small pile that he already started by the closet. He must have felt my eyes burning a hole into his back, because he turned around with a timid look in his eyes. "So, I hope this is okay. I asked the girls at the store for help, and this is what they picked out. I chose the colors, though. It's why I was late today. I just wanted you to have a place of your own here." Jhett was uncharacteristically antsy; he transferred his weight from one foot to the other on more than one occasion.

"So.....this is *my* room then?" My words came out a little harsher than I intended. I appreciated the fact that he took it upon himself to make me feel welcome and I couldn't expect more than that, but I guess I figured out where I stood with him. "I mean, thanks. I really like it. The colors are just like something I would have picked out myself." I flashed him my best half-smile, before turning away to busy myself with the boxes of Cameron's things.

"I'm glad you like it." Jhett left without continuing the conversation and walked out of the room, sucking all the air with him.

Sitting on the edge of the bed, his last few words replayed in my head. *Get it together, Charlie. You're a grown woman. Remember what you told yourself earlier? Just live in the moment.* I nodded at my own private pep talk.

My feet slammed back down on the floor as I ran out of the bedroom door. I held onto the doorframe and I flung my body into the hall. "How come *I* get the twin bed, and *you* get the de-luxe luxury size bed?" My accent was thick, surprising even myself when I heard it. My hip popped out to the side while I rested my hand at my waist.

Jhett stopped where he stood in front of the fridge and watched me with wide eyes. "Well we can switch rooms if you want...." He was unsure how he should react to my forwardness.

I huffed. "Quit acting like you're such a gentleman and just tell me it's okay to stay with you." Frustration lingered in my voice as it echoed through the house.

Jhett continued to stare, making my stomach churn with instant regret. I pushed him too far. "You know what? You really know how to drive me crazy," he replied as he closed the gap between us, backing me up against the hallway wall with each step. Gathering both my wrists in one hand above my head, he pressed them onto the hard wall behind me. "Maybe I should get you riled up more often. I like it when your accent comes through like that." His breath was warm as he spoke into my ear. All my built-up emotions from earlier flowed out of my body with his touch as my mind focused on him.

"It's not polite to say stuff like that to your roommate." My back arched against the wall in protest, attempting to get as close to him as possible.

A stifled laugh came from Jhett, who now held me hostage with very little effort. "Charlie, I think we passed 'roommates' a while ago." He gave me one quick tease of a kiss on my lips, and just as I was about to give in, pulled away.

"Then what are we?" It was a question I needed answered, even though I didn't mean to ask it. It popped out of my mouth as the thought ran through my mind.

"Let me show you." Jhett picked me up again and wrapped my legs around his middle, just like the night before, and carried me into his bedroom. I gave in, and just like that, all was forgotten. This could be a recipe for disaster.

We lost track of time as we lay together in his bed; the only light was the unruly flicker of the candles he lit when we first entered his room. My bare legs stayed intertwined with his, the covers hiding the smallest of parts on our bodies. It was a warm summer night, but nothing compared to Tennessee. These kinds of nights were comfortable and enjoyable, not sticky and miserable. My body stopped where his started while my head found that perfect spot on his chest.

I didn't dare speak; I wanted to ride out this moment of pure bliss for as long as possible. Lazy fingers traced the lines of the images that crawled up the arm that rested across his chest. His other was tucked snugly around my shoulder and back while he tangled his hand in my hair. I silently questioned every piece of art my eyes grazed over. Each one called to me, wanting me to find out their story. I finally stopped at a tattoo I didn't noticed before. There were several teacups and saucers, but all of them were chipped or shattered completely. My fingers tried to continue upwards, but my eyes were fixated on the sad broken pieces of china that littered his skin.

"You can just ask me about them, you know." I glanced up at him shyly as he spoke, feeling like a kid caught with their hand in the cookie jar.

"I thought it would be rude to ask about what they meant, but I couldn't help but wonder if they're all for decoration, or if they actually have a story behind them." A warm smile danced over Jhett's face. Using his arm that was around my back, he pulled me toward him and pressed his lips onto my forehead, sending a rush of heat through my body that only he knew how to do.

"Some of them do, and some of them don't. It's funny that you always seem to be fascinated with the ones that do, though. Don't think I haven't caught you staring at them before."

I listened to his shallow breaths; the rise and fall of his chest a steady beat that I knew by heart. "Why are they all broken? I can't see one that doesn't have something wrong with it." I moved on to tracing imaginary lines that ran through the blank spots on Jhett's chest where there were no tattoos.

He scooped up my hand in his and intertwined our fingers together. "I'll tell you about the teacups if you tell me something *I* want to know." He gave my hand a gentle squeeze as if he were adding on 'please'.

"What is it with you and your propositions? Anything you want to know you can just ask." I said, laughing under my breath as I used his words against him.

"Very funny. So you agree to answer my question, then?" He looked down at me with narrowed eyes.

"Fine. What do you want to know?" I squeezed his hand the same way he did mine.

"What do you want to do with your life? What are your dreams? What are you scared of? I feel like I know so much about you from other people, but I've never heard them from you."

I got up from his side and sat cross-legged as I pulled the covers tighter around me. Jhett quickly propped himself up to lean against the headboard, calming my nerves as he relaxed. "I guess...I don't know. Right now I just want to graduate college." Trying to formulate an answer was difficult, probably because I never really took the time to think about the questions he asked. All I knew was that I had to finish college, and whatever happened after that, I would figure out when I got there.

Jhett raised his eyebrows; seemingly enjoying watching me squirm from his intense stare. "Go on."

I shifted my legs and tried to think about where I saw myself in the years to come. "I want to paint things that make people happy. I want to earn a living without compromising who I am. I want to be happy, wherever that may be, surrounded by the people I love and who love me, too. I don't want to be scared anymore, and that means trying things I never thought I could. I want to experience life and all it has to offer, with no reservations. I just want to be me without caring what people might think." I let my mind take over as I spoke, and when I looked into Jhett's eyes, my chest tightened, making me forget how to breathe. We sat in silence, just taking each other in, while I pleaded with my eyes for him to say something.

Instead he pulled me to him, right back to the same spot on his chest, but this time his arms were wrapped so tightly around me I didn't think he planned to ever let me go. He planted hundreds of kisses into my hair and on my neck. "I've never seen you more beautiful then you are right now. You *can* do all those things, Charlie. I believe in you." His words were raw, and he spoke without reservation. This was the part of Jhett I only caught glimpses of, but I loved each time he let me in. I backed away from him and gave him a bashful smile. He pulled a pillow from behind his head and set it in his lap. I knew what he wanted and I followed his lead, laying my head down and looking up at him.

"Thank you." I couldn't think of anything more appropriate to say. I wanted to thank him a million times, because I never felt as beautiful as I did when he looked at me.

A lopsided smile danced across his lips. "I mean it," he added, as if I didn't understand him the first time he said it. "Now I guess I owe you that explanation." He held up his arm above me, slowly rotating it so that I could see all the white broken porcelain that covered his skin.

"Some of the earliest memories I have of my mom is of her drinking tea out of these beautiful teacups; they were her family's heirlooms. She would sit at the kitchen table after Gracie and I went to bed with just a cup of tea, and do nothing but stare out into the distance. When my dad was still around, sometimes they would fight so loud at night, I knew someone was going to call the cops and we would be taken away for good. He was always throwing something and yelling about how she didn't love him. I didn't know any better back then…I thought everyone's parents fought like that, but no one wanted to talk about it." He paused, remembering his painful past.

"He wasn't like that with Gracie, but with me, he tried to teach me right and wrong with his fists. I was terrified that he'd hurt her if I stopped caring about the pain, so I tried to fight back. The night he finally left, he shattered my mom's entire china cabinet. I woke up to him slamming the door, while my mom cried on her knees on the dining room floor. She was never the same after that night. That's the night I learned that just because you clean up all the pieces, sometimes things still remain broken no matter how hard you try and fix them. " Jhett was lost in his mind as he looked out into the quiet bedroom.

Reaching up to his face, my hand rested on his cheek while rubbed my thumb over his rough five-o-clock shadow. His features were stiff and hard as he relived the memories from his past. I was immediately struck with guilt. My upbringing was much different and I knew I would never experience that type of pain.

"Sometimes I wonder if I'm going to turn into him." Jhett looked down at me; his eyes dark with the burden of his father.

"You're not him, Jhett. You're so much more than he ever was. Look at everything you've accomplished already." My eyes flicked back and forth over his, trying to see what he was so scared of. I never felt safer than when I was around him. "I mean, take me, for example. I've known you for almost a month - and you haven't done or said a single thing to hurt me." I dropped my hand and he took a deep breath with its release.

"Not yet…" he whispered as he broke eye contact with me; his thoughts enveloping him as he stared off into the distance again.

My heart broke for him. This was an entirely new experience for me, and I wanted nothing more than to take all his pain away like he did mine. Sitting up, it was my turn to embrace him. I wrapped my arms around his neck and pulled him close to me. He was unresponsive for only a moment before the stiffness of his body gave way, and his arms wrapped around my waist.

We stayed like that for a long and silent few minutes. Finally I whispered in his ear, "You won't turn into him. You wouldn't hurt me. I believe in you, too."

SEVENTEEN

Charlie

"Come on! We're going to be late." I heard Jhett yell across the front yard to me. I knew that we had plenty of time, but that was Jhett – forever in a hurry. Locking the door behind me, I bounded down the porch steps and across the concrete path to the driveway. He sat in the driver's seat of my Jeep, the engine already humming as I jumped into place next to him. As much as he joked about the bright yellow color, it was hard to keep him out from behind the wheel. I didn't mind either way; I just loved having the top off. The way the salt-tinged air whipped past us as we drove was my own personal slice of heaven.

Jhett gave me a quick glance to make sure I was ready before he backed out into the street. It took days of nagging to convince Jhett to let me visit him at the restaurant where he worked. I tried every trick in the book to find out the details of his job, but the end result was always the same: vague descriptions and non-answers. The only solid fact I had to go on was that he got the liberty to create items for the menu. I found this out only by default – he used me as his guinea pig.

My head fell back against the grey leather seat my muscles loosen with relaxation. The sun beat down on us through the opening in the top of the Jeep, and it warmed my skin almost instantly. I closed my eyes, reveling in the contentment that overcame me recently, as my thoughts drifted to the man in the driver's seat next to me. After our conversation the other day, there was no reason to keep second guessing each other's feelings, and even though mine were new and something I never experienced before, it wasn't strange. Being around Jhett became second nature. Even his snarky remarks grew on me.

Jhett's fingers laced with mine. The roughness of his hands brought me face-to-face with the intense eyes I just couldn't seem to get enough of. I stayed with my head turned towards him, my chin resting on my shoulder, while a satisfied smile crept onto my lips. He gave my hand a quick squeeze before cutting off the engine and hopping out the door. Following his lead, I swung my body out of the Jeep and onto the sidewalk, squinting in the bright light of the sun.

Eagerness to explore filled my chest as I looked over each building around us, trying to figure out which one Jhett worked in. He parked behind a row of several tiny shops, and from the sounds of people shouting and the muffled waves breaking, I knew we were close to the beach.

"You ready?" Jhett's hand found mine again.

Looking up at him I nodded. "Ready when you are. But I still don't know what I'm going to do while you're working. Should I just sit in the corner and make sure to be the biggest pain in the butt possible?"

He shook his head, already leading me towards a door at the back of one of the beige stucco buildings. There were no signs or any indication of what type of restaurant we were entering, not even a name. "I'm sure we'll figure something out," he smirked as he opened the door for me and ushered me inside.

I waited for him to lead the way and followed him through a tiny, bare hallway and into a nice sized restaurant front. I scanned the room anxiously while I tried to make sense of what I saw. The room was completely white, with some booths against the walls and a few tables mixed throughout the black and white checkered floor.

"Well look who finally decided to make it today." Ginger's slender frame appeared from the kitchen located behind the counter, juggling an armful of papers and folders that she unceremoniously dumped on a table. Her eyes zoned in on our joined hands before she looked up at me. Her eyebrows drew up in question the same way Jhett's did when he tried to make sense of something that puzzled him. "I can see why you might have been running behind." She pursed her lips together and took a seat in front of the papers that she spread out before us. Jhett pulled out a chair for me and stood behind it, waiting for me to sit down.

"Don't even start with that, Gracie." Jhett gave her a look of warning.

I ran my fingers through my hair and eyeing them both in confusion. "Does anyone care to tell me what the hell is going on here? I thought you worked at a restaurant? Well, I'm looking around, and I see what *could* be a restaurant, but no one is working. In fact, it looks like no one has worked here in quite some time." My eyes flicked back and forth to each of them, neither one jumping the gun to answer me.

"You didn't tell her?" Ginger narrowed her eyes at Jhett, accusation staining her voice. She backed Jhett into a corner for me. I was going to have to thank her later.

"I didn't exactly *not* tell her," he spat at her. "I may have just left out a few tiny details. Technically, I *do* work here. But I also own it as well. And you're right. I am nowhere near opening the doors to this place. But that's why I have the most wonderful business partner here to help me with the paperwork and financial end of it." He flashed a smug look in Ginger's direction.

"Well I thought it was about time I did something useful with all that college someone forced me to attend. Why not help my little brother out?" Ginger's sarcasm was something I could get used to. She reminded me a lot of Hannah when she spoke. "So what do you think, Charlie, now that all of this has been sprung on you?" She asked the question as if she were a news reporter interviewing a witness to a crime.

I cautiously lowered myself into the chair next to Jhett's. My mind was still reeling as I tried to wrap my head around all the details he failed to mention earlier. All eyes were on me, filled with the anticipation of my reaction. "This is... *awesome!*" I let out with an excited breath. "I just don't get why you didn't tell me sooner. It's not like you're burying dead bodies in the back. This place has so much potential, and with your cooking, it's going to be phenomenal – ooh, and I can totally work the tables as a waitress." I was practically bouncing in my seat, ready to take on the world.

"Well she took that much better than I expected. Most girls wouldn't enjoy this kind of thing being unloaded on them. I think you underestimated her." Ginger smacked Jhett's arm playfully, making him shove lightly into my side.

Jhett never broke away from my stare as he responded to Ginger. "I'm starting to realize she's not like most girls." I couldn't help but get lost in the desire that radiated from him.

My pulse quickened at his word. I was still not used to his constant flattery.

"I'm so glad you two worked out whatever it was that you had going on, but we do have some paperwork to go over today." Ginger was picking out the papers with multi-colored flags poking out from the sides, sliding different ones in front of Jhett for his signature.

"I'll take that as my cue to go explore while you do your grown up things." I pushed away from the table and stood up from my chair, not bothering to look at them as I made my way over to the floor-to-ceiling windows that lined the front of the building. Leaning up against the glass, I strained my vision to see what else was around us. Being a corner lot, I could see a clear path down the street to the beach. I couldn't spot any other restaurants around. There were an unlimited number of clothing stores, a few surf shops and one tattoo shop. There was no question in my mind that Jhett could make this place successful.

I found myself drifting towards the corner opposite where Jhett and Ginger sat. Taking a few steps back, I stood and admired the rest of the restaurant and embraced the beauty of its potential.

"I told you he wasn't so bad." Ginger's hair shone brightly out of the corner of my vision as she ambled over to me. "I'll be honest. It's kind of strange the way he looks at you. I mean, I noticed it the first night I met you, but I wrote it off because he doesn't like to see girls upset. But now...I've never even seen him hold someone's hand, and it's kind of weird for me to even admit that about him. I have to say it though...be gentle with him."

I thought about what she just told me. "Is this the 'I'm-his-

sister-and-I-have-to-tell-you-I'll-beat-you-up-if-you-hurt-him'
speech? Because believe me, I think you'll win in a fight, and
I'd rather not try and prove that theory wrong." I gulped, the
thought alone intimidating me. Ginger was about the same
height as me, but the way she carried herself screamed that
she could kick your ass and wasn't afraid to try.

"Yeah, right. Don't think I didn't notice the same look in
your eyes, too." Her elbow jabbed into my ribs, which made
me stifle a giggle with my hand. "That's what I thought. You
make him happy and I can't argue with that. *Someone* around
here deserves to be happy. He's spent enough time trying to
fix me and my problems, so I'm glad he has something else to
focus on." The painful look she always seemed to get when
she spoke about Cameron flooded her face. I didn't know
what to say to comfort her, so I decided to stay silent. She
shook her head from side to side, trying to rid him from her
thoughts, and forced a smile to appear instead. "So tell me
about the evil plans you have for this place. I know you didn't
light up for no reason when Jhett showed it to you."

I rocked back on my heels and double-checked that Jhett
was still busy with the mountain of paperwork Ginger left
him. He was bent over the table with his back towards us,
scribbling on a notepad in between the shuffling of paper. I
leaned in close to her just to be sure Jhett couldn't hear us.
"What do you see when you look around the room?" I asked
her.

She followed my lead and scanned the room wall-to-wall.
"Walls and windows?" Suddenly her hand shot straight up
into the air. "Oh, I know - an ass ton of work?" she replied
sarcastically.

"I'm being serious. You want to know what I see? A blank

canvas. There are so many possibilities here. When do you guys plan to open?" I asked.

"If we start actually getting things done around here - and fast – I'd say two weeks, give or take a few days. Why? What are you planning?"

An evil grin fell over my lips. "I just have some ideas of my own." I smiled at my secret. Ginger's face fell when she realized I wasn't going to let her in on my plans."What'd you do to Gracie to get her looking like you just pissed in her Cheerios?" Jhett appeared beside me unexpectedly and gave Ginger a playful shove. "Turn that frown upside down." I became so wrapped up in my conversation with Ginger, that I totally forgot to check and make sure that Jhett was still busy.

"Charlie was just telling me that she didn't think you'd want to go to the bonfire tomorrow night." I shot her an accusing look, but she just winked at me in return. At least I knew she could keep a secret. "She said you would be too busy 'playing scrabble.' Whatever that means - I don't *even* want to know!"

My mouth fell open from shock. "I did not." I looked at Jhett. "I didn't say that. I swear!" I knew my face was bright red from Ginger's innuendo. The girl was vicious.

Jhett's whole body shook as he laughed. "Are you sure? Because that *really* sounds like something you would say, and *nothing* like what Gracie would say." I could finally breathe once I realized he caught on to her charade.

"Okay, so maybe she didn't say those words *exactly*, but you guys should come. It'll be fun!" She dragged out the 'n' sound in a sing-song voice. "Besides, everyone is dying to meet you, Charlie, and they promised to be on their best behavior. But you better get there early before we're sloshed, because after that, I can't guarantee anything." She brought her hands together and then threw them apart, indicating that she wouldn't be responsible for anything else that happened. "I expect to see you there. Same spot as usual," she told Jhett, before gathering her things off the table and pushing open the front door to leave.

EIGHTEEN

Jhett

I sat on the edge of the bed with my acoustic guitar resting on my lap, while the faint sound of the running shower echoed through my ears. It was bad enough that my mind constantly wandered to Charlie, but knowing that she was naked *and* dripping wet less than five yards away from me was absolute torture. She was like a drug to me, and I was addicted. Not that I had to worry, because I knew from the way she touched me that she felt the same way.

I continued to strum the strings of my Taylor with the accompanying vocals playing only in my mind. I drowned out the sounds around me as the music pulsated through my body and into my ears. It was a long time since I felt inspired to play something from the heart. My muse stood in the next room, and no matter what horrible things I experienced, I knew that I must have done something right for her to end up here with me.

Charlie's body was still steaming from the shower as she drew in close to my bare back and snaked her hands around my waist. "When are you going to let me listen to this super secret song you've been working on?" she asked. I grew to love how she always wanted to hear me play. It didn't matter where we were or what we were doing. She would happily lie in bed, on the couch, or outside in the yard while I sang to her. She was the one person who actually enjoyed my singing.

"I told you - it's a secret for a reason. But I promise that you'll hear it when it's perfect." I turned to kiss her cheek, which rested just inches away from mine over my shoulder. The soft vibrations from her laughter traveled all over my body.

"Let me try, then." I got up to face her on the bed. She sunk back onto her heels, giving me the most innocent and pleading look, and grabbed the guitar from my hands.

"So what? You think you're Taylor Swift now?" I looked down at her as she returned my question with a convincing pout.

"Don't hate me 'cause you ain't me," she teased back. She adjusted her legs beneath her so that she sat cross-legged. The light chestnut outline of the guitar hid just as much of her body as the threateningly loose towel wrapped around her chest did.

I walked around the bed, careful to never let my eyes fall from her body. She ran her fingers down the strings, attempting to imitate what she watched me do countless times. The sounds that came from her fingers were nowhere close to being classified as music, but it didn't matter to me. Every second she played around without my help gave me more time to admire the sight in front of me.

I took advantage of the sudden lull in her strumming to climb onto the bed behind her. I felt like a tiger stalking his prey. If I didn't keep myself in check, I would be down one less guitar, because all I wanted to do was throw it and the towel off of her and make her mine again.

"Put your fingers like this." Even though I was taller than her, I knelt on my knees behind her to give me enough room to easily reach around her shoulders. My hands guided her fingers around the neck of the guitar. "Good. That's called a G. Now strum," I spoke into her ear.

She did as she was told, and created only a slightly off-key sound. She turned her head up to mine and flashed me her best 'I did it' grin. When she moved, I said a silent thank you for remembering to wear a belt, and rubbed it against her towel. It created just enough friction to make it fall loose around her waist. "Oops!" I held both my hands up in the air. "It wasn't me. I swear."

"I know your game now, Tattoos, and you really gotta get some new moves." Her attention turned back to the guitar. "Teach me another one," she demanded.

I gave in with a sigh. I would never admit it out loud, but she sure knew how to wrap me around her tiny little fingers. I leaned against her completely exposed back to reposition her fingers in a new chord. "That's an E."

She picked the strings again, but this time the sound she produced was unrecognizable. "I'm terrible." She exhaled loudly and slumped her shoulders against my chest.

"Throwing in the towel already? Don't leave me feeling like a failure as a teacher." She tilted her head to the side, exposing the soft skin of her neck. She knew my weakness and I took the bait, planting tender kisses right under her ear.

"I think I just like it when you play better…" She let go of the guitar, and I tore my concentration away from her delicate skin. Catching the neck in my hands, I swung it around her body to rest next to me. "Your turn." Charlie flashed me a satisfied smile as she slipped her undressed body beneath the white sheets. She laid her head down directly in the middle of the pillows, which left me only a tiny spot next to her top half. She wasn't a stranger to this routine that seemed to happen at least every other night.

"What will it be tonight?" I asked, settling down next to her with my back against the headboard.

"Ummm..." Charlie put a finger to her lip to think, driving me crazy with the simplest actions. "You pick tonight. Pick a song that makes you think of me." She smirked. She was delighted with her own cleverness.

I inhaled a deep breath through my nose, letting the song choices run through my head. I adjusted the guitar in my lap one final time before nodding to her. I knew the perfect song to play. "You are my sunshine, my only sunshine. You make me happy, when skies are grey. You'll never know dear, how much I love you. Please don't take my sunshine away." I sang to her from my heart, amazed that such a basic children's song could express so much of what I felt for her. The look on her face told me she felt the same way.

"Why'd you choose that one?" She narrowed her eyes and rolled onto her side to face me. "My dad used to sing that to me when I was little. It was our own special little 'thing.' He told me that one day I would light up the world with just a smile..." Her words trailed off as she got lost in her own memories.

I set the guitar down next to the bed and climbed to the familiar spot beside to Charlie; my jeans now the only thing between she and I as the sheets settled down around us. I lifted her chin up with a finger, giving her nowhere to look but directly into my eyes. "He was right, you know. I know you've got a lot of things going on in your head that you don't want to talk about right now, but I just hope you understand that I'll always be here for you, no matter what you need." I pulled her close to me and kissed her forehead, trying to push all the love I felt into her.

She grabbed my hands away from her face. "I need a key to the restaurant," she pleaded.

I pulled my head back from hers, hoping some space would help me process what she just asked me. "You what? But I…I mean, why do you need a key? We can go there whenever you want," I said, while trying to control the shocked expression I knew was written all over my face.

Charlie knew how to get what she wanted. Not in the way that most women used, batting their eyelashes and trying to take advantage of you. No, Charlie went straight for the kill when she wanted something that was important to her. Her lips met mine with such passion, that even I was taken back a little. She raked her fingernails up my arms and around my neck until she found her way into my hair, grabbing gentle handfuls as she explored my mouth with her tongue.

She broke the kiss first, careful to avoid eye contact in an act of fake coyness. "I just thought that maybe I could start painting the walls or something. The white is so…sterile. It's like a hospital in there, and they give me the heebie- jeebies." She wrinkled her nose, causing her freckles to dance on the bridge of her nose.

"I would love for you to paint every inch of that place, but we still have a lot more to do before painting can even begin." I tried to let her down as easy and honestly as I could. It's not that I didn't want her to have a key, because truly, she was the only woman I could ever have dreamed to be by my side when I finally opened the doors.

"So that's a no?" She looked up at me with her bright blue eyes and waited for me to crack. Damn her. She called me out.

"It's not a yes or a no. It's a 'we'll figure it out when we get to it'." I wasn't used to her manipulation attempts, as innocent as they were.

She sighed heavily. "Fine. But can you at *least* tell me what your vision is for it? How do you see it a year from now?" I assumed that she gave up, because she was soon snuggled tight against me; her cheek pressed to my chest on the spot right under my jaw.

I thought for a few minutes and tried to put myself into the future. What *did* I want? "When I first thought about opening my own restaurant, I knew that I wanted something unique. I want people to have the ultimate experience. Someplace where you can walk in off the street while you're enjoying a day at the beach, and try something unexpected and new. I want to serve all types of burgers and sandwiches and have a whole wall full of bottled sodas and drinks. Kind of like a modern day burger joint slash deli." Charlie lightly grazed my chest with her lips, bringing my cravings for her front and center in my mind. Her little tease of a kiss was not good enough for me.

"That sounds just like you, if only the place sprouted legs and a pompadour," she giggled. "Have you named it yet?"

Her laugh was the final straw. In one fluid motion I rolled her from her side and onto her back, catching her wrists above her head. "I was thinking maybe you could help me with that." I ducked down and starting to trail wet kisses from her chin down to her collarbone, eliciting a squeal from her parted lips.

"It's kind of hard to think when you have me in such a compromising position." She wiggled beneath my grasp. I never held her hands down too tight or against her will, but I figured out what she liked, and it was exactly that.

"I could guess one thing you're thinking about right now." I let go of one wrist, which left me free to explore the curves underneath me that continued to drive me wild. My hands slid down her chest and side, blazing a trail straight to her thighs. Her unsteady breaths let me know that enjoyed every minute of the sensuous torture I planned for her.

Charlie's hand slipped up to my face, and she locked her eyes onto my own; the deep blue color acting as my kryptonite. "I've only got one thing on my mind…" The soft pad of her thumb ran across my bottom lip, sending a shiver down my spine. She caught me off guard as she pressed her lips on mine with only the slightest amount of pressure, causing me to breathe in deeply through my nose.

"How many hours of sleep you're going to get after I rock your world all night?" I couldn't even recognize my own voice anymore. It was deep and husky, filled with a kind of need and lust I never heard come out of my mouth before.

Charlie took my earlobe into her mouth, running her teeth lightly over it before she released my sensitive flesh and spoke directly into my ear. "What bathing suit I'm going to wear tomorrow at the bonfire…"

I immediately snapped up as the shock of her words set in, which gave her just enough time to slip out from underneath me. She was so pleased with herself; she wasn't even trying to suppress her laughter. She pulled a dresser drawer open and grabbed a black t-shirt from the folded piles, sliding her arms and then her body into one of my giant band t-shirts.

I sat on the bed and simply stared at her in disbelief. She just teased me - practically to the point of no return - and now she had it coming to her. She busied herself with her hair and ran her hands expertly through it as she formed it into a braid. I saw my chance as she basked in her tiny victory. I launched myself off the bed toward her, grabbing her around the waist with both arms.

"Jhett! Not fair.'" She shrieked as she tried to escape my grasp, but I only pressed her back into my chest tighter. This was just another game of cat and mouse to her.

"Oh, you have *no* room to talk about playing fair!" I already figured out my plan. I wiggled my fingers into her side, knowing that she was incredibly ticklish. Payback was sweet, especially when it was with her. "Say it," I yelled between gulps of air and my laughter. "Say '*Jhett's the King*'."

"NEVER!" She screamed, and twisted her body in such a way that made me lose my hold on her. She ran out of the bedroom and down the hall into the kitchen without even looking back.

I felt like I was back in elementary school chasing the girl I liked around the playground. I followed her, meeting her face-to-face across the island. "You're in trouble now, *Charlotte*."

She grimaced when I said her first name. "Ugh." She rolled her eyes at me while we countered each other's moves for a while; each time one moved, the other would try and outsmart them but would inevitably fail miserably.

"Say it, and I'll leave you alone. Last chance, Blondie." My hands were flat on the countertop as I hovered above it, my elbows forming a perfect ninety-degree angle. Charlie's ice-cold eyes narrowed as she looked me up and down, and then she took off around the island one more time. This time I had a plan I knew would work.

I only took a few steps before I collapsed on the floor in pain. I rocked back and forth, holding onto my knee with a death grip. Charlie was instantly at my side, kneeling down next to me in my too-big-for-her shirt.

"Oh my goodness, Jhett! What happened? Are you okay?" Her voice was ragged with worry as her hands inspected my knee; she tried her best to get a handle on the situation. The concern she showed for me started to border on panic, which almost made me feel bad about what I had done.

With one fast sweep of my arms I laid Charlie flat on her back again, this time right on the kitchen floor. Her moans of frustration only fueled my desire for her. "Hey, remember - I don't get even, I get ahead," I smirked as she crossed her arms in a last ditch attempt to try and get out of losing.

Her shoulders dropped in defeat. "Fiiiiine," she sighed. I knew that I had her right where I wanted her. I sat back on my heels and waited for her to admit that I won.

Without warning, Charlie turned the tables and threw all her body weight against me as I tumbled backwards. It was her turn to straddle me; her bare legs falling on each side of my torso while her hands held my wrists against the cold floor, just as I did to her earlier. Her golden locks were a wavy mess; her braid never stood a chance. But there was a new fire burning behind her eyes that I never saw before. She enjoyed the sudden shift in dominance. In her eyes, she won our little game.

"Say it," she demanded, only inches away from my face. "Say *'Charlie's the Queen'*." She was challenging me. I should have known to stop underestimating her. She never ceased to amaze me.

"You're *my* Queen, Charlie," I told her, my voice just above a whisper. It was worth it to give up; it wasn't often I got her riled up like this.

I watched her features soften as my words hit her. "That's...That's not what I told you to say." She was flustered as she stumbled to find the right words, causing her hold on my wrists to loosen.

I sat up, easily breaking my hands free to reach around and support her back, as she sat upright in my lap. She pressed her forehead to mine and closed her eyes in contentment. "But it's the truth. And you deserve to know the truth."

The thing about Charlie was that she was passionate in everything she did. Whether she was happy, sad, mad, or excited; it didn't matter. It was one of the things I admired most about her, because you always knew how she felt. As her lips crashed down onto mine, there were no words that had to be exchanged. I knew how she felt about me; I could feel it emanating off of her. I only hoped that I could live up to what she needed me to be. I never wanted to be the reason for her to feel anything less than the way she did in that very moment.

NINETEEN

Charlie

"This was a horrible idea. At this rate, we may not ever make it to the beach." I detangled my limbs from the pink beach cruiser beneath me. We barely made it a block from the house, and I already fell down more times than I could count. I stood up, threw my hands in the air in frustration, and turned to face Jhett behind me.

"Is this a bad time to remind you that it was *your* idea to ride our bikes to the beach?" He stopped in the middle of the sidewalk with both feet planted on each side of his blue bike; his hands still gripped the handlebars instead of helping me. I guess he gave up sometime after the first five wipeouts.

I pulled my bike back upright and rolled my eyes. "Yeah. It's probably a really bad time. Especially when *you* were the one who planted the idea in my head. 'Oh yeah - we normally ride our bikes to the bonfires, but we can drive if you want.'" I was bobbing my head from side to side as I mocked Jhett. I didn't have to turn around again to know that he probably had the biggest smirk on his face. It was no secret that he enjoyed this greatly.

"Blah, blah, blah," I heard him say behind me, this time

mocking me. "You're over-thinking it. Just let your mind go free and you'll be fine. We're almost there, and then you can relax." Jhett was just a blur as he took off and passed me, taking the lead in our bike caravan.

The sun was still high in the sky above us as I tried to follow his advice. I pushed off and peddled forward, making sure that my eyes stayed straight ahead. This time, I let my shoulders drop and I relaxed. With each turn of the pedals under my feet, my mind slipped further and further into the sweet memories of the night before. Apparently that was all I needed to distract me since I managed to stay upright long enough to finally enjoy myself.

I wove in and out of the busy pedestrians on the sidewalk like a pro. My confidence blew through the roof with just that minor accomplishment. It may have taken me almost a month, but I finally figured it out. I could ride a bike. I could do anything now – even take on the world.

Jhett slowed down in front of me as he rounded a corner and hopped off his bike with little effort. Despite the fact that we were going to be on the beach all night, he still wore his usual cuffed jeans; only switching up the color of his shirt from white to black. He was busy setting up the locks for our bikes when I finally rode up and hopped off, only slightly less gracefully than him.

"Did you see me? I didn't fall once." I found an empty slot in the bike rack and rolled my bike into the metal grate, kneeling next to Jhett to help him with the locks.

"I knew you could do it. Must have been the amazing view you had." He wiggled his eyebrows up and down with the last clicks of the locks. "There. Now we've got to figure out where everyone is. Can you text Gracie for me and ask?"

He grabbed my hand and led us to the concrete barrier. There were already quite a few fires started up along the shoreline, and I got a feeling that we might have to walk the entire beach to find her.

With my free hand, I sent Ginger a text. Within seconds she responded, except that I needed some type of decoder to figure out what it said. I handed the phone to Jhett, who just shook his head. "Does that mean she started the party without us?" I asked him. There was barely enough vowels the message to consider it a sentence.

"I think that's exactly what it means. However, I am fluent in 'Drunk' and I think I can us to where everyone is at." Jhett slipped his shoes and socks off as I kicked my flip-flops off in front of me. He grabbed them before I could pick them up and put them into the same hand as his own. He laced his other hand with mine and gave it a small squeeze.

I followed next to him with my eyes glued to my feet, carefully watching my step in fear of falling on my face, as we approached the wet sand. I instinctively trusted that he would guide me where we needed to go. Things once again changed between us. I guess that was the beauty of my new life: I held the power to decide which direction I wanted it to go in. Jhett may not have been part of the plan when I first arrived in San Diego, but he sure was a huge part of it now.

The sun set quickly behind us as we raced the night with each step. "THERE'S MY GIRL! THIS IS HER, GUYS!" an extremely shrill and slurred voice rang across the beach. I grabbed onto Jhett's side like a scared child. I was never good with being the sudden center of attention, especially with a group of people I didn't know from a hole in the wall.

Ginger finally reached us and dramatically pulled both of

us into a hug. I tried to discern who was in the group of people gathered around the fire pit in front of us. Anxiety swelled in my chest when I realized what her words meant. I was *her* - Cameron's sister. I pulled away from her quickly and hoped that the smell of beer that came off of her wasn't contagious.

"Hey Gracie. I see that you guys have already started. Been for a swim?" Jhett lifted up strands of her damp hair that fell down the front of her sheer white dress, exposing the black bikini underneath.

"You could call it that. Now go find your friends. I've been waiting for this adorable little thing to get here so we could *really* start the party." Ginger linked arms with me and began to pull me up the beach towards the blazing fire.

"Remember Gracie – best behavior!" Jhett shouted behind us. I stole one more glance over my shoulder as he mouthed 'sorry' to me.

I couldn't stand being dragged through the sand away from Jhett. I watched as he greeted a group of guys further away from the rest of the group with a few hugs, slapping each other on the back forcefully. Ginger was deep in a conversation with me that I had no interest in responding to. This side of her made me nervous. She was already unpredictable, but when you added alcohol into the mix, I knew it was bound to be trouble.

"Ladies, I found her. I told you she was coming with Jhett." She led me up to a group of girls who stood around a huge metal container. They all seemed slightly less drunk than Ginger, but each one of them wore the same expression – disgust. She ducked her head in closer to the group, lowering her voice to a whisper. "You know they're like...a *thing* now.

They *live* together," she explained to the circle of girls, like I wasn't being held hostage next to her.

The girls all started to giggle and talk amongst themselves; their eyes darting back and forth from each other to me like I was some kind of zoo exhibit. I yanked my arm away from Ginger's grasp, which caused her to stumble from the sudden loss of stability. I caught her arm and whipped us around so that our backs faced the circle. "I don't know what you've had to drink tonight, but that doesn't give you an excuse to go flapping your trap about me and Jhett. It's not anyone's business what we are, and I sure as hell expect you to respect that!" My voice was low and stern. I meant to scare her. I wanted to have fun tonight - not be a spectacle for everyone to see.

"Charlie, right? Why don't you just have a drink and we'll catch up about Jhett later." Ginger and I both turned around to face the group slowly. I thought I was being stealthy with our conversation, but apparently I broadcasted my emotions to the world. A girl with jet-black hair and blunt-cut bangs across her forehead held out a red plastic cup in front of me, filled with an amber liquid, which splashed over the rim.

Politely, I pushed her hand away. "Oh, I'm not twenty-one yet," I told her. Instead of waiting for her reply I looked over my shoulder, trying to spot Jhett in the crowd of shadows that surrounded us. More fits of laughter made me turn back to the group of girls.

"Three weeks is less than a month, which is close enough to twenty-one for me. Besides, no one here is a cop. Just have some fun with us. Pleeeasee?" Ginger dropped down to her knees with her hands clasped together in front of her. I was speechless – not because of the fact that she threw herself on the ground to beg me to drink, but because she knew my birthday.

"How'd you...?" I whispered to her and reached down to pull her to her feet.

She flashed me an eerie smile before she brushed the sand off her knees. "Hellloooo! News flash! I dated your twin!" Ginger waved her hands in front of my face, making it seem like *I* was the one who was clueless.

Why did I not think about that before I opened my mouth? The girls still stood closely around us, never hiding their nonchalant whispers. We sure put on a good show for the masses.

"Yeah, what Ginger said. In fact, if you start with these, drinking that disgusting beer the guys picked out won't be so bad later." The black-haired girl passed out enough tiny glasses for all of us, while her friend with the almost-white hair produced a tall skinny bottle filled with clear liquid. "Shots of vodka make everything better. You want to show Jhett a good time tonight, right?" She giggled as she passed over each of our glasses and filled them to the top.

I stared down at my hand. The logical part of my brain told me to just walk away. These girls weren't my friends. But unfortunately, another part of me pushed through to the surface. I *did* want to have a good time. When my friends back home drank, they seemed so carefree. I blinked, bringing myself back into the moment. Everyone else already held their glasses in the air together in the middle of our circle.

"To Charlie! And to a night that no one will forget for a long time." I followed their lead and clinked the rim of my glass together with theirs, before tossing my head back and dumping the liquid into my mouth. My throat burned as I swallowed the fiery liquor, and I struggled to keep the contents of my stomach in place. I put my hands on my knees as I bent over in a fury of coughs that wouldn't let up.

Ginger brought her hand down across my back and gave me some harder than necessary whacks. "Have you ever taken a drink before, Charlie? Please don't tell me this was your first shot?" She asked, while I recovered from the feeling of a burning hole in my chest. All eyes were on me, and I knew that each of them wondered the same thing.

"Is that seriously what all alcohol tastes like?" Laughter erupted all around me, which made me realize that I gave myself away. I always envisioned my first time taking a shot as being much cooler; never did I think I would end up looking like a weenie. Before I could react, the bleach blonde took a hold of my wrist and poured second shot for all of us. "Another one?" I asked nervously. My body was still in shock from the first one.

"We've only just started. Think of this as one of *many* for tonight. Cheers ladies." Everyone responded to Ginger this time with a simultaneous 'Cheers!' before clinking their glasses together again and throwing back their heads. This time, I tried to open my throat and let the liquid flow down easily; waiting until the very last possible moment to swallow and relive the fire coursing through my body.

To my surprise, I made it through without even a sputter of a cough. "That wasn't as bad as the first one." I was proud of myself. This was kind of fun. "Maybe we should go ask Jhett if he wants to join us?" I tried to whisper to Ginger, but failed miserably. My voice was still loud enough so that everyone else could hear me.

"Oh, honey. Jhett doesn't drink anymore. But if you *did* get him to drink even after…well…you know, the accident, then I'll place my bet and say that he's in love with you," one of the girls who hadn't spoken yet told me out of earshot of the others.

"Look, now you've got the hang of it!" Ginger danced around me, jumping up and down, while her friends messed with a radio that was hooked up to someone's iPod. "Turn it up, bitches! Now it's time to move onto phase two – dance your heart out. Take this and try not to spill." She shoved the red cup from before into my hand and dragged me out a few feet away from the fire.

The rest of her friends joined us, each of them waving their hands above their heads as they jumped wildly in the sand below us. They were singing along with the lyrics, but I never heard anything like the music that blared through the speakers, almost rendering me deaf. "I don't know how to dance!" I shouted into the group.

They all looked at each other and laughed. "Just keep drinking! You'll figure it out!" the black-haired girl shouted into my ear. I did a quick check to see how I felt. I didn't feel drunk, or at least I didn't feel like what I thought being drunk was like. I was hot, like I had stood in the fire, and was dying of thirst. I gulped down the brown liquid in my cup as a last resort, naively trusting Ginger that nothing bad would happen to me.

TWENTY

Jhett

It was nice to be with the guys again. I wasn't trying to avoid them, but ever since Cameron's accident, things were a little awkward between us. We saw each other every once in a while at Riot Night when we played, but I didn't feel too comfortable being around them anymore. Combine that with having to play babysitter to Gracie for a few weeks, and then everything with the restaurant - and not to mention Charlie falling into my lap when I least expected it - I just didn't have time to hang out like we used to.

"So, stranger. Your sister finally dragged you out of that shack of yours. Thanks for leaving her for us to deal with. I mean, she was bad before, but she's really been out of control lately." Danny, the bartender from The Point, nodded his head over to the group of girls across the fire, where Gracie dragged Charlie. I knew her friends all too well, and I wasn't sure what they planned for Charlie. The only thing that put my mind at ease was that Gracie promised to watch out for her. "And I see that you brought some unique arm candy with you tonight." He was looking in the same direction as me, right at Charlie.

"Hey - let's not even go there, alright? Yes, she's special

and no, she's not just arm candy to me. Moving on." I painfully diverted my attention back towards the group. I was worried that this conversation would be brought up tonight; I just didn't realized how fast it would happen.

Wes, the singer of the band I played with at The Point, shoved me with a laugh. "Uh oh. I think we struck a nerve." Wes was the antagonist between all of us. He was half the reason why we didn't play together on a regular basis anymore, and was walking proof that sometimes people didn't grow up as they got older.

"I just don't think you should talk about ladies like that, Wes. It's not very gentlemanly." I gave him a nasty grin, still secretly trying to keep Charlie in my line of sight.

"What the *fuck* happened to you? Since when do you care about being a gentleman? I don't think I've ever seen you keep a girl around long enough to even know their name." Wes played dirty. Maybe if I had a drink, I wouldn't be so uptight.

"Let's just drop it while we're still sober, you two." Danny attempted to divert the growing tension. "I think we better go throw some more wood on the fire before it goes out on us." Danny's hand landed on my shoulder, giving it a firm squeeze, before pushing me toward to fire.

Sparks arced up in different directions into the night sky when Danny threw another pallet into the flames. I still kept my eyes on the girls while the danced on the other side of the fire. They turned on the obnoxious chick music that we somehow always got roped into listening to during these types of parties. There was something about a heavy bass that made girls dance like they had no worries. It was a phenomenon I would never understand.

I caught glimpses of Charlie swaying her body to the beat that thumped through my ears. She looked like she was having a good enough time, so I didn't feel the need to interrupt. As much of a partier as Gracie was, I trusted her to keep a good eye on Charlie.

"Now that I've got you away from the rest of the dicks over there, when do I get to hear the whole story about her? You know, I met her the night she came down to the bar, and I watched you run out the back door to follow her. Other people might not be smart enough to put two and two together, but I like to give myself a little credit and say that I can." I sat down in a blue camping chair around the fire pit. A few other partygoers mingled around us, but Danny and I pretty much had a spot all to ourselves.

I sunk against the back of the chair and tilted my head towards the night sky. "Nothing ever gets past you, does it?" I didn't look at him as I asked the question.

He shifted in his chair beside me. "I'm a bartender. You think I'm only supposed to make good drinks? No, my job is to read people. And I've never seen you move so fast in your life."

I took a deep breath. "Yeah. I may have had an 'oh shit' moment when I first saw her. I don't know what happened, but I knew who she was and I knew that I needed to talk to her." I couldn't bring myself to explain anymore of the situation to him. It was far too complicated.

"The way Ginger made it sound, you've done more than just talk to her. I can't believe she's still around after what happened. You must talk a good game if she stayed after hearing it all."

His comment knocked the wind out of my chest, and

made me whip my head back in the direction of the fire. It was the first time someone verbalized the exact situation I tried so desperately to avoid. "I just got lucky, I guess." Charlie's eyes landed on me through the flames. Even in the dark of the night, I could see the excitement form on her face when she noticed I was watching her. She leaned in close towards Gracie and pointed in my direction. Gracie followed her finger with her eyes before whispering something to her and pushed her toward me.

"Well speak of the devil..." Danny's eyes were glued on Charlie as she ran over to us, kicking up sand all around her with each step. She was only left wearing her jean shorts and bathing suit, which left absolutely nothing to the imagination. Her red polka-dotted bikini only covered the necessary parts of her body to stop her from being arrested, but the rest of her porcelain skin glistened from the heat of the fire.

"Jhett!! Goodness gracious, Jhett. I missed you. Where have you been?" Just from her words alone, I knew something was off. It wasn't until she let each leg slip through the holes in the chair below the armrest and straddled me, that I knew exactly what was wrong.

"Have you been drinking?" I pushed her up in my lap, but the smell of alcohol on her breath was overwhelming.

"Isn't it so much fun? Did you know I popped my vodka cherry? Oh, and my beer cherry. And I think my rum cherry, too. That's a lot of cherry poppin' for one night, don't you think?" She continued to speak without taking a breath, her eyes never focusing on my face; just flashing from one side over to the next.

Danny stifled a chuckle next to me. I gave him a look of death. "You know exactly whose fault this is. I swear - I can't leave her alone for more than five minutes before she's up to no good." My blood boiled.

"Are you mad at me? Ginger said you wouldn't be mad at me if I drank with her. They told me that you liked to have fun like this." I could hear the sudden shift of emotion in her voice. I forgot how naive she was, and it only intensified with the amount of alcohol she consumed.

Charlie leaned her head down and against my shoulder, nestling under my chin. I stroked her bare back in a last ditch attempt to reassure her. "No, babe. I'm not mad at you. You didn't do anything wrong. You just tell me who told you that."

"It was the girl with black hair. She looks like she could be in a cartoon, but don't tell her I said that. I don't think she'll find that funny. She kind of acts like she has a stick up her ass. Don't tell her that either!" Charlie lifted up and held onto each side of my face with a death grip. Even though I was fuming at the girls, I had to admit, drunken Charlie was kind of cute.

"She does have a stick up her ass. It's called the bitter stick and Jhett-" I cut Danny off before his words turned cute-drunken-Charlie into crying-mess-drunken-Charlie.

"Shut up if you know what's good for you, Dan." I pointed my finger at him beside me. "Hey Kitten, do you mind if I go talk to the girls really fast? Do you think you could stay here with Danny? You remember him, right?" I slipped my hand up into Charlie's hair and forced her to look at me. I needed to make sure that she was still somewhat coherent.

"You've never called me kitten before. I like it. I like babe, too, babe." I lifted her up into my arms with ease as I stood up. Danny gave me a nod and I set Charlie back down on the chair behind us. "Do you think I look like a cat, Danny?" She turned to him, ready to bombard him with her drunken banter.

Once I left Charlie's side, I was a man on a mission. It only took a few steps around the fire before I found the girls I was looking for. "Girls, we need to have a little chat."

As expected, I was answered with a round of groans. "Don't act like you're not enjoying Miss Goody Two-Shoes like that. Have you seen her moves tonight? I know how much you love a naughty girl." Blair stared at me through her thick black hair in a standoff of wills. I knew that our past probably influenced her actions tonight, but they were uncalled for.

"Just because you're still pissed about how we ended doesn't mean you have to take it out on *her*. She's the innocent party here. She's not even twenty-one yet," I shouted at them. I couldn't believe I even needed to have that conversation with them.

"*You* were the one who ended things, Jhett. And I don't think you not calling me counted as ending things on good terms. So soooorry that I got your little flavor of the month drunk, but it was far too easy to get under your skin. Besides, she's an adult. She made her own decisions tonight." Blair said her peace, and with a flip of her hair was gone, back towards her friends.

I had no desire to fuel the Blair fire. Instead, I turned my attention to Gracie. "What the hell, Grace? You're supposed to be watching out for her - not influencing your friends to get her drunk." I was way passed pissed off.

"No, that's *your* job, remember? I've got to go enjoy

myself. Maybe you should grab a drink. You're way more fun when you're drunk. Oh, and you should probably go get your girlfriend before someone else snatches her up from under your nose." She nodded back towards the chairs where I left Charlie.

I stood there trying to catch my breath, before the buzzing in my ears stopped and I could get a grip on my anger.

TWENTY-ONE

Charlie

"You're so funny Wes, you know that? I don't know why Jhett would say those things to you. He's normally such a sweetheart." Everything was suddenly so funny and everyone was so nice. Jhett had such nice friends. First, Danny went to go get me some water, and then Wes showed up and wanted to dance with me. I loved to dance now.

"I bet I'm sweeter if you'll let me show you. Here, drink some more of this." Wes reminded me of Jhett. He was tall and nice. Taking giant gulps from the red cup in my hands, I finished Wes's drink in record time.

"That is *not* yummy. You lied to me." The endless giggles threatened to come back up through my throat. They were on and off all night.

"I didn't say that was yummy. Beer is never *yummy*. And I would never lie to you. You're way too much of a lady to be lied to. You deserve to be shown the world." He stroked my shoulder and down my arm with the back of his hand. I didn't like it when he did it. It felt wrong. He wasn't Jhett.

"You're not Jhett." I tried to focus on his face, but everything became one big blur. My mind was so consumed with Jhett that even the fire in the background started to look like him. Squinting past Wes's shoulder, I swore that I could see Jhett walking towards us and I wanted to be back with him, instead of in someone else's arms. I lost my balance when I tried to walk past Wes and to Jhett, falling over and into the chair I was supposed to be sitting in. Why was I not sitting in it before?

"Hey, Wes?" A familiar deep voice called from behind us. I knew I saw him. I knew Jhett wouldn't leave me like Wes said he would.

I tried to get up out of the chair as Wes turned around to face Jhett, but before I could even realize what happened, Jhett reeled his arm back and punched Wes straight in the jaw and sent him flying to the ground.

There was a blood curdling scream coming from somewhere in the distance, stopping only once my hands covered my mouth. The scream came from me. My vision threatened to go black on me from sheer panic.

Jhett instantly kneeled in front of me as mild chaos ensued behind him. His hands grabbed my face and forced me to focus on his just inches away from mine.

"Charlie, did Wes hurt you? Are you okay? He's such an ass. Where's Danny?" Jhett's forehead was covered in tiny creases as he fired questions at me faster than I could process them.

A groggy smile crept over my lips. I could feel Jhett's staggered breath as I reached out and put my finger to his lips. "You said a bad word, *babe*." I looked down at Wes, who was knocked out on the sand a few feet away, before searching out Jhett's face again. "I think you put him to sleep. You didn't even have to sing to him like you do me. I was tired of him telling me that you weren't going to come back. You're amazing. Thanks for coming back." I flung my arms around his neck and squeezed my eyes shut in an attempt to stop the world from spinning. I didn't want to drink anymore.

TWENTY-TWO

Jhett

I sucked in a deep breath and wrapped myself around Charlie. Despite the amount of alcohol she drank, I could still smell her sweet scent clinging to her skin. I stole a glance next to us as one of Wes's friends helped him sit up. I was thankful that I only needed to throw one punch to knock him out cold. Honestly, I didn't regret anything. He had it coming for a long time before tonight, and I knew that others agreed. I would still be fighting if they didn't.

"I think I want to go lay down. I feel like I've just been on a rollercoaster and wasn't allowed to get off," Charlie whined. I felt bad for her. I spent way too many nights feeling that way, and she didn't deserve it the first time she ever took a sip.

"Let me get your shoes and your bag and I'll carry you home." I leaned her back against the chair and took off towards the fire. Her things were in a pile next to the beer, and I threw everything inside her oversized bag before throwing it over my shoulder. I was going to need both of my hands to make it home with her.

Once again I was by her side. Slipping one hand under

her knees and the other around her back, I lifted her into my arms. Her arm draped around my neck as she rolled into my chest. I leaned down to press my lips to her slick forehead. I knew that once she started with the cold sweats I would have to hurry, or else I would be wearing second-hand alcohol.

I walked in silence with her in my arms until we reached the quiet street of our neighborhood. The bikes would be fine until morning. I paused just long enough to look down and check on her, only to be greeted with the most adoring eyes looking up at me. "Don't fall asleep on me, babe. You've got to stay awake until we can get home and you can drink some water. You're not going to feel all that great in the morning."

"Have I told you that I *really* like it when you call me babe? No one has ever called me *babe* before. Not even my boyfriends. Are you my boyfriend?" My heart stopped. I hoped that Charlie would be lucky and bypass the drunken stage where you say things you didn't remember the next day, especially things that may or may not be what was really in her heart.

"I like being the first one to call you babe," I told her in an attempt to avoid the subject of boyfriends. Relief flooded into me when I saw the house come into view ahead of us.

"You didn't answer my question." She pressed her cheek against my chest, but kept her chin tilted up towards my face.

I sighed. "Do *you* want me to be your boyfriend, Charlie?" I decided avoidance was key if I wanted to stop her from jumping straight off into the dreaded endless-tears-stage at the snap of my fingers.

"I've been telling Hannah that you're my boyfriend. She doesn't believe me, though. She said there's no way I'm telling the truth." Her eyes fought her pending sleep, stuck somewhere between wanting to stay awake and passing out. "Why did the girls tonight say that if I got you to drink after what happened with Cameron, they would bet that you loved me?"

My heart sunk. I thought that maybe, just maybe, those awful girls wouldn't try to start trouble. Well, so much for trying to find the best in people. "I just decided it wasn't worth it for me to drink anymore after what happened." I hoped that she was sobered up enough that she could figure out what I meant, and not ask any more questions.

"You mean because of the drunk driver? I should have thought of that. I think I'm a bad sister," she trailed off as she talked about other things that made no sense or that I couldn't understand. I didn't have it in me to explain things any further.

Finally I made my way up the steps, and after skillfully unlocking the door with one hand, was greeted with a rush of cool air as we entered the house. "We're home. Do you want to go to the couch or the bed?" I asked her, even though I knew she was probably asleep.

"I like our home. I like being here with you. I don't think I want to go back to Tennessee." Once again, she took me by surprise. I decided to go with the couch so I could get her some water and a few aspirin, and still have her within my sight in case she ended up getting sick - which seemed inevitable at this point the way things were going.

"I don't want you to go back, either. You can stay with me as long as you like." I tried not to feed into her ramblings. I honestly wasn't trying to pry her feelings out of her. Drunken confessions didn't count if you couldn't remember them when you woke up. "I'll be right back. Try to relax, and yell if you're going to be sick, okay?" I laid a blanket over her still almost-nude body. Any other day, her lying on the couch in only her bathing suit would have distracted me, but I was kind of enjoying the fact that she needed me to take care of her.

Once I felt she was all right for a few minutes, I went into the kitchen and pulled down two glasses from the cabinet, along with a bottle of aspirin. I took out two pills for Charlie and then filled both glasses up. I turned around to meet Charlie back on the couch, but was stopped dead in my tracks. Before me stood Charlie, completely naked, dancing to the music in her head.

I set the glasses and aspirin down on the counter, making sure that my hands were free in case there was any sudden loss of control. "What…are you doing…?" I asked her cautiously.

My question didn't faze her. She just sauntered over to me as best as she drunkenly could, without dropping my gaze. Her hands took on a mind of their own, and she wasted no time finding all my sensitive flesh. "I know you've been staring at me all night, so now I'm staring at you." Within seconds she found my belt buckle, and with one good tug, she whipped it through the loops of my jeans and tossed it to the side with a bang on the wood floor.

I wouldn't be a man if I said that she wasn't a dream come true, but I also knew how much she drank, and it wouldn't be fair for me to play her games. "Let's just go into the bedroom and see what happens." I tried to grab her hand, but she took off on unsteady feet down the hall without me.

Charlie stopped right before the doorway, turning on her heels in a slow pivot, and let her hands grope her body from her chest down to her ankles. Her eyes darkened with a mischievous sparkle kissing the sides. I knew I should be scared.

She took off in a blur, sprinting towards me down the hall. I only had seconds to throw my hands up before she launched herself onto me; clinging to my front as she wrapped her legs around my waist. "Whoa! Easy, killer." I grabbed at her arms in an attempt to pull her from me, but she refused to let go. That tussle must have fueled her fire, because she was caught up in covering every inch of my exposed skin in sloppy, wet, kisses.

I needed to pick my battles, and at that point, it was easier to let her keep going than to try and stop her. I picked up the pace down the hall, shuffling as she twisted in my arms. I finally made it to the bed in record time, and began trying to untangle her limbs from around my body. After a few seconds of back and forth with her, she landed on the sheets with a bounce. Her hands fought mine for the covers. She was going to kill me by the time I went to sleep. She refused to let me cover her body.

"Fine. Stay like that then. I'll be right back. Just stay there," I repeated. I tried not to let her catch me looking at her, but I couldn't resist a quick peek. She was sprawled out on the bed, on top of the covers like a starfish in all her naked glory, complete with her bottom lip stuck out in a pout. I ducked out and into the kitchen before I could get sucked into feeling sorry for her.

"I'll be ready and waiting to rock your world, *BABE*," she called into the silence of the bedroom after me. I rolled my eyes at her comment. I changed my mind. Thank God, Drunken Charlie wasn't a regular occurrence. Grabbing the water and aspirin off the counter, I made my way back down the hall and into the bedroom.

Charlie's delicate body was wrapped in a web of sheets, and she was curled up on her side in the bed. Her snores confirmed my fears – she fell asleep before I could get anything into her system. I could only imagine what she would feel like in the morning, and I knew she wasn't ready for it. I set the contents of my hand onto the dresser and searched through the top drawer, finally pulling out Charlie's favorite piece of my wardrobe – a white t-shirt.

I shook it out in front of me, then sat down on her side on the bed and slipped it over her head. I wasn't taking any chances after seeing her before she fell asleep. It was one thing to lie next to her naked, but it was completely different thing to lie next to her naked and have her be off-limits. She could wear a trash bag, and even then, I wouldn't deny her what she wanted.

Trying to get her arms into the sleeves was a lot like trying to dress a baby. She was limp and wiggly, even when she was passed out. Flicking off all the lights, I made my way around the bed and under the blanket beside Charlie. A faint glow from the moon shone through the glass doors across from us and landed perfectly on Charlie's soft features.

I propped myself up on my elbow and faced her as she lay silent, with only the sound of her shallow breath filling the room. I ran my fingers through the soft strands of hair that fell around her face. It was something that I found myself doing often and without thinking. She stirred under my touch, rolling towards me and pushing me flat onto my back. In one astonishingly smooth motion, considering her prior state, she melted into my side; her hand finding a death grip on the t-shirt that I wore.

I inhaled deeply, taking in all that she was. I knew I didn't deserve her. I didn't deserve this kind of blissful happiness. Danny's words from tonight echoed through my thoughts, and the guilt that hung in the back of my mind pushed out in full force. I told myself that everything happened for a reason, but I wondered if that reason was worth it. Would she still stay if she knew the truth?

"Don't leave, Jhett," Charlie mumbled as she wrestled restlessly with herself in my arms. Her eyes remained closed as she continued to mumble into my shirt. I pressed my cheek to her forehead, letting my own eyes close, careful not to lose this moment to my own sleep.

"I'll be here until you tell me to leave," I spoke into the night. I knew that she was asleep, but it didn't make a difference. I just prayed that she never changed her mind.

TWENTY-THREE

Charlie

The light was back in the room again. I tried to flip myself over and away from the brightness, but every muscle in my body refused to cooperate. My head felt disconnected from my body, and I felt the room begin to spin. With all other options exhausted, I pried my eyes open to try and convince myself that I wasn't on a boat and about to get seasick.

I finally managed to sit up and drag myself to the edge of the bed, when I noticed the oversized t-shirt draped on my body. The whole night was a blur. It took everything inside of me to choke down the burning sensation that crept up my throat. I shook my fingers through my hair and tried to regain some type of composure, or at least a tiny shred of memory about why I felt like a bus hit me in my sleep.

Tiny droplets of sweat sprouted all over my body as I tried to tame the sounds coming from my empty stomach. It only took me seconds to realize that the gurgles were coming up whether I wanted them to or not. I jumped off the bed and raced into the bathroom as fast as my broken-down body could carry me. I reached the toilet mere seconds before my stomach decided to empty the burning liquid that remained.

Once every bad decision I made the night before was

flushed down the toilet, I scooted along the bathroom floor and leaned my back against the cool wall behind me. I thought I was never going to feel normal again. Even though there was nothing left inside me, I swore that my body was ready to gear up for round two. "Oh dear Lord," I moaned into my hands. Why did I ever think that taking shots was a good idea? This was absolute hell.

The only thing worse than puking your guts out was the aftertaste in your mouth once you finished. I became desperate for my toothbrush, and crawled across the bathroom floor on my hands and knees. I threw all my pride out the window, not caring if Jhett happened to walk by and see me. I was going to brush my teeth one way or another; the only problem was I could barely manage to stand on my own two feet.

I kneeled in front of the sink and scrubbed the inside of my mouth with unsteady movements as I silently tried to convince myself that I wasn't going to be sick again. Reverse psychology worked, right?

Jhett's raised voice caught my attention. "I don't know how you think you can come in here, and just *assume* that everything is going to blow over and be fine. Some things can't be erased from your memory. And seeing Charlie passed out naked and snoring on the bed right after she threatened to rock my world happens to be one of them."

"You can't be mad. You should be thanking me. That sounds like a good night to me." Irritation flared through my body. I recognized her voice immediately.

Ginger. Hazy flashes of the night on the beach began to flood my memory, and Jhett and Ginger's argument became background noise. I groaned again, and then fell back onto my butt on the floor. I was *that* girl last night. I probably said a whole lot of things I would regret when someone reminded me of them today.

"Charlie?" Jhett called to me from the bedroom. Was he crazy? I had no intention of yelling back to him, for fear that if I opened my mouth I would be sick again. I could tell he found me anyway, judging from the sound of his footsteps on the tile floor. "I take it by the looks of things you don't feel very good?" he asked as he squatted down next to me on his heels.

My eyes met his with a questioning look. Did he really ask me that? "I feel like someone tied me up and dragged me behind their truck from my hair. This can't be normal." I rested my forehead against his leg in front of me. "Make it stop. Seriously, how do people do this every night? I don't think I'm going to regain my normal thought process for at least a few days. I think I'm still drunk."

Jhett reached down to grab my hands and gently pulled my body up next to his as we stood together. I refused to let go of him for fear that I wouldn't be able to stand on my own, with the way my head was still spinning. "Come on, let's go and get you at least semi-fixed up. And just to warn you, you have a visitor who won't leave. Believe me when I say I've tried all morning." He didn't hide his irritation.

With my arm wrapped around Jhett's middle, I shuffled next to him and into the kitchen, not even bothering to glance in Ginger's direction. Instead, I leaned my body weight against my arms on the island counter. It wasn't that I was mad at her – I made my own choices – but I was irritated that she kept me going, instead of at least having the decency to cut me off.

"Nice threads. Glad you got so dressed up for me." Ginger sat on one of the barstools, her head resting on her propped up arm. I gave her the same miserable look I gave to Jhett earlier. "Feeling that good, huh?" Ginger joked. "I'm surprised you're not a zombie right now after last night. You're a riot to party with."

Her voice echoed through my skull. Why did she have to be so loud? "Did you come all this way just to harass me some more, or do you actually have something important to contribute to the conversation? Maybe like….saying *I'm sorry?*" Both Ginger and Jhett's mouths fell open. "*WHAT?*" I yelled, as I threw my hands out to my sides and stood up.

"Did she hit her head last night, too? I didn't think a few drinks would make her that angry," Ginger asked Jhett. He shook his head and laughed while he sat a glass of water down in front of me next to a couple of tiny, white pills. I didn't take my eyes off of Ginger.

"Maybe I'm just irritated that no one even considered telling me to stop? Did that ever cross that little mind of yours? Or was it just too much fun watching me make a fool out of myself in front of all your friends? *'Oh, look at poor Charlie. She can't handle herself.'* Is that what it was?" If my life were a cartoon, smoke would of shot out my ears.

The color drained from Ginger's face. It may have been the traces of alcohol still in my blood, or my unnaturally harsh anger at her behavior, but I burned hot again and wasn't tolerating anyone's bullshit.

"You were having fun. It feels good to let loose every once in a while. In fact, you were the one who kept asking for refills. I didn't know you had it in you." She spoke fast as her words hit me hard.

I got a funny feeling she was telling the truth. Guilt overwhelmed me as my audience looked at me with confusion. I was ashamed in the way I acted. I pushed myself off the counter, a sudden rush of blood going straight to my head. My balanced wavered, just as my stomach tried to make its way up my throat again. Every muscle stiffened in an attempt to stop myself from being sick.

Jhett was at my side the instant he knew something was wrong. "You don't look good, babe. Why don't you go back into the-"

I couldn't choke it down anymore. Flinging my hands out and pushing Jhett to the side, I ran to the closest door I could find. I made it past the wood deck and into the bushes before my stomach emptied itself again. I dropped down to my knees onto the damp ground, while hot tears ran down my face as I continued to heave. This was what hell felt like.

Large hands rubbed my back as I gasped for air. My cheeks became even hotter at the realization that he probably was there the whole time while I retched up the nothingness left in my stomach. Real cute, Charlie. There's a reason mama told you drinking was for fools. "I'm so sorry," I mumbled into my hands. It was all I could manage to say to him.

"Don't apologize to me. You don't know how many times I've been where you are and believe me, I remember just how badly it sucks." Jhett pulled me up by my elbow and we walked over to the deck steps together. He didn't hesitate to tuck me into his side, vomit breath and all. "You know, I think those rose bushes needed watering anyway. They'll thank you for the extras you gave them."

I moaned into his chest. I was never going to live this down. "Really? You couldn't have waited a few more minutes after I hurled all over the backyard to make fun of me?"

Jhett's chest rumbled with laughter. "I couldn't help it. Besides, after everything you said last night, I deserve to poke some fun your way." I knew I went too far the night before, but I still couldn't remember a thing. "I think my girlfriend still owes me a lap dance, seeing as how she passed out right after she promised one to me."

Jhett's words made me stiffen. I couldn't possibly have heard him right. "Excuse me?" I pulled back from his shoulder, allowing enough room between us so that I could look directly into his eyes.

A knowing smirk crept over his lips, and his eyes danced with a matching mischievous glow. "You can tell Hannah she's wrong." Jhett leaned in and kissed my forehead. My pulse instantly raced as the fuzzy light-headed feeling took over again. I once again choked everything back down. I refused to get sick. I might have been thinking like a lovestruck teenager, but hearing the world 'girlfriend' come out of Jhett's mouth was butterfly-inducing for me and he knew it. My mind couldn't formulate a response. I just bit my lip and tried to stay calm. "Let's get back inside," Jhett offered. "You're the lucky one. You get to stay home and recoup. I, however, have to go deal with super bitch Barbie all day. The rest of the kitchen shipment is supposed to arrive, and then we can start getting ready for opening day."

I rose to my feet with him still at my side and slipped my hand into his, letting our fingers lace together. "I know she's your sister and all, but that doesn't mean I have to forgive her just yet. I made my own decisions, and I accept that, but I just wish she could have stopped me at some point," I explained, as we walked through the open patio door and back into the kitchen. Ginger was nowhere to be found, and I was glad that she might have actually got the hint.

When we were completely inside, Jhett reached up underneath my arms and set me on top of the counter next to the sink, and was gone back down the hall before I could respond. Within moments, he returned with my toothbrush, ready for me to use. I raised my eyebrows. "Are you trying to tell me something? I mean, I know I just yakked all over the rose bushes, but...."

"But, nothing. Brush your teeth. I know how you girls are about that stuff, and it's killing me to not be able to kiss you." He began to dig through the fridge and cabinets, pulling out pans for breakfast.

I turned towards the sink and cleaned my teeth; careful not to let him see the smile that appeared on my face. He was right. There was no way I wanted my face close to his after what just happened.

He continued to talk while I finished at the sink. "As for Gracie – you're right. You both are somewhat to blame for last night. She told me she would be on her best behavior, yet she didn't stop you from getting worse once you slipped past the point of no return. And because I know how bad you're hurting right now, I'll spare you a lecture, but you should know that she already got an earful from me. She's probably dreading spending the rest of the afternoon with me, now."

I kicked my feet underneath me. "Yeah. I guess I'm just more upset with myself than at her. I don't have many girlfriends out here, you know? I would have looked out for her if the roles were reversed, but I think she may just have a troubled heart right now," I thought out loud, the free space in front of me consuming my vision.

"I know that you like to find the good in everyone, but don't let her get off that easy. That's what she's used to." Jhett planted a quick kiss on my cheek while he finished making my favorite breakfast – bacon and eggs.

Maybe Jhett was right about Ginger. Maybe she really did expect people to feel sorry for her, and that's why she acted the way she did; she was constantly on a back-and-forth roller coaster of being happy and being miserable. I didn't know how she could live her life that way. I couldn't stand for people to feel sorry for me after Cameron died, but she thrived on it. I had no plans to tell either of them, but I already forgave her. It may be one of my weaknesses, but the good-hearted Ginger was in there somewhere if Cameron was able to love her the way that he did, so could I.

TWENTY-FOUR

Charlie

I practically fell into a booth from exhaustion. We spent weeks of nothing but manual labor and tough love, trying to get the restaurant looking like an actual working shop instead of an abandoned building. This also meant that I was face-to-face with Ginger on days that I helped. She had yet to apologize to me and we tried to avoid each other at all costs, which was easy, seeing as how she was known for skipping out and leaving multiple times during the day. Even though I forgave her in my own mind, I was still left with mixed feelings about her. I couldn't understand how one minute she was so happy for Jhett and I, and the next she was a diabolic mastermind. Something changed in her, but I quickly learned, thanks to the recruited help of Jhett's friends, that I wasn't the only one she burned her bridges with recently.

The high-speed fans drummed in my ears as I closed my eyes and relaxed against the wall behind me, letting my feet extend over the red seat. The heat of the summer was in full swing already and I was miserable. I was used to the sticky heat of Tennessee, but this was a different kind of humid all together. We were only about a week away from the fourth of July, the prospective opening date of the not-yet-named restaurant. The planner in me couldn't stand that Jhett didn't have a name. It wasn't because there was a shortage of names being thrown around – no – it was because Jhett couldn't settle on the 'perfect' one.

The clanging sound of metal falling to the ground made my head snap up.

"Dammit. It shouldn't be *this* hard. These directions don't make any sense." Jhett roared behind the counter, making it hard to suppress a laugh. Danny and Jhett spent the past hour trying to figure out how to install the metal surface of the bar behind the counter. I was actually impressed that Jhett even attempted to look at the directions. He was definitely a figure-it-out-as-you-go guy.

I laughed as the two of them fired insults back and forth at each other. This was a normal life for all of us now, and I got a feeling that things would get even crazier once we opened for business. I agreed to help Jhett work the floor during the day, as long as he worked in the kitchen. He even hired a few other people to help fill in the gaps, but overall, it was just the two of us. Ginger made it clear that she was only there for the business end of things. But honestly, it was the most normal I ever felt in my whole life.

A buzzing noise echoed across the finished checkout counter as Jhett's phone went off. "Charlie, can you do me a favor? I need you to run back home and pick up some paperwork from the kitchen counter and meet Gracie with it." Jhett's greased head of hair popped up from behind the counter in the kitchen.

Meeting his eyes, my nose wrinkled at the mention of Ginger. "Does it have to happen right now?" I complained. Usually I wasn't whiny, but I was so tired lately that no amount of sleep made a difference. Combine that with the fact that I needed to do something nice for his sister, and I was just not in the mood.

Jhett's features hardened. "I know, believe me, *I know.* I just really need you to do this for me. Please?" He leaned against the almost finished metal countertop on his elbows, while flirtatiously batting his eyelashes the best he could in my direction.

"Oh, alright. Just because I like you, I'll do it. But only paperwork…that's it." I pointed my finger at him accusingly. He wore his best up-to-no-good smile that sent my stomach into knots. I got up from my seat in the booth and met Jhett in the hall right before the back door. When he finally reached me, my arms tangled around his shoulder as he pressed me up to him and twirled me around in a circle. A childish squeal escaped my lips. Being in his arms was pure bliss.

Before setting me down on my feet again, he planted a tiny kiss on the tip of my nose. "Have I told you how gorgeous you are today?" he asked, his hands resting comfortably on my hips.

I shook my head and looked down at the floor playfully. "I'm covered in sweat and grime. This is anything but cute." I shifted my weight from one foot to the other and looked up into his eyes.

"Just the way I like you." Jhett leaned down and playfully nipped at the tender flesh of my collarbone. I let out a soft but muffled moan next to his ear. "Keep doing that, and we're going to have to christen the bathroom…" he warned; which had the effect of making my legs practically give out underneath me before I pulled myself closer to him with more force.

"I'm not even going to argue with you this time. I'll do anything to keep from having to be alone with your sister…" A chuckle came from Jhett, which caused me to pull back away from him. "What? I'm serious." I threw my hands out in frustration.

"I know. Now go play nice and have fun. I'll have Danny drive me home when we're done." He swooped in for one more quick kiss before turning to go back to the kitchen.

I sighed as I mentally prepared myself for what was about to happen. Have fun? Who was he kidding? Make sure I come out with less scratches than her was more like it.

Irritation pulsed through my veins when I walked up the steps to the door of Jhett's house. Ginger was supposed to be there waiting for me, but in true Ginger fashion, she was nowhere to be found. She would probably end up strolling through the door in an hour or two, and try to act like *I* was the one who was late.

Once inside, I shut the door and tossed my keys and purse onto the table in the foyer. In a way, I was thankful for the change of plans. This meant that I might actually get a much needed nap in. Reaching in the fridge, I grabbed a bottle of water, when a sound from one of the rooms down the hall left me frozen in fear.

Panic quickly spread throughout my body. Someone was in the house. It was my worst nightmare. Frantically, I searched the kitchen for the closest sharp object, producing a butcher knife from the block on the counter. I held my breath as I crept on my tiptoes down the hall.

Another boom caught me off guard. It came from 'my' room. I hadn't spent much time in there since I moved in, because things with Jhett escalated pretty quickly. I reached for the doorknob with one hand and raised the knife above my head with the other. Squeezing my eyes shut with hope that I could figure out how to defend myself, I flung the door open with my shoulder.

"DON'T MOVE! I HAVE A KNIFE!" I shouted into the dim room. My adrenaline spiked so high, I could have been one of those people who tossed cars around with one hand. I scanned the room furiously before my eyes landed on a small, shadowy frame in the corner.

"Seriously? That's what you would do if someone broke in? *'Don't move. I have a knife.'*" Laughter spilled out from the mocking figure that stood in front of me. I was so scared and confused that it was difficult to focus. I just stood there stupidly with my mouth to the floor. "Okay, let's just put this knife away before you hurt someone, Rambo."

I blinked, trying to make sense of what happened. "HANNAH!" I slammed the knife down flat on the dresser and tackle-hugged her, causing both of us to fall backwards onto the bed. "How did you -? Why are you -? Heavens to Betsy, I almost killed you!" I shrieked. I didn't realize how much I missed her until she was next to me.

"I highly doubt you could've done *anything* to me with that knife. As for how and why – apparently you've got a birthday coming up and I'm your early present," she beamed, bouncing her shoulders up and down in excitement. There were so many more questions I wanted to ask her, but none of them mattered. I finally had my best friend with me. Life couldn't get any better.

We settled onto the bed, folding our legs under us as we sat across from one another like we were back in high school. I tried to go over everything since the moment I stepped off the plane. Hannah heard most of it already, but she demanded a play-by-play with no details left to the imagination. A week or so had passed since we talked, and now I knew why. Hannah was horrible at keeping secrets. She definitely would have let this one slip.

"You're joking. I can't believe she would do something like that. It just doesn't add up." She tried to figure out the story about Ginger and the bonfire.

"What about her is confusing you? She's batshit crazy." Maybe I was over-exaggerating, but she wasn't on my nice list at the moment.

"Because *she's* the one who called me and bought my ticket out here. She even picked me up from the airport and dropped me off. She said you were feeling homesick, and since it was almost your birthday she wanted to surprise you." Hannah's bright eyes shone under her chestnut bangs. I couldn't tear myself away from the sincerity in them.

"That *doesn't* make any sense...." My mind worked in overdrive as it tried to put everything together. Maybe Ginger wasn't so bad after all. "I still don't know..." I trailed off in thought.

"What's there to know? I'm here in sunny California with you while you're shacked up with some hot Adam Levine look-a-like, and you're *happy*. I've been your friend for as long as I can remember, and I don't think I've ever seen you like this. You're glowing, girl." She grabbed my hand and pulled me up off the bed to spin me around. I couldn't help the giddiness I felt at her being there, so I happily obliged. "Now where's this hot hunk of man meat?" She peeked her head out the bedroom door, as if anyone else were there to see us, and took a look around before dragging me back down the hall towards the kitchen.

I choked at Hannah's comment. "Um, first of all his name is *Jhett*, and he's still down at the restaurant, working. When I left he said he would have his friend drop him off later." We made an abrupt stop at the end of the hall.

Hannah looked around with wide eyes. "I saw this place when I first got here, but jeez, it's like a schizophrenic hippie lives here. Are you sure he's a musician?" She laughed to herself as she walked around the counter in the middle of the kitchen, letting her hand run along the edges.

"This is just so crazy to me, Charlie. You know, your mom and dad are really ticked at you. They've only told my parents where you are. Everyone else thinks you're at some elite summer program for college. I mean that's how you know you're on their shit list – they're lying to the country club about you!" She finally made her way into the living room and flopped down on the couch.

I decided to ignore her comments about my parents. I was simply too happy to let them rain on my parade from over two-thousand miles away. "So how long are you staying? Tell me you'll be here for my birthday. Jhett keeps trying to convince me that we need to have a party, but I really just want to have a nice dinner. Wait until you try Jhett's cooking. Oh my gosh, Hannah, you've never had anything like his food before." I went on giddily and settled down onto the couch across from her.

"Well, you're stuck with me for the next week and a half.

And you can bet your sweet ass we're having a party. My best friend only turns twenty-one once." I gave her an unenthusiastic look. "Well okay, party pooper, you don't have to drink - but I sure as hell will. When in Rome, do as the Romans do, right?"

I bit my lip to keep from laughing. "Whatever tickles your pickle, Hannah." I put my arms behind my head while Hannah made herself at home and found the remote. She turned on the TV, flicking through the channels until she stopped on some wedding show. I rolled my eyes; thankful she couldn't see my sassy gesture.

I couldn't believe this was all Ginger's idea. A pang of guilt hit me harder than I expected. As much as I didn't want to, I needed to tell her thank you. I debated with myself for a few seconds before I pulled out my phone and sent her a text.

Thank you for my birthday present. It was perfect.

I left it short and sweet, knowing that I could go into detail with her later.

"Everything okay?" My breathing picked up when my nerves rose. Nothing ever got past Hannah.

I nodded to her reassuringly before she rolled over and returned her attention back to the TV. It didn't take long until that familiar heavy feeling weighed down my eyelids. As much as I tried, I just couldn't fight it anymore.

"She sure is cute when she sleeps."

"Mmhmm. I could watch her all night."

"Good God. Yeah, like *that's* not creepy at all. Does she

actually buy into that stuff?"

Their voices made themselves known before I could open my eyes. I moaned internally, thinking about Hannah and Jhett meeting for the first time while I was knocked out. "Yes, I do. I think it's sweet, creeper. How long have I been out for?" I asked as I stretched out. Hannah was perched at my feet and Jhett sat on the arm on the couch, his arms folded across his chest, looking down at me with a smile that could melt my insides.

"Well, Hannah and I have been able to chat and start dinner....so I'd say at least two hours." Jhett got up and slipped in next to me, letting me head rest of one of his legs.

"Are you serious? I didn't even do that much today." I glared at Hannah. "Why'd you let me fall asleep? I have so much I want to do with you. And, hey – wait - why are you not freaking out that Hannah is in the living room?" I questioned Jhett as I looked up at him.

Jhett pulled his shoulders up in a shrug. "I may or may not have known about it...."

"So you knew that Ginger planned this whole thing...?" I raised my eyebrow at him, hoping that he had some answers.

"I did. I told you she wasn't one-hundred percent evil. She honestly felt bad about what happened, and she wanted to make sure that your best friend was here for your birthday. I only pointed her in the right direction. She may not be good at saying she's sorry, but she really did try hard to make it right in her own way," Jhett explained, giving Hannah a slight nod. She smiled at him from her spot on the couch. She was just as dazzled by Jhett as I was when I first met him.

I caught a whiff of dinner that made me shoot straight up. "Are you making what I think you're making?" I asked Jhett, grabbing onto his t-shirt with both hands like an eager child.

He pursed his lips together. "Mayyybe. This is a night for celebrating. Not only is Hannah here, but we can officially open our doors at the restaurant on July fourth." Jhett beamed from ear to ear with pride.

The excitement was too much for me; I couldn't hold myself back any longer. I threw my arms around Jhett's neck and covered his entire face, including his lips, with short and sweet kisses. "Jhett! That's so exciting. It's actually happening."

"Yeah, that is something I will *never* get used to seeing…" Hannah interjected from outside the happy bubble Jhett and I created.

I kept my arms around Jhett and scoffed at her. "She's just jealous because I was forced to deal with her doing this to every guy and their uncle for years." I stuck my tongue out at her. "Now, I'm ready for some 'Kill Ya Spaghetti and Meatballs'!" I jumped up with Jhett's hand in mine and ran over to the kitchen, lifting up the lid to the sauce. I dipped my finger in and tasted it.

"'Kill Ya Spaghetti and Meatballs'?" Hannah asked as she followed behind us.

"Charlie named it that because it's pretty spicy, and if you eat too much too fast, it'll damn near kill ya," Jhett chuckled while checking on the meatballs in the oven.

"Sooo…speaking of birthdays, I'm with you on this one, Jhett. She needs a party. And we've only got," Hannah paused, looking at her wrist where a watch would have been theatrically, "a few days to plan one before this fine piece of ass has her big day." She certainly was her over-dramatic self, and I knew she wouldn't let this birthday-thing go.

"I've told you both, *no party*. We can have dinner here, just the three of us. I'm completely fine with low-key. Believe me." I leaned my back against the kitchen counter. I was not ready to repeat the bonfire episode anytime soon.

Jhett kissed my forehead before turning towards the stove. "Maybe a low-key party would be okay?" He made the smart choice to avoid my evil stare.

"Really? Whose side are you on, here? Traitor." I playfully shoved his shoulder with a laugh.

"I'm not on anyone's side. I just think that we have a lot of reasons to celebrate, so why not have a party where we can celebrate all of them? And maybe we'll squeeze in a tiny happy birthday song in there somewhere?" He covered his face with his arms in an attempt to block any further punches from me. When I didn't answer him, he peeked out from behind his wrists. "I'll take the lack of violence as a maybe."

I let a deep breath out through my nose and threw my hands up in the air in frustration. Between the two of them, I knew I would never win. "Fine. We can have a non-birthday party with minimal birthday festivities. But that's it! Got it?" I raised an eyebrow at both of them to make myself clear.

Hannah was clearly amused, judging by the way she jumped and clapped like a seal. She once again got her way with only a little help from Jhett. That was just the start to a night filled with never ending laughter. We sat outside on the patio and enjoyed dinner. I couldn't help but take in the whole scene in wonder. This was it. This was the moment I sought out for as long as I could remember. All I wanted was to be happy and content with life, and sitting there on the patio, I knew I finally was. There was only one problem – it seemed that during every practically perfect moment in my life, there was always something that threatened to ruin it. But I wasn't ready to accept that fate for me this time. I changed so much in such a short amount of time; I thought that maybe I could remain this way.

Music began to trickle through the backyard. Hannah found the outside stereo system and led me out into the grass. The backyard was strung with white lights that draped above us, which illuminated the trees that grew in the corners of the yard. Jhett watched from the porch while Hannah and I jumped around to the beats on the radio. I was fixated on him while I danced; he always seemed to draw me in, no matter how far apart we were.

"Thank you," I mouthed to him. I knew Ginger wasn't the only reason why Hannah had come.

"You love him, don't you?" she whispered in my ear as our bodies still swayed in time to the beat.

Hannah's question caused a fire to rise through my toes and up into my chest. I never thought about what loving Jhett would be like. I only knew that I didn't want to find out what life was like without him.

"I knew it!" she accused me. My response was a short, knowing smile and nod in her direction. "He loves you, too, you know."

I turned to Hannah and searched her eyes; I wanted to find the truth to her theory. There was a longing in them that told me she was envious, which made me wonder - was she right?

TWENTY-FIVE

Charlie

I sat up from the sweaty towel beneath me and dug my toes into the hot sand under my feet. I could easily pick Hannah's laugh out of a crowd without even looking for her. She pranced in and out of the waves as they crashed down around her. She didn't look out of place for one second on the beach, with her naturally glowing skin and the caramel curls that cascaded down her back. She came prepared, practically packing enough bikinis for every day she stayed, and not one of them went to waste yet. With only a token reassurance from Jhett that they could handle getting the rest of the restaurant ready without my help, Hannah and I spent our days exploring the beach and the surrounding attractions.

I couldn't complain about the time off. I happily welcomed the vacation and the chance to have some real girl-time with Hannah. It was one thing to talk on the phone, but there was so much I missed about having her around in person. I also didn't mind the small feeling of home that accompanied her. I didn't realized how homesick I felt. It wasn't that I missed my family – I was happy being free from the restrictions and the smothering – but I missed the slow and steady pace of life.

As if reading my mind, Hannah emerged from the ocean, looking like she was stepped out of a movie scene. I was envious; somehow I always managed to look like a drowning puppy when I went into the water. She wrapped a towel around her shoulders and plopped down in the sand beside me, close enough to lean her head on my shoulder.

"You have that *look*. I don't like it. What's up, buttercup?" she asked, never moving from the spot on my shoulder as her wet hair soaked through my shirt. Instead of being concerned about it, we let the warm heat of the sun radiate down on us from high in the sky.

I had to give it to Hannah. She really knew me too well. "I was just thinking about how you being here has made me realize how much I've changed since I left Tennessee. You're like, the only little piece of home I can stand to be around. It's going to be weird if I go back." Apprehension began to swell in the pit of my stomach. This was a topic I tried so hard to push to the back of my mind, but I needed to think about it sooner or later.

Hannah jolted straight up, looking like an alert bloodhound. She was obviously intrigued by where the conversation was headed. "You're coming back? I definitely didn't think you were ever coming home, especially after seeing everything here with my own eyes. You're a completely different person, and I feel like I barely know you anymore – but in a good way. How are you going to just up and leave? You know your mom is still pretty miffed at you about the way things went down...." Her voice lowered; she knew what a tender spot my parents were for me.

"I just....I don't want to leave, not really. I know this is going to sound crazy, but I feel like I owe Cameron so much. I don't think I ever would've found the strength to do anything unexpected like this without him. I realize he's gone, but maybe he didn't die in vain. Maybe this was all part of some weird universal plan. Jhett told me how bad Cam wanted me to move out here, but I never would've before. I never had the drive to do anything outside of what I knew was expected of me, but the pain of losing him changed that. Now, even *I* don't know what to expect from me. It's like I'm finally free to do whatever I want, and I don't have to be scared anymore." I paused, letting the words that spilled from my lips sink in. I never got the chance to speak them out loud, not even to Jhett. I looked out into the water. "You know - I applied for a transfer to San Diego State University?"

Hannah gasped. "You *WHAT*?" She reached out and grabbed my face with both hands, turning it to make me look at her. "You're serious? Did you get in? What does Jhett think?" She dropped her hands and tucked them quickly under her chin, still fixated on me as she fired off her questions.

"Yes, I'm serious. No, I don't know if I got in. And I haven't told him yet. We have conveniently avoided the topic of me going back home when school starts again, since we first met. I just wanted to see if I would get accepted. It could change everything for me."

Hannah flung her arms around me without warning. "Charlotte Caroline Jennings – I've never been so proud of you. It's like watching my little baby bird grow up and fly away. I want nothing more than for you to be happy, and I think that means staying here. Look at everything you've got going for you. You're *going* to get into college here. You have somehow stumbled into the arms of a guy who is so madly in love with you, it's kind of sick, *and* he's opening this amazing restaurant that without a doubt will be successful, *and* he chose you to be by his side through all of this. Do I even have to *explain* what it is that you have waiting for you back in Tennessee?" She paused. "One set of pissed off parents and a miserable existence at some snotty-ass prestigious college. That's not you, Charlie, and it's never been you. You were made for so much more than that. Cameron saw it – we all saw it. The only person who didn't see it was you." Her hands remained on my shoulders as she stared into my eyes; her own reflected back with the truth of her words.

Hot tears threaten to spill down my face. I knew in my heart that everything she said was true, but hearing them come from her made it a reality. It was my turn to bring her in for an embrace. "Thank you, Hannah. I don't know where I would be without you by my side. You couldn't have come to visit at a more perfect time. Thank you so much." I bit my lip, making sure not to turn myself into a blubbering mess of emotions.

"Good riddance, girl. I didn't expect so much of this mushy crap today. I love you. You love Jhett. Let's all eat, drink, and be merry." She winked at me as she chucked her towel off her body and onto the sand behind her.

Hearing the words 'Jhett' and 'love' in the same sentence again made my pulse race. I've never been in love with anyone before. Lust, maybe, but definitely not love. This was new and different and somewhat scary.

Before I could let my mind wander anymore, Hannah pulled me up and towed me behind me down the sandy path and into the water, leaving me no room to argue. I honestly didn't mind swimming through the salty waves. I was thankful for the chance to act like a kid again; we splashed each other and screamed as the waves knocked us down. It had been forever since I got to have this much fun with Hannah, and I wasn't quite ready for it to be over just yet.

"SHHHH!" Jhett lifted his finger up to my lips to try and suppress my laughter. I still wasn't used to the idea that there was another set of ears in the house. Jhett and I were soaking wet after our shower, neither one of us taking a chance to dry off from our escapades before he chased me into the bedroom and left me in a fit of post-ecstasy giggles.

I nipped at his finger playfully. "Maybe if you didn't do things like *that* in the shower I wouldn't have to be shushed!" I threatened him as I climbed under the soft sheets of the bed. He followed behind me and we soon found the familiar grooves that were made just for each other, as I wedged myself up next to his side. There was no greater feeling than being in Jhett's arms at the end of the day.

"You've been asking for that since you left this morning. Don't act like you didn't like it." He leaned down and planted a sweet kiss on my forehead. "I know you're having fun with Hannah, but I'm going to have to steal you away for a night. Even though you said no making a fuss for your birthday, with all the craziness that will happen once we open, I want to make sure we get one night to ourselves before it all starts. I guess what I'm asking is, can I have the pleasure of taking you out on a date this Thursday?" he asked.

I was lost in the love that shinned in his eyes. Maybe

Hannah knew what she was talking about. "You're asking me out on a date? Like a real, get-dressed-up-and-go-someplace-fancy date? And on my actual birthday, at that?" I realized how ridiculous I sounded, but I didn't care. I could think back to the plenty of times we went out together, but I guess none of them could be considered an official `date', since we ended up doing things a little out of order.

Jhett's now-famous smirk spread across his lips. "Yes, like a *real* date. I'll even wear a suit for you, but you have to find something equally as smashing to wear." His eyes began to burn with desire at the mention of me getting dressed up.

"I think I can manage to clean myself up for you. But, you *do* realize that it's the day before opening night, right? You won't have stuff you need to finish up?" I finally settled my head back down against his chest; the soft beat of his heart echoing in my ear and soothing my soul.

"We were cleared to open during the inspection today. The only thing left to do is wait." I could hear the pride in his voice, making my heart swell in my chest.

"So does this mean I'll finally get to find out the name? It's been torture not knowing. I don't get why it's such a big deal to keep it a secret," I pouted, and let my hand explore the soft skin of his bare chest.

"It just is. You'll find out before everyone else, anyway. You have to be patient." His voice shuddered when I started to blaze a trail of kisses from his waist, up his chest, and to his lips.

"I hate being patient. Distract me," I demanded. My craving for him was already far too intense to control myself. Jhett didn't need any further prodding. I already knew he was fighting himself about going in for round two, and he loved to use my need for him to push me over the edge.

TWENTY-SIX

Charlie

It didn't matter how long I stood and looked in the mirror before me, there was no way I knew the person staring back at me. Hannah kicked Jhett out of our room for the afternoon while she tweezed, poked, prodded, and painted me up for my date tonight. She outdid herself.

"You're gorgeous, Charlie. Jhett's not going to know where to keep his hands when he sees you." She stood behind me, beaming with obvious pride at her work.

The way the butterflies flew around in my stomach, I thought I might have regressed back into a teenager again. Jhett and I slept together – hell, we lived together - so why did tonight feel so different?

I gave myself another hard look from head to toe. Hannah insisted she come with me to pick out my dress, which ended up being an adventure in itself. It took about three hours to convince her that I didn't want to look like I was going to prom, nor did I want to look like Malibu Barbie. In typical girl fashion, I made up my mind on what I was going to wear before I fell asleep the previous night. That was the easiest part of this whole thing.

I smoothed my hands down the front of the perfectly

pressed fabric that fell from my waist and down over my hips. Black polka dots danced across the red cotton that clung to every curve of my body. My long, golden hair was pinned up in rolls on top of my head, while the rest was left to fall in soft curls down my back. Hannah painted my eyes and cheeks with minimal make-up, but my fire engine red lips were the real game changer.

"I look like I stepped straight out of the fifties…" I whispered under my breath in amazement.

"I believe that was the point, genius," Hannah spouted off. The soft ring of my phone on the bed next to her caught our attention. She cautiously looked from the screen to my face. She scooped the phone up and handed it to me. "It's your Dad…"

I heard Hannah when she said who it was, but the white letters on the screen weren't registering in my brain. We hadn't spoken since I left. I never ever gave them my new phone number. My mind swirled with questions. With every once of courage I could produve, I slid my finger across the screen and brought it up to my ear.

"Happy Birthday, Baby Girl." His warm voice was just like I remembered.

"Dad? How did you get this number?" My limbs shook from the cocktail of emotions that ran through me. I was scared he was upset, but also elated that he put aside his pride and called. *That made one of us.*

"You know your mother has her ways, but she doesn't know I'm calling you right now. I just couldn't let a birthday go by and not talk to my favorite daughter, no matter what the circumstances may be." He spoke in a hushed tone, and I envisioned him tucked away in his office, away from my mom and her super-sonic hearing.

"Dad...Thank you. I'm sorry about-" He cut me off. I was silently relieved.

"Don't do that. I didn't call to talk about that. You do what you have to do, but know that I love you. No matter what, you will always be my one and only baby girl. Enjoy your birthday, Charlotte."

The conversation ended just as quickly as it started. I gripped my phone in my hand as it fell down to my side. Hannah's forehead was creased with worry. I flopped down next to her on the bed. "He just wanted to wish me a Happy Birthday..." It was the only coherent sentence I could form.

Hannah took my hand. "It's because you're the soft spot in his heart. He could never stay mad at you when we were kids, either." She bounced off the bed, taking me with her as she moved. She stood me up straight to admire her work one last time. "Tonight is *your* night, so be happy you got to talk to your dad...but don't forget there's a gorgeous man waiting for you in the other room."

I missed Hannah's pep talks. She was right; there was no reason to pout over a good phone call like that. I just needed to remember that next time, it was *my* turn to be the adult and call home. Until then, I had a date to go on.

"Chop, chop. Don't want you to be late and have your gorgeous dress turn back into rags at the stroke of midnight," Hannah teased, pushing me towards the bedroom door once she was satisfied I was finished with my self pity party.

I walked out into the hall with timid steps. Before I made it past the wall and into the open area of the kitchen and living room, I stole one more glance behind me to Hannah. "Happy birthday." She blew me a kiss and then sprinted across the wood floors and into the other bedroom.

I sucked in a deep breath through my nose, and stepped out into the open space. Jhett leaned against the arm of the couch, fidgeting with something in his hands. Fire ignited in his eyes when he looked up, eyeing my body me up and down.

"Charlie, you're…Wow…You look absolutely stunning." He closed the gap between us and scooped me up around my waist, pulling me up off the floor into him. My feet kicked as they dangled in the air.

I let out a satisfied squeal before he set me back down on the ground. His hand found mine, and he lifted them above our heads, giving me a tiny push with his free hand. "Spin for me," he told me. I did as he asked, turning on my toes under his grasp like a little girl. When I was done, I looked up at him through my eyelashes, giddy with nerves. Jhett remained silent next to me.

"Well? Are you going to say something, or are we just going to stand in the living room all night in silence?" I teased, as he dropped our hands and snaked his arms around my back once more.

"Charlie, don't get me wrong, you are *the* most gorgeous woman I've ever laid eyes on, especially in this vintage get-up. But tonight, I'm in awe that you would even go anywhere with me. In fact, I'm beginning to question whose birthday this really is, because I would love to unwrap you like a gift of my own right now." He leaned in, painfully slow, before planting a soft and tender kiss on my cheek.

"Well, you don't look too far off from the fifties yourself there. You look…*sexy*. Is this how you got all the girls to fall in love with you on tour?" I motioned with my hands, following up and down the length of him.

Jhett's eyebrow raised just enough to match the smirk on his lips. "Why? Is that what's happening to you?"

I pursed my lips. It was my turn to give him the once-over. I took a few steps back, as he mimicked the same pirouette he made me do. He wore a dark grey, long sleeve button down shirt with a black vest on top, black pants with the trademark cuffs on the bottoms, and a pair of black Chucks to complete the look. But it was his hair, slicked back into a pompadour that made my heart melt. "I haven't started screaming your name and crying yet, so I think I'm safe for now." I reached for the clutch that Hannah picked out for tonight, so that I wouldn't have to wear my shoulder bag.

"We have all night to try and change that." He winked at me as I followed behind him and walked through the front door to his truck. He insisted that we not take the Jeep, just for the night. I learned not to argue when he had his heart set on doing things his way, and tonight was all him.

Jhett opened the door to the truck for me, and I managed to jump in fairly gracefully considering the amount of fabric I wore. I scooted across the leather seat and into the middle, so that I could ride next to him. That small feature was my favorite thing about the truck; I took every chance I could to be close to him.

Jhett filed in next to me seconds later and situated himself, letting the engine roar to life. Without warning his hand went to my cheek as he guided my face towards him; his lips met mine with a hunger neither of us could deny. He pulled away first, leaving me to bite my lip. Tonight felt like we were experiencing every first all over again. It was strange and enticing, and I got a feeling that Jhett's actions had something to do with it.

"What was that for?" I asked, my hand finding its way to his, our fingers lacing together as I tried to hide the smile that I couldn't make disappear.

"Because after this, you're going to be mad at me." I gave him a questioning look, but he left me no time to argue. "You have to close your eyes until I give you the okay to open them." My mouth fell to the floor. "Just trust me, babe, okay?"

I pouted for a few moments before relenting and squeezing my eyes shut. "Okay, but only because I *do* trust you." I wiggled my back against the seat behind me as the truck started to reverse.

"Good. No peeking!" Jhett said before we arrived our destination. I tried to pay attention to which way we were going, but after a few turns, I was completely and utterly lost. I had absolutely no clue where we ended up. I did trust Jhett, but the fact that I really was in the dark for what he had in store killed me. Even Hannah didn't know what he had up his sleeve, which meant that Jhett really wanted to keep it a secret.

"Only a few more minutes until you can open your eyes, I promise. I'm going to be right back, but you *have* to keep your eyes shut. I'm just warning you, there will be severe punishments if I catch you peeking." Jhett laughed at his own words and slammed the truck door shut, leaving me alone in the silence of the night.

It was only mere seconds before the passenger door opened and Jhett's voice drifted into my ears. "Ready, birthday girl?" There was something about not being able to see him when he spoke in his low, husky tone that made everything feel more intense.

His hand grabbed mine once more, pulling me to the edge of the seat and helping me down out of the truck. "I don't know how you managed to convince Hannah to let me get out of a normal drunken twenty-first birthday. You must have used your charm on her, because there is no other way possible that I could have escaped that." Jhett placed my arm on his own, my hand grabbing onto the inside of his elbow as he led me to what sounded like a doorway.

Even though I couldn't see him, I knew the playful grin that danced across his face. "Yeah, it was something like that. And besides, there's always tomorrow night at the grand opening. You know she wouldn't let you get off that easy." Mentally I rolled my eyes. He was right. But at least I got one night of relaxed celebration. Jhett steered me into a quiet room as the doors shut behind us with a loud clang of metal.

He withdrew from my side; the lack of his warmth created an eerie feeling as I stood by myself in a room I couldn't place. Just as soon as he left my side, I felt him behind me again, his arms lying softly on top of mine around my stomach. "You can open your eyes now..." Jhett whispered into my ear; sending a rush of goose bumps to flutter down the right side of my body.

My eyes eagerly blinked open, taking me a few seconds to adjust to the dull lighting. I looked around as my breath caught in my throat. I knew where we were. It was hardly recognizable in its current state. There were candles placed all around us, which cast shadows on the tables and chairs that were pushed to the sides, leaving just enough room for the extra large blanket that laid in the middle of the room. My hands darted up to my mouth in surprise as I turned in Jhett's embrace to face him. "The restaurant? I had no idea. It looks so different like this. It's soo…"

"Romantic? Charming? Bad ass?" He asked, looking down at me with a satisfied grin. I could only answer with a few quick nods. "Good - that's what I was going for, because tonight, I get to break in the equipment and we get to enjoy the first meal ever served here together." Jhett beamed with pride as he spoke. "Are you hungry? Because I've got a few recipes in the works that I've been saving for tonight."

"I'm starving." I laughed. He wasted no time as he dragged me into the kitchen, flicked on a few lights and other knobs on the grill, and gathered the ingredients he needed out of the massive silver fridge that sat in the corner. He set out a chair for me behind him, leaving only the back of him in view while he worked his magic with our dinner. There was something about watching him do what he enjoyed that made him even more attractive than he already was.

We sat in a comfortable silence while Jhett cooked; stopping only to ask me a few questions before turning around and engulfing himself back in his work. The aroma that filled the restaurant was beyond a tease to my stomach. I made mental guesses as to what Jhett was going to present me with, but every time he added a new ingredient, a different idea popped into my head. Even while cooking, he kept me on my toes.

All at once, Jhett clicked off all the knobs on the grill and turned to face me. "I'll meet you in the other room in a second. We're eating picnic-style on the blanket." He flashed me a sly wink and he turned his back on me once more.

Reluctantly I followed his directions, passing through the hall before finding my way to the blanket. I giggled at myself as I struggled to find an easy way to sit down. I wasn't used to wearing such poufy dresses, and the girls I saw wearing them before certainly made it look a lot easier than it was. I settled for shifting my legs to the side next to me, and let the red fabric fall around me on all sides.

Jhett's footsteps crept up behind me. He appeared with a plate in each hand, skillfully bending down and sitting on the blanket beside me. Reaching over, he placed a plate in front of each of us. Before me was the juiciest, most mouth-watering burger and skinny French fries I witnessed.

"Here - don't forget this, too." Jhett pulled out two champagne glasses from the basket behind him, and I took one from his hand when my nerves finally settled in. I didn't want a "normal' twenty-first birthday because I was scared I wouldn't be able to stomach any alcohol. Jhett's face dropped when he noticed my panicked expression. "Do you really think I don't listen to you? You said no alcohol, so I got us something even fancier." I narrowed my eyes, watching him intently as he produced a celadon-colored bottle. I recognized it from when I was younger – sparkling apple cider. As he filled both our glasses, the butterflies returned in the pit my stomach. Jhett did listen, and obviously planned this night for quite some time. He was impressive.

He held his glass up in front of him as if to propose a toast, and nodded at me to follow suit. I brought mine up to meet his, making sure to never take my eyes off of his. There was something different behind them tonight that I couldn't quite pinpoint. "Happy birthday, Charlie. Thank you for letting me steal you away from Hannah for one night to come out on a date with me. Thanks for taking a chance on me. I know how hard it was for you to trust me, but you've put the light back into my life. I only hope one day you realize what a beautiful woman you are – inside and out." Jhett took a deep breath in through his nose. "Cheers." He clinked the edge of his glass with mine.

"Cheers," I responded, and took a sip of the cider. I smiled as I swallowed the chilly, bubbly liquid down my throat, and Jhett's words swam around in my mind. There was so much I wanted to tell him. I wanted to tell him exactly how I felt, tell him I was falling in love with him, and that I wanted to stay and never go back to Tennessee. That even though the spot in my heart for Cameron would never be fully healed, he eased that pain and gave me the courage to be the woman he saw before him.

"Are you going to try your burger? This is one of the specials I created with you in mind. I want you to taste it before I tell you what's in it." His words interrupted my thoughts, but his child-like eagerness made him easy to forgive. Noting in the world existed right now, except for what was happening between the two of us.

I raised an eyebrow at him in question. "Well I know it's not spaghetti, so now I'm curious…" I picked up the massive burger with both hands before taking an enormous bite. Egg yolk dripped down the sides of my lips as I chewed a mouthful of bacon, egg, avocado, cheese, and meat. I stifled a giggle as I used the back of my hand to wipe my mouth. "A breakfast burger? This is perfect. What did you make for yourself?" I glanced over at his plate while I devoured the rest of my meal.

He took a bite of his own burger, chewing before he spoke. "A 'Bring the Heat' burger - Hot sauce, bleu cheese, and some bacon. You know I like spicy things." His grin instantly made my stomach tighten. The rest of the night was going to be trouble – I could feel it. It was already difficult for him to keep his hands off me before we even made it to the restaurant. There was only one difference about tonight – I wasn't going to stop anything that happened. It was my birthday, and I was ready for a little celebration.

We finished the rest of our meal, joking and laughing with the easy-going banter that I enjoyed between us. Jhett cleaned up our plates and disappeared back into the kitchen. "You ready for dessert?" he called from behind me before he came around the corner singing Happy Birthday. In his hands he held a much larger than normal cupcake, complete with a single lit candle sticking out of the top.

My heart pounded from sheer excitement. He took his place next to me on the blanket again, and held lowered the plate in front of me at eye level. "Time to make a wish…" Jhett spoke in a hushed voice.

I squeezed my eyes shut and held my breath as I ran through a list of ideas in my head before deciding on one very special wish: I wanted to stay this happy forever. I sucked a deep breath in, and blew the candle out in one quick exhale. Jhett placed the plate on the blanket next to us and gripped a small cupcake morsel in between his fingers. I knew what he wanted me to do. I leaned in toward him and opened my mouth just wide enough for him to slip the piece of cupcake inside my mouth.

My hand went up to my lips out of habit. "This night keeps getting better. This is the best cupcake I've ever tasted. And it's strawberry cake with white frosting? How'd you know this was my favorite?" I asked him, while scooping up a piece in my own fingers and holding it out toward him.

He leaned in the same way I did and took my fingers into

his mouth, sucking the cupcake and lingering frosting off with his tongue. "I can't take credit for making it – one of the best bakeries in town did. I do, however, remember you mentioning your love for strawberry cupcakes one night. I told you before, I *do* listen when you talk." He licked his lips while he watched me take another bite into my mouth.

"I never said you didn't listen. I'm just enthralled, that's all." His eyes were fixated on my lips as I spoke. I wiped the sides of my mouth nervously. "Is there something on my face?" I asked, mid-wipe.

"You've got a little...frosting..." He chuckled as he brought his hand up to my cheek and ran the gentle pad of his thumb over my now parted lips. He inspected his work and frowned. "I don't think I got it all..." His voice was a low growl as he leaned in and kissed the corner of my lips; trailing feathery kisses at a teasingly slow place down to the center of my bottom lip, before sucking it all the way into his mouth. He nibbled on it softly while he tangled his hand into my hair and deepened the kiss. I was leaning into him, craving more of his touch with each second that passed.

Jhett brought his other hand up to my cheek, cupped my face with both hands, and broke the kiss. I let out an unexpected whimper as he drew my forehead in to his. "Any more of that, and we won't make it to the rest of your birthday presents," he said between breaths.

I sat back and folded my hands into my lap. "Well, if we get to do *that* again as one of them, I'm all about it," I smirked at him.

"Close your eyes," Jhett commanded. I groaned next to him, but followed his direction anyway. He shuffled around in the same basket that held the apple cider loudly. "Okay, open them."

Eagerly I opened my eyes and focused on Jhett sitting across from me, a tiny, opened grey jewelry box in his hand. Silence fell between us. The only noticeable noise was the sharp intake of our breath. My hand was drawn to the box like a magnet. Lifting the gold chain from its resting place on the velvet pillow, I held the necklace up to the light in front of me. A delicate gold seashell with a miniature pearl that hung in the center of it was attached to the chain.

I let out the air that was stuck in my lungs. "Jhett…" I finally formed the words that lingered on my tongue. "This is gorgeous. I'm just…speechless…" I tore my eyes from the necklace and back to him. "Thank you. Will you put it on me?" I asked, transferring the necklace into his hands and turning my back to him. I gathered the curls that lay down my back to easily expose the rest of my neck. He reached around me with both arms and draped the necklace so that it lay perfectly in the center of my chest.

Jhett didn't speak as he clasped the necklace together and let it drop on to my skin. My hair stayed gathered to the side and down the front of my chest as I let go to finger the seashell lying delicately on my neck. I never was particularly fond of jewelry, but there was something about this necklace that made me never want to take it off. Maybe it was the fact that it came from Jhett, or that it reminded me of so many things I had grown to love. Whatever it was, I wanted to stare at it for hours.

A soft pair of lips pressed to my neck, which caused my eyes to close in pure pleasure while I soaked up the entire moment. Jhett continued to trail down to my shoulder while he let his fingertips rake up and down my arms. My body shivered in response to his touch, lighting all of my nerve endings on fire. I leaned back into the arms I never wanted to leave, and felt his solid form press against me. My eyes met his. "Jhett...I...." I stumbled on my words. Why was this so hard? I knew what I felt in my heart, but I couldn't bring myself to say it.

TWENTY-SEVEN

Jhett

I held Charlie in my arms, the glow from the candlelight reflected off her necklace that draped around her neck. I wasn't one for romance, but I was willing to try and do anything for Charlie. That was the funny thing; the whole night was about her, but somehow, I felt like *I* was the lucky one. I knew it as soon as she stepped out of the bedroom in her dress. I was done for when it came to her. She could have asked me to give her the world, and I would've died trying.

She finally looked up at me through eyes that reflected the soft warmth of the candles that surrounded us. "Jhett...I...." She paused, obviously waiting for the right words to come to her. She was the picture of perfection, but the pause in between her words told me one thing – she wasn't ready to say those three words that I was dying to tell her all night. As much as I would have loved to hear them, I wanted her to be completely comfortable telling me on her own. Not because she felt like she should.

I put my finger up to her lips to stop the rest of her words from escaping. Her body relaxed in my arms and I knew that I made the right decision. Love was a funny thing, especially when it came too fast. There was no doubt in my mind of my feelings for her, but I never wanted her to think that I took advantage of hers.

She placed my hand in hers and brought it up to her mouth, leaving a quick kiss on the inside of my palm. "Does tonight really have to end? It's been absolutely perfect."

A grin crept over my lips. "Well, don't write it off as done just yet. We've still got one more place to be." I ignored the stunned expression on Charlie's face as she sat up and watched my every move as I grabbed my backpack from one of the tables and slung it over my shoulder. With quick steps I walked around the restaurant, stopping at each candle to blow them out.

When I was done, only the glow from the moon as it shone through the glass front of the restaurant illuminated the room. Charlie stayed still on the blanket, looking lost in her own mind. Her hand hadn't left the necklace since I put it on her. Just watching her made my heart race. "Time to go." I held my hand out to help her to her feet. She steadied herself and followed me out the doors and onto the sidewalk of the busy streets.

We waited at the corner of the busy intersection that the restaurant sat on for the light to change and we could cross the street. She slipped her hand in mine, and once again I was struck with awe that she was all mine. The night was cooler than usual, but still warm enough for us to make the trip down to the beach comfortably.

When we reached the concrete barrier, we both took off our shoes. There were only a few people that littered the end of the beach, mostly people walking back from dinner or walking to the bars for the night. I stepped out onto the gritty sand, looking back only to make sure that Charlie followed.

"The beach?" she asked, gingerly placing her feet onto the sand. "What are we going to do here? The sun already went down, so we can't possibly be watching the sunset…" She continued to rattle off ideas as to why we were there, but my mind was lost on what was coming up next. The plan sounded great in my head, but it all depended on her reaction. The end result could go either way – good or bad.

We walked until we were just a few feet above where the tide stopped in the sand. I knelt down and unzipped my backpack while Charlie stood in front of me, curiosity getting the best of her as she tried to peek down and investigate what I was doing. I pulled out another fresh blanket and laid it smoothly on the sand behind us. I shuffled through my bag once more, and produced out two white paper packages and a lighter that I stuffed into my back pocket.

Charlie watched me with growing suspense. "So I don't have to close my eyes for this surprise?" She bounced on her toes as she teased me.

"Only because for this one, you'll need to keep them open for the magic to work." I took one of her hands into mine and ran my fingers over her knuckles. "You haven't mentioned anything about it yet, but I want you to know, I didn't forget it's Cameron's birthday, too. He would be so proud of you. He's probably looking down and having a drink just for us. I didn't want you to think that you couldn't remember him tonight. He'll always be your twin brother." I watched Charlie's face for the slightest reaction. Her stare was intense, and she bit her lip, looking down when a timid smile teased the sides of her mouth.

I dropped her hand and expanded the two white paper lanterns, which resulted in a gasp from Charlie. I ignited them both with a flash from the lighter. "I don't know about you, but I never really got the chance to remember him the way I wanted to. And what better time to do it than on his birthday?" Charlie managed a short nod while she reached out and held onto one of the lanterns with a death grip. Turning my attention back to the one that remained in my hand, I slowly raised it into the air, letting it hover above us for a few seconds before releasing it onto its own path in the salty sea air.

"Happy Birthday Cam. I hope you're somewhere surfing the killer waves in Heaven. Just don't be waiting to kick my ass for dating your sister. You were right – she's beyond amazing. I miss you, buddy." I watched as the white light slowly disappeared into the night and Charlie wiped her cheeks with the back of her hand beside me.

"My turn?" she asked with a strain in her voice that made my heart ache. She was hurting. I tried to be the strong person she needed, and nodded at her to go on. Her shoulders rose with her chest and she took a deep breath in; closing her eyes as if she was having a silent conversation with herself. Eventually, she exhaled and let the lantern go. We both watched together while it drifted up into the sky. "Happy Birthday, big brother....I miss you so much. I swear not a day goes by that I don't think of you, wondering if I'm making you proud, if you'd be happy with the person I'm becoming. I wish you were here with me right now. There are so many things we didn't get to do. But I promise, I won't let you down. I hope you know that I'm finally happy with the way things are going. It kills me that you can't be here to be a part of that, but I finally have someone by my side that pushes me, just like you did. It's weird how alike you guys are sometimes, but you already knew that. Anyway…I love you, Cameron. I'm so sorry…" Tears rolled down her face when she finished.

It only took me to turn my body toward her before she buried herself in my arms, tucking her cheeks against my chest. I said a silent prayer that this wouldn't end in the way I dreaded. I pulled her closer to me as she sobbed, her whole body convulsing with each breath. The guilt that lingered inside me tried to push its way to the surface as she clung to my shirt. There was always the thought that somehow, this was all my fault. I caused all of her pain. I wanted to tell her that I should be the one who was sorry, but there are just some things that words can't explain.

I ran my hand into her hair, and tipped her head up towards mine. Leaning down, I kissed the spots of flesh where her tears remained. "You're too beautiful tonight to cry."

Pink rose to the surface of Charlie's cheeks and she looked away from me; a slight smile tracing her flushed lips. "I'm not upset, I promise. Overwhelmed, but not upset. I'm just beyond thrilled that you remembered Cameron. I've been trying to pretend like I could be strong and not let it ruin this beautiful night you made for me, but he's always there in my head." She finally looked up and pressed her lips to mine, leaving a tinge of salty tears when she pulled back. "I can't thank you enough for everything, Jhett. This has honestly been the best birthday ever." Her hands moved to her necklace once more, contentment rising inside me that she was happy.

"You don't have to thank me. I only wanted you to feel special. But I am glad that you liked your gifts. I noticed you couldn't keep your hands off of this one." I took the golden shell in my palm while Charlie beamed up at me.

Grasping my hand, she pulled me to the blanket, waiting for me to sit before climbing onto my lap and straddling her legs around my waist; her face just inches from mine. "It's just that no one has ever gave me a gift like that before. It's so…personal. But you didn't tell me why the seashell and pearl?" Her hands absentmindedly played with the collar and buttons of my shirt.

"You're going to make me tell you the whole sappy meaning behind it, aren't you?" I asked her. Her breath was warm on my neck.

"Uh huh. Down to every…last…detail." Charlie ran her fingers up my chest and down my back, essentially making me putty in her hands.

I sighed as I thought about the true meaning behind the necklace. "You've got a beach lover's soul, Charlie. You may not be from here, and you might not even stay here, but it's in you, just like it was in Cameron. I don't want you to forget that piece of you. So now you can always have a little bit of it with you, no matter where your heart takes you." I held in my breath while I waited for her reaction. We never brought up what would happen in the future – if she would stay here or go back home.

Charlie leaned back as she adjusted herself in my lap, gripping my shoulders with her hands. "You mean when I have to go back home?" she asked, her eyebrows knit together with questions.

"We don't have to talk about it tonight. There's still time to figure things out. I just wanted you to have this." I picked the necklace up off of her chest one more time in an attempt to distract myself. All I really wanted to do was scream at her not to ever go back to Tennessee. This was her home now. But it was selfish to think that she would stay for me, because truthfully, I was scared as hell as to what I would do when she was gone.

"I'm sorry, Jhett. I don't want you to think I'm leading you on." I could feel Charlie's heartbeat speed up underneath my hands on her chest.

"Let's just save this conversation for another time. No more apologies tonight. There are only a few hours left until it's not your birthday anymore. We've got to make them count, right?" I lifted my hand under Charlie's chin. A coy smile danced across her face and put my worry at ease, at least temporarily.

"Are you trying to seduce me, Mr. Hudson? And right here on the beach in *public*?" She straightened her body up against mine, pushing her chest into me. I had been good all night, and now was not the time to play games with me.

"Don't act like you aren't enjoying this, Miss Jennings..." I let my hands roam down to the smooth curves of her ass, eliciting a high-pitched yelp of pleasure from her. The layers of clothing between us were enough to drive me insane. I needed to feel the warmth of her milky white body on mine. Brushing her hair away from her neck, I found the fabric that held the top part of her dress in place. All it took was one swift tug and the soft fabric fell down, exposing the tiniest piece of skintight fabric that kept her chest one step closer from being exposed.

She frantically covered the top half of her body with her hands. "Jhett! We can't do this here. There are people around," she exclaimed, fidgeting with the tie of her dress.

I looked around dramatically before tearing her hands away from the red fabric. "I don't see anyone....And right now, there's only a few more layers of clothes between me and what you've had me thinking about since the night began, and I fully intend to make that screaming happen." I could sense the urgency coming through my voice as I spoke, but the burning in her eyes told me that she felt the same way.

Without any more hesitation on Charlie's part, her hands went to work on my belt, letting it out just enough so that she could undo the button and zipper of my pants with ease. I loved when she was like this. She was no longer the nervous girl I met a few months ago. She was the woman who wanted me just as much as I wanted her.

I laid back against the blanket in the sand, lifting my hips with little prompting from Charlie as she wiggled my pants off my hips and down my legs. I couldn't stand one more second of her being so far away from me. Sitting up, I grabbed her by the hips and pulled her back on top of me, the ends of her dress flowing around us. She snatched my wrists and brought them up above my head like I often did to her, and laid her body on top of mine.

Her mouth crashed down on my own; the hunger we had for each other was never more intense. I wanted to taste every inch of her mouth as her tongue slid in and out of mine. I couldn't get enough of her sweet flavor. She pulled back just long enough to flash me one of her enticing lip-biting smiles, before she dipped back down and found the spot right under my ear; biting it softly.

This time it was my turn to let out a moan of pleasure. I fought my hands loose from her grip and reached under her dress to the soft flesh of her thighs, digging my nails into the curves I wanted so badly to be exposed. My hand ran around the side of her hip and up the inside of her leg, seeking out the last piece of fabric that stopped me from being inside her…but found only the soft folds of her skin.

"No panties?" I asked her, as she sat up and let out a soft giggle. She didn't need words to respond. Instead, she lifted herself up slightly before easing herself down onto me. I pushed the stray curls of hair behind her ear. "God, you're beautiful," I whispered to her, as the moonlight shone down and illuminated her body in all the right places.

She rocked her hips against mine, our eyes locked together as we moved in sync with one another. She let out a raspy moan and fell against my chest, while her hands held on to the back of my neck. The entire time, I felt like I was watching it happen to someone else. I was never more in awe, or in love, with Charlie.

Her breath was hot and sticky against my cheek as she rocked faster against me. In between her moans she left damp, sweaty kisses along my jawline. "I love you," she finally whispered into my ear, and I felt her body give way as she entered into her own world of passion.

Her words were all I needed to send me over the edge. "I love you, too, Charlie," was all I could manage between my ragged breaths as I turned myself over to the ecstasy she brought me.

I wasn't sure how long we laid like that, Charlie on top of me; neither of us wanted the moment to end. When her breathing eventually mellow out, she let herself fall against my side and rested her head on my chest. I managed to slip my pants back on quickly enough to still enjoy the feeling of passion that lingered in the air from the words that we exchanged.

"Did you really mean it?" Charlie finally broke the silence, her voice quiet and shaky.

I pulled her closer to me, still craving as much contact with her as possible. "I've never meant anything more in my life. Those aren't words I just throw around loosely," I told her.

"Good. Because you're the first guy to ever hear them from me." She gave my hand a gentle squeeze.

"I wouldn't change that for the world, Charlie." A smile she would never see spread across my face. I looked out into the sky, thanking all my lucky stars for bringing her to me.

TWENTY-EIGHT

Charlie

The faint sound of laughter drifted over me and I stretched my leg up and over Jhett's. Reflexively, he wrapped me tighter in his arms, tucking me closer into him. I wasn't ready to get up and have last night officially come to an end.

The laughter returned, only this time, it sounded as if it were right next to us. In an attempt to shield my eyes from the sun, I rolled over onto my elbow, using my other hand to block out the light. I saw two pairs of tiny, sandy feet before I looked up and took in the giggling little girls staring down at us.

"Holy Hell, Jhett! Wake up!" I flipped around, completely ignoring the girls. I clutched the top of my dress to my chest and tried to quickly tie the back into a messy knot before turning my attention to Jhett, shaking him in a panic. Jhett shot up like a bat out of hell, blinking the sleep from his eyes and startling the two girls, causing them to run away in a continued fit of laughter. What a show we must put on.

Jhett's panic didn't let up as he took in his surroundings. He pulled his backpack to him and began to rifle through it. Watching him made my heart practically beat out of my chest; half from panic, and half from the memories of last night that came back to me in a flood of emotions. Finally, he sat back and let out a sigh of relief. I was still frozen as I stared at him with wide eyes.

I fell apart at the seams when he finally looked up. The ridiculousness of the whole situation caught up to me, and I couldn't hold back the nervous laughter anymore. Jhett's features finally relaxed and he joined me, pulling me back next to him.

"I can't believe we actually fell asleep on the beach! I feel like we may be a part of a romantic comedy or something. This just had to happen to us." I wiggled my body between Jhett's bent legs, resting my elbows on his knees. "Oh my God! We've got to get moving. The grand opening is tonight, and we *still* have so much stuff to do." I twisted my body so that I faced him and sat back on my heels while my dress spilled around me.

"You know what?" He paused to wait for my reaction. "I love you."

Even though we both said the same three words last night, hearing them again in the light of day made everything that much more real. "I love you, too. I don't think I'm ever going to get tired of you saying that." I pressed my lips to his for only a quick second, before rolling back on my heels and standing up. "But we really need to go home and get ready for tonight. And I'd rather not stick around and get caught by anyone else. Having those little girls as our personal wake-up call is something I prefer to never to experience again."

Jhett chucked to himself as we shook out the blanket and folded it up into his backpack. Together we walked the short distance back to the restaurant, hand-in-hand like we did last night. As we weaved in and out of the tourists and surfers, I let my thoughts get the best of me. Yesterday was a game changer for us, and eventually we were really going to have to talk about the future – if I would stay, or if I would go home to Tennessee at the end of summer.

Jhett stopped me when we reached the double doors. "Before we go in, I just want to say thank you for everything that you've helped out with around here. You didn't have to do anything, but I hope that you know how much I appreciate it. Now - go on so you can be the first person to step into 'The Voodoo Kitchen', since tonight we open."

A smile that matched Jhett's spread across my face. "Did you just tell me the name? Jhett! *The Voodoo Kitchen*? That's amazing. I love it!" I threw my arms around his neck and pulled myself as close to him as possible. Jhett's dreams were coming true, and I was perfectly happy to sit by and watch them happen, because I knew that when the time came, he would do the same for me.

"Seriously Hannah, we've got to go. We're not walking the freaking red carpet here." I hissed at her while I paced the length of the bed. As the time to head over to the restaurant drew closer, the more my anxiety grew.

"Shut your pie hole, Diva. You got to play dress up last night, and now it's my turn. Besides, if *someone* hadn't made love until all hours of the morning and then fell asleep on the beach like something out of *The Notebook*, we wouldn't be rushing to get ready, now would we?" She popped out of the bathroom entryway with her tongue stuck out, teasing me like always. She was practically ready – she wore an all black dress with a black lace panel that went from her chest, up and around her shoulders to her back, leaving a keyhole cut out down her lower spine. Her chestnut hair fell loosely around her face, but it was the red heels that pulled the whole look together. She could really put herself together.

"Just hurry up." I shouted at her, and then fell back onto the bed and began to stare a hole in the ceiling. I had my fair share of fancy dresses after last night, so I settled for something more comfortable – a strapless dress with red and white stripes across the top, and a knee-length navy blue bottom from the waist down. I even sucked it up and wore a pair of brown wedges after some persuasion from the fashion queen herself.

The bed shifted under Hannah's weight as she climbed next to me and let her face hover just inches above mine. "I'm ready, and you're just laying here relaxing? Jeez, you would think that you weren't excited to go to this shindig. At least *I* can be excited. Food, drinks, and a band? Seriously, who gets a better birthday present than that?" she asked, and then yanked me up off the bed.

My hands sought out my necklace. I could think of a few things better than this party, I thought to myself. "For the last time, this *isn't* a birthday party. It's to celebrate the grand opening of the restaurant. You agreed to that, remember?" I glared at her as I slung my purse over my head and onto my shoulder, letting it drop next to my hip.

Hannah shot back an equally sassy look, her lips pursing as we walked to the Jeep. Even though we were only a few blocks from the restaurant, Hannah insisted that we blast the radio the entire ride there. When 'Want U Back' by Cher Lloyd came on, I couldn't resist myself anymore. Screaming at the top of my lungs, Hannah and I sang every word in the most awful, off-key voices. But it didn't matter, because this was my happiness.

I pulled around to the back and parked close to the door, before throwing the keys in the glove compartment. From the sounds drifting out into the parking lot, it seemed like the party was already in full swing. I was right – we were late. Hannah jumped out of her seat and joined me around the back of the Jeep. I stalled before going inside.

Hannah ran her fingers over the fresh vinyl signs that now decorated the doors. "The Voodoo Kitchen? Nice name. Sounds like my kind of place. Now suck it up, soldier, and let's get inside and find that lover boy of yours." She winked at me, put her hand in mine, and dragged me behind her through the back door and down the hallway into the main room.

I definitely had a case of Déjà vu when I looked around the restaurant. There was a band set up on a makeshift stage at the front of the room, and I recognized a few people from the bonfire dancing in front of it. The rest of the room was full of people engrossed in their own conversations and eating an assortment of burgers and sandwiches – Jhett's specialties.

Hannah already wandered off and over to the dance floor. There was something about music that just drew that girl in. She couldn't turn down any song as long as there was a beat she could move to. I, on the other hand, was much more content to sit back and watch from afar. I scanned the room and my heart sank when my eyes fell on a head full of bouncy, bright red hair as she twirled around under the arms of a guy I didn't recognize. We still hadn't talked much since the bonfire. I knew I was going to have to be the bigger person and say something to her tonight. We couldn't ignore each other forever.

A pair of familiar arms encircled my body from behind. I inhaled deeply as I took in his woodsy smell and let all my worries fall into the back of my mind. We stood without exchanging any words, just watching everyone move around the room and enjoy themselves. Finally Jhett took my hand and spun me away from him, twirling me this way and that as I followed his lead. When he was done, he held my waist and dipped me backwards, with a satisfied look that spread across his entire face.

"Well, I'd say this turned out to be a success," I told him as he set me back down on my feet. "You look like you've got your work cut out for you tonight. There are lots of mouths to feed. Are you ready for that?" I teased, and playfully pushed his shoulder.

"Babe, I was born ready. But speaking of mouths to feed, I better get back there and finish helping out. Don't want anyone to jack up my cooking mojo while you're out here distracting me." He mimicked me by pressing a finger into my chest. "Now *you* go out and enjoy the party. Remember, it's half yours, too. If I see you moping around again, I'm going to sic Hannah on you before you have a chance to run away. I saw her out there dancing already." He swooped in for a kiss on the cheek, before turning his back on me and disappearing into the kitchen.

I decided to try and make the most out of the night and attempt to enjoy myself, instead of worrying about what birthday surprises Hannah might have planned. She was far too mischievous to simply let tonight be laid back like I wanted. I found her sitting in a booth with a few girls I was thankful I didn't know. She was mid-bite into a burger when she saw me and waved me over.

I slid into the booth next to her and stole a fry off her plate. She began to introduce me to the girls across from us, when something else caught my attention. Dressed in a skin-tight purple dress was Ginger, and she was headed straight for me. The anxiety rose in my throat. I changed my mind. I wasn't ready to be the bigger person.

"Hey Charlie. Do you mind if we talk for a second?" she asked, with a tinge of coyness in her voice.

I got up from the booth and followed her over to an empty space in the corner of the room. I bit my lip with anticipation and she fidgeted in her black heels. "I'm just going to say that I'm sorry. And I hope that you've been able to enjoy some time with Hannah. She's actually not the most terrible person on the planet." She shifted her weight and waited for my response.

I tried to choke back a snort of laughter. She may have liked Hannah because they were almost the same person, minus Ginger's super psycho split personality. "I forgive you. And thank you. You brought her out here at the perfect time." I hesitated to continue the conversation. The way her eyes darted back and forth as she swayed made me uneasy.

"Well...alright then..." She was gone in a flash, her heels clicking against the floor as she vanished into the crowd.

I stood in shock for a few seconds before Hannah's voice pulled me back into reality. She stood next to me and motioned toward the dance floor. "Did that look as weird as it felt?" I asked her.

"Um, yeah. That was beyond awkward. Let's never do

that again." She laughed as we made our way through the small crowd of people and to the front of the restaurant. When we reached the mini-stage, I recognized a few of the guys playing. I searched out their faces more intently in an effort to find Wes, but when I came up empty handed, I relaxed and let Hannah dance with me just like we did the night she arrived. Once I finally let loose and allowed the singer and the upright bass to sing to my soul, I knew I could have stayed dancing like that all night.

It felt like I had been out on the floor for hours when a sudden lull fell over the band in front of us. I stopped swaying to the beat I started to finally to enjoy and glanced at Hannah, who looked equally confused.

"I hate to cut this song short, but a little birdy told me that the man of the night would like to say a few words. Let's give it up for Jhett and The Voodoo Kitchen!" The singer started up a round of applause as he backed to the side and Jhett jogged up the stairs to make his way up on stage. I couldn't help but let excitement wash over me; seeing him up on stage reminded me of the very first night I laid eyes on him.

Jhett took the microphone from its stand and began to walk from one side of the stage to the other like a natural. "I promise I won't keep you guys from dancing for too long, but I wanted to tell everyone thank you for coming out and celebrating the grand opening tonight. Many of you heard me talk about opening my own restaurant for years now, and I finally got my act together and made it happen. But all this wouldn't be possible without a lot of help from you guys – so thank you! Tonight is also a night to celebrate the birthday of someone very special to me. It doesn't feel like it was only a few months ago that I was playing on stage and she literally stumbled into my life. But I wouldn't change a single thing that's happened since that day. And as one last birthday present from me and someone else close to her heart, I want to play her a song."

Hannah's hand was in mine, but I couldn't focus on anything other than Jhett and the guitar that now rested in his lap. He placed the microphone back in its stand in front of him, and adjusted it to be level with his lips. I hung onto every second with anticipation, until he started to strum the six strings of the acoustic guitar and nodded to someone behind the crowd. It wasn't until the words began to play around me that my knees threatened to go out beneath me. The voice I heard wasn't Jhett's – his mouth was closed. It was a voice I didn't think I would ever hear again. Cameron's voice sang along to the music that Jhett's hands created.

> *You belong among the wildflowers*
> *You belong in a boat out at sea*
> *Sail away, kill off the hours*
> *You belong somewhere you feel free*
>
> *Run away, find you a lover*
> *Go away somewhere all bright and new*
> *I have seen no other*
> *Who compares with you*
>
> *You belong among the wildflowers*
> *You belong in a boat out at sea*
> *You belong with your love on your arm*
> *You belong somewhere you feel free*

Run away, go find a lover
Run away, let your heart be your guide
You deserve the deepest of cover
You belong in that home by and by

You belong among the wildflowers
You belong somewhere close to me
Far away from your trouble and worry
You belong somewhere you feel free

It was Jhett's voice that filled in the gaps where Cameron's went silent, but he didn't stop playing until he made sure I wasn't going to look away. He didn't have to worry though; nothing could pry me away from looking into those eyes that glowed with a fiery passion. I didn't even try to stop the tears that flowed down my face, nor did I notice the hush that fell over the crowd. There was complete silence, but the only person I could focus on was the man who sat before me.

Jhett tucked the guitar behind the stool he sat on and let out a heavy sigh. "Cameron asked me to help him with recording this song for you. We never got a chance to finish before his accident, but I knew he would want you to hear it tonight." Jhett only took a few steps before he bounded off the stage and wrapped me in his arms; applause roared around us.

There was no way I could ever repay him for the gift he just gave me. I clung to him, afraid that I really would pass out at any given moment. I finally recovered my voice and pulled away from him letting my hands rest on each side of his face. "How did you...? When did you...? That was the most amazing thing I've ever heard," I said in between choking back more tears.

Jhett wiped my cheeks as they fell. "That's what I've been working on in the studio. Cam used to say that Tom Petty must have wrote that song about you, and I don't think he could be more right. It took some piecing together on my part, but in the end, it was all Cameron." He looked down at me with nothing but love in his eyes, and I knew without a doubt that mine were reflecting back the same thing.

TWENTY-NINE

Jhett

My heart thumped as it tried to explode from my chest. All the years of performing in front of crowds twenty times larger than this one could never have prepared me for playing Cameron's song for Charlie. I knew just the impact it would have on her, but I never thought it would affect me like it did. The best thank you she could have given me was the love she had for me when she looked into my eyes.

A few small gasps drew my attention away from Charlie. Gracie made her way up to the side of the stage and walked straight for the microphone. Anger rose into my chest.

She tapped the mic a few times before she grabbed it with one hand and looked down into the crowd; her dark eyes landed on Charlie and me. "Woooow…That was something, wasn't it? All that just for little 'ole Charlie. How nice of Cameron to think of her for her birthday, right? Isn't that so sweet? Well news flash for you all: He's dead! Do you really think he cares about any of this right now?" She spat out her words without ever leaving Charlie's gaze. I could feel Charlie's pulse speed up under the grips of my hands.

That was the final straw. I let her get away with so many things - making excuse after excuse for her - but not anymore.

Not after that. "I'm so sorry, Charlie." I let go of her hand and brushed past the rest of the crowd, all still staring in awe at the events that just unfolded in front of them. I clenched my fists to try and control the beast that raged within me, and marched up on stage and directly to Gracie. With little effort, I slung her over my shoulder and shoved back past everyone as I made my way toward the back door.

When I knew we were alone and away from prying eyes, I set her back down onto the pavement. Lacing my fingers together, I put my hands behind my head and closed my eyes, leaning back towards the sky.

"Care to explain what's got you in a huff, Mr. Hudson?" Gracie screeched as she walked toward the back of the parking lot.

"Oh no! Don't even try and play dumb with me. What the *fuck* was that in there?" I threw my arms in the air. She stuck her bottom lip out, pouting as I took a calming breath. I was really trying to not jump down her throat, but having a older sibling meant that they knew all the ways to push your buttons. "Do you care to explain why you took it upon yourself to get up on stage and not only embarrass yourself, but me too? You had *no right* to say any of those things to Charlie. I thought we talked about this? Tonight *nothing* would happen. You were going to stay sober so that you could actually *pretend* to be a normal, functioning adult."

A smug grin danced across her face. "I kept my promise, little brother. I'm sober as a skunk. But *you* had no right to do something like that. Everything is always about Charlie and Cameron, but no one remembers *I* was his girlfriend. And seeing you two in love like that just makes me sick. You don't deserve a love like that – especially not with *her*. Don't forget, sometime soon she's going to go back to Tennessee, and you'll be left all alone. I already know how it feels to get your heart ripped out of your chest, so I was just trying to prevent you from making the same mistake as me." Without missing a beat, she swung around and headed to her car.

"Are you telling me that Cameron was a mistake? He didn't *choose* to leave you, Grace. He died!" I couldn't control the anger anymore. The person I was scared to become leaked out through my words, not caring what kind of damage it resulted in.

"Exactly Jhett! He *died*. Meaning he's *never* coming back. And you know exactly why he's gone. Because you were a drunk asshole that couldn't hold it together, and *you* needed your best friend to come save you from getting into any more trouble than you were already in. So it's *your* fault, Jhett. *You* called him to pick you up, and you knew he would come because he always had your back. So please forgive me, because maybe I am a little bitter that you get to be the one who's happy and in love, and for no reason other than because my boyfriend died and she happened to be his sister that you promised to look out for. Hell - that's the only reason you even got to meet her, isn't it? How is *that* fair? I didn't even get to tell him that I wanted to spend the rest of my life with him before you ripped him away from me and yet because of that, you get the whole damn fairytale. You don't deserve to be in love, because it's *your* fault you took my love away from me." Her chest heaved up and down as tears stained her cheeks.

It all started to make sense. The reason why Gracie struggled so much was because she blamed me for Cameron's death. I was being selfish, because I knew that if I told Charlie, she would blame me too. All the self-hatred and guilt I shoved away for so long came back to me. I was frozen in place as I watched Gracie run back into the restaurant and right past Hannah and Charlie, who stared at me with eyes so full of hurt and betrayal, I almost wished it was me who died that day instead of Cameron.

THIRTY

Charlie

They didn't realize that we stood there and listened while Ginger spat all of Jhett's secrets in his face. I couldn't will my body to turn around and just walk away…I needed to hear what made her so angry, that she would say such hateful things to me in front of so many people like that. But I was never prepared for the words that came out of her mouth. Everything in my stomach threatened to come back up my throat. I couldn't think clearly. I tried to comprehend all the details that began to fill in the blank spots around Cameron's accident.

It's your fault, Jhett. I wouldn't believe those words on any other occasion. But as Jhett stood there only a few feet away from me, I could see the sorrow written all over his face. He knew that I discovered his deepest, darkest secret; Cameron was in the car the night of his accident because of him. Not even ten minutes ago I was utterly and completely amazed at the depth of love he had for me, and the whole time he was keeping secrets from me.

Jhett was the first to move and approach us. "Charlie, I'm so sorry. I was going to tell you, I promise. That night you fell asleep at my house I tried, I really did - but I was so scared that it would shatter you even more, and I already couldn't stand to look into those broken eyes of yours. I promised Cameron I would look after you, and I couldn't do that if you hated me and -"

Hannah cut him off. "I think you should just stop. I'm not going to let you stand there and hurt my best friend. Save it for another day, buddy." She stepped between Jhett and I as she tried to defend me, as usual.

"Go back inside, Hannah." I reached out and shoved past her, putting myself face-to-face with Jhett.

"But I -" she protested.

"I *said,* go back inside. I can handle this on my own." It wasn't like me to be so harsh with her, but I didn't feel like myself. I heard the door close behind me as Jhett and I stood in a Mexican standoff. When I knew we were alone, I let everything I felt spill out.

"That's what this is all about, isn't it? You keeping a promise to my *dead* twin brother? Where did that get you, huh? Is everything you told me a lie, or is it just bits and pieces of the past two months together? Did you really want to get to know me after you first saw me, or was it just the *promise* you made with Cameron that kept you around? I can't believe you! I thought I pegged all wrong, but I didn't. You were just using me to try and make yourself feel better about all the guilt you carried on your shoulders." I was no longer just upset. I was downright fuming.

Jhett grabbed my hand, pulling me into his chest like he did so many times before. Only this time his touch disgusted me. "Don't touch me!" I yanked my arm free from his grasp and took a few unsteady steps backwards. I looked into his eyes one last time; all the love that I felt in them was fading fast. I took a deep breath and tried to pull myself together, slamming into his chest with my shoulder, and raced past him in an attempt to get to the driver's side of my Jeep faster than he could.

"Just give me a chance to explain," he pleaded with me, as I got into the front seat and found the keys I left in the glove compartment. "You don't know how it feels to live with that kind of guilt. But then you walked into the bar and you were even more amazing than Cameron ever explained, and I didn't want to lose that, Charlie. I couldn't lose you when I only just found you." I stared straight ahead, my own heart tearing in two. Not only had I lost my brother, I now had to let go of the man I had fallen deeply in love with. My heart was raw with loss all over again.

My clenched fist rested on my legs and I let the keys dangle in my fingers. Finally, I returned his gaze. "The sad thing is Jhett, I probably would have forgiven you if you'd just told me yourself. If I've learned anything recently, it's that most things happen for a reason. I don't think it's your fault that Cameron got into that accident. You weren't the one driving the other vehicle. But it *is* your fault that you didn't think enough of me to tell me the whole story, even when you knew how badly I wanted to know it. I let you in. I took a chance on you, and you didn't even have the nerve to be honest with me. That's what people do when they love each other, Jhett. They tell each other the truth." I turned the keys in the ignition, choking back tears with the realization of what I needed to do. I threw the Jeep in reverse and then drove straight out of the parking lot and onto the main street, my tires squealing as I rounded the corner.

As soon as Jhett was out of sight, I gave in to the

mountain of tears that built up behind my eyes. I knew I had a few minutes to let it out while I waited for the left turn arrow to change at the stoplight in front of the restaurant. Neon green finally lit up the night before me. Pressing my foot lightly on the gas pedal, I turned the wheel to the left, but something in the corner of my eye caught my attention.

For just a moment, I could have sworn that I saw Cameron standing on the corner of the street, smiling at me as he glowed in the moonlight. He watched me as he stepped off the sidewalk and into the street, before the blinding white headlights of an oncoming car drowned him out. Terror consumed my body and I reflexively slammed my foot down on the brakes, screaming out Cameron's name as the car went right through him and instead, barreled straight in my direction.

My whole world crumbled around me. I was acutely aware of what happened, but had no control to stop it. Each one of my body parts jerked in a different direction while the sound of broken glass and crunching metal filled my ears. I couldn't see anything; my vision was once again filled with the blinding white light I saw just moments before. I braced myself for the crushing pain again, ready for my limbs to snap from my body, but it never came. Instead, a warm rush of liquid pulsed through my body and the flash of light engulfed me, leaving me to float in the warmth of it in peace.

THIRTY-ONE

Jhett

I failed. I promised to take care of her, and I failed her. Not only by leaving out the most important parts of Cameron's accident, but by letting her get hurt. I let her get into the Jeep and drive away when I knew she was upset. I made it through the restaurant just in time to meet her at the intersection, but she never saw me standing there. She never heard me screaming her name, and she wasn't conscious when I tried to get her out of the mangled metal that surrounded her. I couldn't get to her. There were arms around me dragging me back as I watched the EMTs pry her practically lifeless body from the yellow cage that trapped her inside.

Tonight was my punishment. It was my living hell. Anything that happened now, I deserved. The florescent lights of the hospital didn't let me forget where I was and the reason I was there. I wasn't sure how long I sat there on the sterile green plastic chair. I refused to acknowledge anyone but the doctor who ushered Hannah and I into the family waiting room.

I knew Hannah was just as torn up inside as I was, but I couldn't be that strong person she needed when I was already so broken myself. There was nothing left inside me but the tiny flicker of hope that Charlie would be okay. It didn't matter anymore if she wanted me or not – I just had to know she was going to be okay.

I already memorized the intricate lines that spread across the speckled floor tiles when Hannah finally spoke; her was voice just as tired and broken as I was. "You know, she's a fighter. She'll be okay. She's going to walk away from this." Her voice was hushed, as if she didn't believe her own words.

I looked up at her through my arms that rested on my knees. "She wouldn't have to fight if it wasn't for me. *I'm* the reason she's laying on a bed somewhere fighting for her life." I snapped at her. Hannah recoiled and adjusted her position on the seat next to me so she was as far away as possible. I knew it was only seconds before the tears returned to her eyes. My hand went to the back of my neck, rubbing it out of frustration with myself. I sighed and draped my arm around her shoulders to bring her back close to me.

That was her cue to let go. All her fears and worries drained from her eyes, and she clung to my shirt like a helpless child. It was then that I did something I hadn't done in years. I cried, too. The guilt of the entire situation was just too much for me to handle. I was always taught that a real man didn't cry, but I now knew that wasn't true. A real man worried enough about the woman he loved to cry for her.

"You know her parents are going to be here tomorrow, right? I already talked to them on the phone, and I don't think they're going to be too pleased with you being around when they get here," Hannah said as she sat up; wiping the tears from under her eyes and resting her head on my shoulder.

I leaned back, rubbed my face on my sleeve to rid my

cheeks of the wetness that still lingered, and took a moment to think that far into the future. For me, tomorrow was a thousand years away. "The thing is, I'm going to be here until they kick me out. I'm not leaving until I know she's going to be okay. Then if she wants me to go, I'll go." The painful truth of reality stung me down to my core. She was leaving me when she left the parking lot. She was ready to say goodbye, and that meant she might still feel the same way when she saw me again.

"Mr. Hudson? Miss James?" A man in a white coat, whose face I didn't recognize, stepped out into the waiting room through the double doors in front of us. Both Hannah and I jumped out of our seats without any hesitation. The doctor shook our hands. "I'm Dr. Miller. I've been the attending surgeon working on Charlotte. We finally got her in stable condition, and she's recovering in her room. She's lost a lot of blood and suffered a few broken bones, so she's in a highly sedated state right now. I've spoken with her parents and they gave you both permission to see her; however, there's only one visitor allowed back at a time." He paused to gauge our reactions.

Hannah and I looked at each other with confused expressions. I couldn't understand why Charlie's parents would give me permission to see her, especially after what happened between them. But whatever the reason was, it didn't matter right now.

Dr. Miller apparently wasn't a man who liked to be kept waiting. "Miss James, why don't you go first? One of the nurses will escort you back." He made the decision for us. I watched as jealousy raged inside me while Hannah walked with a nurse and vanished behind the double doors – the doors that kept me from being with Charlie.

"Why don't you sit down, Mr. Hudson. There's something we should talk about before you see her." The pain that laced the doctor's voice was enough to cause every fear I had about Charlie to bubble to the surface. I knew I wasn't prepared for whatever he was about to tell me.

THIRTY-TWO

Charlie

No matter how hard I fought, I couldn't get to him. I could no longer count the number of times I was stuck in the same dream over and over again. My limbs refused to work, and he stood just out of my reach. I remember seeing Cameron step off the curb, but he looked as if he didn't have a scratch on him. Now he stood before me, fading in and out of the white light. He refused to speak, but I knew that he heard me crying out for him. If I could just get to him, maybe I could save him. When I was finally able to take control of my arm and reach out for him, he was gone before I faded back into darkness.

"She's going to be okay. The doctors told us it could take a few days before we'll be able to see any improvements." I knew the man's voice. I struggled to open my eyes and see my dad for myself, but I couldn't. Just like in my dream, my body refused to cooperate.

"It's been almost a week. Something's not right, I can feel it," a woman's voice responded. Was that my mother? And was she worried about me? The sound of muffled sobs filled the room. "I can't lose her, too, Michael. I won't let it happen."

I'm right here. I'm okay. Please just let me open my eyes. I'm going to be fine. Just let me get up – I can show you.

I tried to speak, but the only noise I could produce was an inaudible gurgle. I wanted to see my parents. I needed to see someone – anyone – just to make sure I was still alive.

A pain in my side hit me out of nowhere. It was searing hot, and every way I tried to move, I couldn't escape it. I wanted to cry out, to tell someone to make it stop, but no words came. It took all my strength to force my mind someplace else and away from the pain. I focused on the first thing that came into my head...a memory of Jhett and I standing together on the beach while we watched the sunset. But with that memory came a whole new type of pain.

The white light appeared again and forced its warmth onto me once more. I allowed it to suck me in without a fight. I wanted to feel the numbness of nothing again. This time, I welcomed it.

THIRTY-THREE

Jhett

I paced the waiting room; the white walls and tiled floor became my new home over the last week. I stayed true to my word – I wasn't leaving until someone made me. I only went home to shower and eat. I was lucky to be able to stomach any food before I was sick again. But even that was at the urging of Charlie's dad, Michael, who was surprisingly welcoming given the current situation. Mrs. Jennings, on the other hand, was the complete opposite. She refused to even acknowledge my presence, often relaying messages to me through Charlie's dad.

Despite the stories that Cameron and Charlie both told me about their parents, it was clear that they loved their children. There was no blame placed on anyone in particular, even though the guilt I experienced was enough to drive me to drink. They usually kept to themselves, but I did have a few rare, hushed conversations with Charlie's dad. Mrs. Jennings only left her bedside when I entered the room. There were a few occasions when she lingered in the background, but I didn't care. Any extra time I got to sit with Charlie was worth the hate she burned into my back. I knew she didn't trust me – but it was probably within good reason.

Hannah left a few days earlier. I was the one who drove her to the airport and listened to her cry the entire ride there. I knew she didn't want to leave her friend, but there wasn't anything else she could do except wait in the wings with me. It was bittersweet to say goodbye to her. I finally knew why Charlie kept her around, because despite her crazy nature, she had a kind heart. She loved Charlie like a sister, and regretted saying goodbye to her when she didn't know if she'd ever get the chance to say hello again.

Charlie's parents appeared in her doorway and made their way into the hall. It took a few strides to approach them before I stopped in front of her dad. Her mom continued down the hall, careful to never bat an eyelash in my direction.

"We're going to go downstairs and get some lunch. Why don't you keep Charlotte company while we're gone for a few hours?" He extended his hand out for me to shake.

I gripped it firmly as I looked into his eyes. "I would love to. Thank you, sir." He let go and turned to follow his wife. I watched to make sure they were gone, but he only moved a few feet before he turned back around. "And son, don't forget. If she wakes up, please let us know." He gave me a hard nod and finally continued down the length of the hallway, before disappearing down one of the stairwells.

It was my first chance to see Charlie all day. Mrs. Jennings seemed to enjoy keeping me on a once-a-day schedule, but I didn't let it faze me. I still stuck around as long as they let me. Reaching her door, I pushed it open, careful not to let the hinges make too much noise. The only way to rationalize my fears was to act like she just sleeping.

I found my usual seat already pulled up next to her bed. As I sat down, my eyes wandered over her frail form while I did my daily mental inspection. Each day she seemed to look better, but she still didn't look like the glowing Charlie I knew and loved. Her bruises were turning yellow and green, and she no longer needed a tube down her throat to breathe for her. Her right arm was in a cast up to her elbow – a pink one that made me wonder who picked it out, since I knew yellow was her favorite color. At least she always looked peaceful. I don't think I could have handled watching her suffer in pain.

I took her left hand in both of mine, squeezing them together as I placed a soft kiss on her forehead. "Hey Charlie. It's Jhett, again. Your parents left to go eat some lunch, so I guess we get to spend some time together today. You know the drill, if you can hear me just squeeze my hand." The nurses told us we should talk to her, that she could hear us, but she probably wouldn't be able to respond.

I continued to talk to her about my day and how things with her parents were going. I joked that they were freakishly nice to me, and that I must have hit my head, too, because I fully expected the wrath of them to come down hard. But they never did. I told her that they loved her so much, and that they always made sure someone was with her; she was never alone.

I apologized to her countless times. I explained how I hoped that somehow she would understand and forgive me, but that I knew there was a chance she wouldn't, and I wouldn't blame her for it if she felt that way. I told her that I meant every word I ever said to her, including that I loved her, because I would never know love or pain like this ever again.

After an hour or so of my one-sided conversation, I leaned forward on her bed and rested on my elbow next to her. I shoved my other hand into the pocket of my hoodie and pulled out the same box I presented to her just a little over a week before. I snuck the necklace out of the bag of her possessions before her parents had the chance to go through them. The EMTs broke the chain as they worked on Charlie, but now it was as good as new.

I held it up and let the seashell spin around in the air. "I don't know how you're going to feel about me when you wake up, but I hope you don't forget everything you felt about me." I let the necklace fall into her now open palm and closed her fingers around the gold chain. I shut my eyes and reveled in the moment.

My heart stopped. There was movement underneath my fingers for the first time. My eyes flew open in disbelief, and I looked down at Charlie's pale hand still clenched around the necklace. "Babe, please prove to me I'm not crazy and do that again." As if she heard every word, she responded back with another faint squeeze. "I knew it. Charlie, open your eyes. Let me see those beautiful eyes of yours," I urged her, her squeezes becoming more frequent and stronger.

And then it happened. She blinked her eyes open for the first time since the accident. I knew what I was supposed to do, but I couldn't bring myself to leave her side. I didn't want to share this moment with anyone else. This moment was ours.

THIRTY-FOUR

Charlie

It took a few minutes for my eyes to adjust to the florescent light around me, but almost instantly I could feel every ache and pain I was, for the most part, blissfully unaware of take over my body. I groaned as the new sensations ran through me.

"Charlie?" A shaky voice spoke next to me on the bed.

Seeing Jhett's sleep-deprived face staring at me with disbelief was more than I could take. I broke down around myself. I didn't care about anything that happened. I just wanted things to be okay again. "I could hear you…" was all I managed to choke out from my excruciatingly dry throat while my whole body shook from crying.

Jhett didn't leave me to cry alone. His arms found their place around me, careful not to get caught up in any of the wires that extended from my body. The strength in my arms disappeared as soon as I tucked my head into his chest.

He pulled away from me disappointingly soon, his face still white and pale; I thought he might be the one to pass out instead of me. Neither of us spoke. I don't know if it was because there were no words to explain how we felt, or that we were scared that one of us would confirm the other's fears, but looking into the terrified face across from me, I knew I couldn't turn away from him ever again.

"I'm so sorry." The words spilled out without hesitation.

Jhett stopped me from continuing almost immediately. "Don't - just don't. You have no need to apologize. *I'm* the one who should be sorry. You were right, Charlie. I should have told you that I was the reason Cameron went anywhere that night. If it weren't for me, none of this would've happened. Cameron would still be alive, you wouldn't be lying here like this in the hospital, and the baby would still be okay. I did all of this." His body sank into the back of the chair, and he let his guilt consume him.

The room began to fade in and out around me. The medicine they pumped into my body must have messed with my head. Jhett's words didn't make any sense. "What are you talking about? What baby?" Flashes of the accident passed through my thoughts again, causing me to gasp. "Was there a baby in the other car? Oh my God – are they okay?" A rush of adrenaline pulsed through my veins and I sat straight up in bed.

Jhett's face fell. Something was wrong, very wrong. "Charlie, I'm so sorry…" He watched me intently, as if I was going to break at any given second. "You couldn't have known…the doctors said it was so early…there was nothing they could do." Jhett's voice started to fade away, and soon was replaced with a high-pitched ringing in my ears.

My whole body went numb. I watched in slow motion as my palm opened and the necklace Jhett placed into my hand fell onto the floor. I understood what he meant me, but it couldn't be true. There had to be some mistake. There was no way I was pregnant. I thought we were cautious. "You're lying. Stop it," I screamed at him, my throat raw from the sudden overuse of my voice. I couldn't hear Jhett's response over my screams. "Just stop it! You don't know what you're talking about." I continued to yell over and over.

Suddenly the room was filled with people rushing in every direction around me. I refused to look at any of them. I didn't want to do anything but continue to scream and cry, until there were no more tears left in my body. I couldn't speak. I couldn't think. There was nothing anyone could do to make everything okay again.

THIRTY-FIVE

Jhett

A solid set of arms grabbed me and yanked me backwards from where I stood next to Charlie's bed. I fought hard against them as they attempted to pull me from the room. There was no way I was going down without a fight, and this time, I had something to fight for. It wasn't until I recognized that the hands I fought against belonged to Charlie's dad, that I stopped throwing reckless punches into the air.

"What the hell is *wrong* with you? What happened to letting us know if she woke up? What about everything the doctors said? You think that just because you're some punk ass kid with tattoos, you can do whatever the hell you want? That's *my* daughter in there screaming because of you!" Charlie's dad hovered a few inches above me. He was a broad, thick man, and his attitude did a complete one-eighty. The thing he didn't realize was that I was so far gone; his words couldn't hurt me anymore. The only pain I craved was physical.

"And that's the woman *I* love in there; the woman who lost our child. *I* should be the one who's in there with her. Not anyone else." I shouted at him and spectators began to poke their heads out of rooms to witness the scene that unfolded around them. I knew that it was only a matter of minutes before my anger really took over and things got nasty.

"You saw what happened when you were in there just now. I don't think that's a good idea," he threatened me.

Mrs. Jennings appeared in the hall, quietly slipping out of Charlie's room and letting the door click shut behind her. It was difficult to look at her for too long – Charlie was the spitting image of her mother, minus about thirty years.

"Jhett, I think you should go. Charlie doesn't want to see you," Mrs. Jennings spoke her first complete sentence to me since she arrived. I stared at her in disbelief.

"Then I'll come back tomorrow, when she's ready." I stood up tall in an attempt to match her dad's stature, and took a step forward. I wanted them to know that I wasn't going to back down.

Charlie's mom was the one to stop my advances this time. "I think it's a good idea if you go home and forget about her completely. She's already been through enough, and she doesn't need to be distracted anymore by some love-struck child. If you come back again, I will have security escort you out." Her words cut through me like a knife. I just witnessed the unpleasant part of Charlie's mom that all of her childhood stories consisted of.

"I'm not a child and neither is she. I love your daughter, and if you don't see that she needs me by her side now more than ever, you're not just blind, you're crazy, too." I couldn't stand there and fight with them any longer. It was pointless, and I knew that I had to get out of that hospital before I lost it completely. "This is bullshit!" I reacted the only way I knew how. My fist made contact with the wall as I walked down the hallway.

I heard gasps from the nurses and shouts from a doctor as I passed, but I kept walking towards the exit. I ignored the security guard as he followed closely behind me. All I knew was that I had to make it to my truck and back home. It killed me to leave Charlie, but if I stayed any longer I would have laid out anyone who stood in my way, and I wasn't sure how well she would react to that news.

The drive home was a blur. My focus wasn't on the road in front of me or on the cars around me; it was on the fact that I left my heart behind in that hospital room. I let Charlie down. I let our baby down.

The silence that consumed the house finally made me snap. The hall table was the first to go. I only had to grab it with one hand before it flipped over and slid across the wood floors with ease. The chairs that Charlie and I ate our meals at every day were next in line. Each one shot across the floor at a different angle, the sound of cracking wood echoing through the house.

With one sweep of my arm, everything that littered the counter was dumped on the floor. Glass shattered as the bowls hit the ground and mixed with the mail I let pile up over the past week. My chest tightened when I looked around and my worst fears were confirmed. I had become my father.

I slammed into the wall with my back and slid down, holding my head in my hands. A beige envelope sat between my legs. I couldn't break my gaze away from it. It was addressed to Charlotte Jennings.

Without even thinking, I grabbed the envelope and tore it open within seconds. My eyes scanned the typed words before me.

Congratulations on your acceptance to San Diego State University for the Fall Semester.

My blood flowed hot through my veins. I hated myself. I hated everything I ruined for her. She never planned to go back home. She even tried to tell me on her birthday, but I stopped her...and for what? Bow, everything would be different.

Things weren't supposed to be this way. I didn't realize how much I craved the normalcy of a relationship, but I would trade my whole life to see her she graduate from college, or hold our children for the first time. But she wouldn't - because I took that from her, too.

THIRTY-SIX

Charlie

The view of the parking lot from my hospital room's window was my only glimpse into the real word. I was awake for just a few days, but apparently that was deemed enough time for me to recover, as the doctors no longer saw a need for me to stay in the hospital. I looked down at my arm, now wrapped in a yellow cast and held snug to my chest with a sling.

"The nurse should be here any moment with the papers for you to sign. Are you ready to go home?" My mom had not left me alone since I woke up. She continued to hold conversations with me, even though I refused to respond. I only ate enough to keep me full, and fell asleep any extra moment I was given, even though I continued to cry and yell in my sleep. It angered me that none of this concerned anyone. I turned everything off.

It wasn't the physical pain that bothered me – I could handle that. It was the gaping hole in my heart that hurt the most. I never expected to learn that I was pregnant and that I would never meet my baby, all in the same day. I also never expected for Jhett to turn his back on me the way he did. He hadn't even come to see me since he broke the news to me. I needed him. I couldn't do this alone.

It was my mom who finally made me realize it. She told me about how he flipped out after my dad dragged him from the room. She wouldn't tell me everything, but she made it clear that he said he was done. Just like that - after everything – it was over. It was karma, though, my payback. After all, I did the same thing to him. I turned my back on him for something that seemed so insignificant now.

I clutched the necklace with sweaty palms in the pocket of my hoodie. There was nothing left in San Diego, but I couldn't stop Jhett's words from replaying in my head; telling me that my necklace was a little piece of the beach that would always be with me. It was like he always knew I couldn't stay.

"You know - you should stop sulking about that boy, Charlotte. If he really loved you, he would have come by to see you after your little outburst," my mom chimed in again from the chair in the corner of the room. Despite her daughter's near-death experience, she still lacked any form of compassion.

I continued to stare out of the window while what was left of my heart crumbled. "Heaven *forbid* my outburst be because I was upset over the fact that I *lost my baby*. Or does that not count on your list of things to be upset over?" I finally turned to face her; my renewed hatred for her becoming the only emotion I could stand to feel.

A short, bald nurse saved us from having it out in the middle of the room. He explained the details of my recovery, and how I needed to follow up with a doctor in a few weeks. I was only half-listening as I signed the papers, because I knew that once I stepped outside those hospital doors, I would only have a few more days before I left everything in California behind.

I fidgeted in the wheelchair I was forced to ride in while I waited in front of the hospital for my dad to pull their rental car around. When the gold car made its way up through the driveway, my body went numb. This was it.

"Time to go, Charlotte." My mother held the back door open for me. I refused to let her see the internal battle that raged inside of me as I slid onto across the cool leather seat. My mom reached across my chest and clicked the seatbelt into place. I had no desire to protest her help. I just wanted to get moving.

"Ready, kiddo?" My dad turned around from the driver's seat before my mom made her way into the car. His unconcerned demeanor caught me by surprise, but it was his knowing smile that really confused me. I could only nod my head in agreement.

I folded my free arm against the one in a cast and watched the buildings move at an agonizingly slow speed, as we made our way to the hotel. I could point out every place we passed by – I went all over these streets with Jhett. *Jhett*. His name made my emotions real. I couldn't think about him without feeling as if I made the wrong decision somewhere down the line.

"Are you excited to get back home? Everyone really missed you while you were gone." My mom made a half-hearted attempt at small talk.

I scoffed at her. "You mean while I was actually out living my life? I bet they missed me because then there was no one around for you to take all your anger out on, was there? Who did you pick on while I wasn't there?" I could feel myself breaking; I was tearing in two. As much as I hated the thought of going back to Tennessee and resuming the mind-numbing routine that my parents had for me, staying in San Diego alone wasn't exactly the best option either. Whichever route I took, I knew my heart would never heal.

"Now, now, Charlotte. I've turned a blind eye to your little beach adventure and forgave you for getting caught up with that tattooed mess of a man - but the moment we step off that plane, things *will* return back to normal." Her perfectly painted face never changed as she stared at me over her shoulder and pushed me to the point of no return.

We passed by a neon sign that to anyone else would have just been a blur in a restaurant window. But I read it as if we weren't moving at all. *The Voodoo Kitchen.* Something inside me snapped. All my scrambled thoughts finally fit together. I realized that there was no life for me if I went back with my parents. If I went down that road with them, I wasn't really living, I was just surviving.

"Stop the car!" I shouted to my dad as I grabbed the headrest in front of me, startling him into tapping the breaks in confusion. "Hurry! Stop the car!" My voice continued to rise with each word as I shook the seat beneath my grasp.

My mom turned completely around in her seat and slapped my dad on the shoulder as she faced me. "Michael, You will *not* stop this car! Do you understand me?" Her cold stare finally landed me, but it was too late. The car was already at a complete stop on the side of the street. "Michael, what are you doing? I thought I told you not to stop the car?"

My hand was on the door handle, ready to escape into the

life that waited for me, but my Dad's newfound backbone kept me from pulling the trigger.

"I heard what you told me to do, Roz, and I'm choosing not to listen." He didn't look at either of us as he spoke. It was as if he was having a conversation with a ghost in front of him.

My mother completely ignored him, as she did with anyone she didn't agree with. "Charlotte Caroline Jennings! You will NOT get out of this car if you know what's good for you."

She just threatened me like a child for the last time. With one last deep breath, I flung the door open and stepped onto the sidewalk, shutting the door with unexpected force. That door was the breaking point for my mother. I made something snap inside of her, tpp. She immediately got out of the car herself and walked toward me. Without warning, she grabbed the elbow of my good arm and started to drag me back towards the car.

I pulled out of her grasp, completely unaware of the scene we caused. There was only one thing on my mind – it was time for me to stand up for myself the way I should have done years ago.

"You know what, mother? I think you're right. I should start taking your advice and doing what's best for me – not what's best for you. I'm not the same person that left town a few months ago. I'm a grown woman, and I make my own choices now. It may have took me this long to realize it, but I never wanted to choose Tennessee. I should have followed Cameron when he left, because at least he wasn't scared to take chances. And I'm not scared anymore either – not of you, or the future, or whatever else comes my way. Right down the street there's a man who I love, and I don't know if he even loves me anymore, but I refuse to run away like the scared little girl you think I am, and never find out." I tried to catch my breath. I wasn't sure when my dad joined my mother on the sidewalk, but now I stared at both of them, not ready or willing to back down.

"Michael - don't just stand there! Do something with your daughter." My mother, Rosalyn Jennings, had officially lost control, and she knew it. She never enlisted the help of my father.

I braced myself, ready for whatever plans my father had in store for me. Ever since I was born, I was Daddy's little girl...but I knew that when having to choose between my mother and me, it would always be her.

My father stepped forward, wrapping his thick arms around me and pulled me into his chest. I was frozen in shock. "Go to him. Don't walk away from something like the two of you have. I'm so sorry for everything. He loves you. I'm sure of it." He gently placed his hands on my shoulders, pushing me in front of him so I had nowhere to look but into his eyes. There was nothing but confusion written all over my face, but my dad's reflected something else back at me. It was regret.

"What? What are you sorry about?"

"Charlotte, don't listen to your father. He doesn't know what he's talking about. That boy will only ruin you - trap you - someplace you don't belong." My mom's voice echoed around us, but I couldn't tear myself away from my dad.

His hands dropped from my shoulders and he turned to face her. "Why keep lying to her? Maybe *that's* your problem,

Roz. Maybe you need to start listening to your daughter instead of talking for her. We've already lost one child. Do you really want to lose another one? I can't do that. I can't sit by and watch you break her, just like you broke Cameron." My mom stood there in a stony silence, stunned from his brute honesty. Finally, his attention turned back to me. "Jhett fought to see you every day you were in the hospital. He never gave up. It was us who turned him away, and for that, I know you may never forgive me. But you're a fighter, too, Charlie. Go and fight for what you want. I love you." I could almost see my parents' hearts breaking, both for different reasons, but both because they knew they were letting me go.

I shuffled backwards in disbelief. My mother's shrill screams of obscenities could be heard down the entire street. I silently mouthed `Thank you` to my father, before turning my back and racing in the direction my heart already knew. It didn't feel right leaving my dad behind after all he just sacrificed for me, but I was never going back. The only direction I wanted to go was forward.

Streets signs didn't matter, because I knew exactly where to go. It took every ounce of endurance left in my beat-up body to push myself to keep going. Each step forward was a struggle, but some things were worth fighting for, even if it meant you had to get hurt every once in a while. I finally realized that all the pain was worth it, as long as you had someone by your side.

As I approached the white picket fence, reality set in. The yellow one-story house that stood before me became my true home, even in just the few short months I lived there. I learned how to let go and grieve inside those walls. But I also learned how to love - not only myself, but also a man who would do anything to make me happy. My only hope was that he still felt the same way.

I inhaled deeply once I stood before the maroon door. I was out of breath and still slightly damaged, but I was fighting for what I wanted. And in the end, that's all that really mattered to me. I didn't make it this far just to give up on myself now, or on the love I felt for the man who made me realize the strength that roared inside of me.

With shaky fingers, I reached out and pressed the doorbell, anxiously counting down the seconds until I was forced to find the words to express what I felt in my heart.

Jhett appeared in the doorway, looking just as broken as I felt. Our eyes met, and we stood there staring at each other in disbelief; the only sound between us was the thumping coming from my chest.

"Hi." That was the only word I could think of to say to the man I loved before me. I wasn't sure what was going to happen once I made it inside, but I knew in my heart that it was where I was supposed to end up.

TO BE CONTINUED...

PLAYLIST

Music has always played a big role in my life, and when it comes to writing, it plays an even bigger role. I can hear a song and instantly think of characters or scenes, which is half the reason why this list is so long. I did make it in order of the book, from start to finish, so if you're feeling adventures, you can try and pick the songs you think go with what scene. You can always see my playlists on Spotify, but please check out some of these amazing artists!

We The Kings – Just Keep Breathing
Jeff Buckley – Hallelujah
Jace Everett – Bad Things
The Rolling Stones – Sympathy For The Devil
The Who – Baba O'Riley
Sum 41 – With Me
The Corrs – Summer Sunshine
Kings Of Leon – Sex On Fire
Cults – Go Outside - Menahan Street Band Remix
Young the Giant – My Body
Dropkick Murphys – Forever
Edwina Hayes – Feels Like Home
A Rocket To The Moon – You're My Song

OK Go – Get Over It
Tristan Prettyman – Shy That Way
Nicki Minaj – Super Bass
Ron Pope – A Drop In The Ocean
OK Go – Here It Goes Again
The Script – Walk Away
Blue Foundation - Eyes on Fire
The Civil Wars – Poison & Wine
Ron Pope – Perfect For Me
Vampire Weekend – A-Punk
Yellowcard – Empty Apartment
Josh Turner – Firecracker
Florence + The Machine – Dog Days Are Over
Josh Record – For Your Love
Never Shout Never – Happy
Norah Jones – Turn Me On
OneRepublic – Feel Again
Bob Marley & The Wailers – One Love / People Get Ready
Calvin Harris – Feel So Close
Alien Ant Farm – Smooth Criminal
Icona Pop – I Love It
Train – Hey, Soul Sister
OneRepublic – Good Life
Jake Coco – Love Is a Verb
Birdy – Skinny Love
Labrinth – Beneath Your Beautiful
Owl City – Good Time
P!nk – Raise Your Glass
THEME SONG: Tom Petty – Wildflowers
Fall Out Boy – My Songs Know What You Did In The Dark
Shaun Reynolds feat. Laura Pringle – Stay (originally by

Rihanna)
Hurts – Stay
Ron Pope – Please Come Home
Angus – Just A Boy To Me
Lupe Fiasco – Battle Scars
Counting Crows – Colorblind
Tom Petty – Free Fallin'
Train – To Be Loved

ACKNOWLEDGEMENTS

I want to start off by saying there's no way I could have done this alone. I may have written a book, but many people have stood by my side during the last six months. I feel like there are so many people to thank for helping me get through this journey, so be prepared to sit back and stay a while. Also, because I love everyone on this list in some way, shape, or form, there's no order to these. Just saying.

Mom, thank you for everything. I feel like I have told you many, many times this same simple phrase, but there are no others words to express the gratitude I have for you in my heart, and not just for helping me become an author, but for everything you have done for me since the day you knew I existed. You have constantly pushed me to be a better person, even when I was a fairly miserable teenager, but all of that has made me into the adult I am now. Just remember, that no matter how old I get, I will forever take pride in the fact that I will always be your little girl.

To my husband, Bradley, even though you escaped the craziness of this whole experience, I appreciate every moment when I was too distracted or up to my elbows in edits and you were understanding and let me get off the phone and back to work. I know how badly you wished you were home for this, but I'm just glad to know I have a husband who supports me when I tell him about my crazy ideas. But hey look – I actually did it! And now you get to be home for the *real* craziness to begin!

To my Indie Troublemakers – Tess and Michele – how boring would Facebook and my life be without you three?

Tess, you have been there since *Promise Me This* was just a laughable thought. Thank you for being my cheerleader, critique partner, person to bounce my ideas off of, writing partner, and friend. The late night and early morning text messages will be one for the history books, for sure. I'm beyond blessed to find such awesome people in the world all thanks to our mutual love for books.

Michele, my writing BFF, it sure has felt like you've been around since the beginning. So much in fact I can't really remember when our continuously open Facebook chat started. I am so glad that it did, though. Having you to go through this with has been just been something else, and I am so excited to see what is in store for us Troublemakers.

Amy Bartol, I have to include you close to those fabulous ladies up there. I like to joke that you are the reason we all were able to come together – it was a love for your books that did it! It's like six degrees of Amy. But I also have to thank you for being my role model, because even from afar, you have been a constant source of inspiration as a writer and a person.

Stacy Sanford, I'm pretty sure you need to change your job description, because you are far more than an editor to me. You have put up with my many wee hours of the night freak-out emails and how you read through some of the stuff I have written in my half asleep stupor, I will never know! I appreciate all of the red pen, laughs, feedback, and advice you have given me, but most of all, I need to thank you for jumping right on board to this crazy train, time constraints and all. You told me we could do it if we worked our butts off, and I'd say we worked out sweet asses off, and did it!

M.R. Polish, I think you are pretty amazing. Thank you for letting me badger you with all of my questions, fears, exciting news, and just being there to talk. You are someone I look up to and as you know, still fangirl for, too. I appreciate you taking the time to critique for me and essentially help me through this whole crazy thing. I'd probably still be crying in the corner somewhere without you!

Kristin Day, I may not have told you, but you have been an amazing cheerleader. Since the first tweet you told me you believed in me and couldn't wait to read my book, I have been in awe, and each time after that has been the same. You have pushed me through the dark blurb days where I thought I was going to suck big time and between you and Stacy, I might have peed myself a little bit with your back and forth Facebook comments.

Cathleen McLaughlin, it's hard to find words to describe us. Soul friends, maybe? I think that one works. You have played a huge part in not only this book, but my life as well. I truly think that everything happens for a reason and you were one of them. Thank you for letting me blast your picture and beautiful face all over the place as Charlie, and for all the late night burger-eating, wine drinking, banana pudding indulging, brainstorming sessions. Thank you for freaking out with me every time I wrote a new part or when I got good news. #donteverletgojack #BFFforlyfe

To my fantastic group of Beta Readers – Karen McIntosh, Kayla Hargaden, Bieke Paesen, Shona Lawrence, Kellee Fabre, and Ren Reidy. You ladies have rocked it hard, short notice and everything. Thank you for letting me pick ya'lls brain and interrogate your thoughts. Hopefully I wasn't too annoying and you all still love me after this, because I know I'm going to need help again! I valued each one of your opinions and suggestions to make *Promise Me This* everything that it is and more. You guys made that happen. Thank you! Dragon Hussies, you killed it again. We make a great team.

Chad Spann, you made Charlie and Jhett's story truly come alive. I have been completely blown away with your enthusiasm and support since day one and I can't tell you how amazing that has been. I'm such a big fan of your photography and I look forward to all the new and exciting shoots that are yet to come! We're not stopping here!

Steven Mathew, or should I just call you Magic Mike? Or maybe Jhett? I'm so glad you agreed to be a part of this journey with me! I know the whole thing probably sounded like you were being Punked, but I couldn't ask for someone better as Jhett. I hope you know how much I appreciate you letting me load your hair up with grease and dealing with my weird beard requests, but I'm glad to have made a new friend though the whole thing.

To the Dropkick Murphys, thank you for influencing the first half of the book with your music and giving Jhett the perfect song to sing. And to Tom Petty, thank you for giving this book a reason to be. *Wildflowers* made so much of Charlie, Cameron, and even Jhett come to life. There's so much about that song that made this book possible.

And finally, but not any less appreciated, you guys – the readers, fans, and bloggers who have shown me so much love and support since day one. I have cherished every comment, message, and tweet leading up to release day and I will continue to value each and every one of you after that. You are the driving forces that continue to make me want to write.

ABOUT THE AUTHOR

My husband and I live in Tennessee with our four dogs and when I'm not writing, I am working during the day in a pottery studio. I enjoy being outdoors and going fishing, camping, kayaking, swimming, and hiking. I also love to curl up any given night and just let a book suck me in. But that doesn't mean that the next night I'm not all hopped up on Mountain Dew and watching The Vampire Diaries or YouTube while fangirling like a crazy person. I'm somewhat of an introverted extrovert, you could say.

I am the creative child that refused to grow up. When I was a little girl, I would steal my mom's tapes and make up my own dance routines to perform for my parents after dinner. I remember my brother and I used a handheld tape recorder and a tape player to create our own radio show skits.

My Uncle was the first one to introduce me to the wonderful world of Broadway, and after that I performed in a handful of plays and participated in choir from Elementary School until my junior year in High School. I guess I have been a storyteller of some sort since that first performance in my parent's living room.

That love of stories stayed with me into college, and I ate up every English class I took. I would finish the required readings within days of receiving the assignments and bust out long-winded essays the night before they were due, but I didn't care – I loved to read and write. A few years ago I started keeping track of the amount of pages I read during the year and then I began to blog. I started getting told that people enjoyed my blog and my writing and since I love to read, why not write my own book?

I laughed at them. I could never write my own book. But the more I thought about it, the more these characters started to appear, and pretty soon I wrote the first chapter, and then I hit 10,000 words, and when I finally decided to announce that I was actually writing my own book, I was blown away by the response. I still am to this day.

If I have learned anything throughout this whole experience, it is that being exactly who you are will get you right where you are supposed to be in life. Each day I am faced with challenges of many different kinds, but in the end, I get through it because I know I am strong enough to do it. Charlie may have discovered who she really was throughout *Promise Me This*, but I also did, too. I have never been happier now that I am pursing my dreams.

I love to hear from all of you. Always feel free to email

me, Facebook me, tweet me, etc! I always try and respond back!

http://www.sarahashleyjones.blogspot.com
http://www.facebook.com/authorsarahashleyjones
Twitter: @Sarahashjones
authorsarahashleyjones@gmail.com

STACY SANFORD
Editor for Promise Me This

Stacy Sanford is passionate about the written word in all its inventive, descriptive glory, and is a grammartastic editing diva; dedicated solely to making authors sound fabulous, no matter what stage in their writing career they find themselves in. She is honest, not snarky, and maintains a professional working relationship with all she encounters. And she loves bacon. Stacy has worked with both Young Adult (YA) and New Adult (NA) novels, but is open to editing anything with words. Or bacon.

You can contact her at her blog
http://www.thegirlwiththeredpen.blogspot.com/
or through Twitter @GirlWithRedPen

JULIE TITUS
Formatter for Promise Me This

You can contact her on Facebook
http://www.facebook.com/JTFormatting

SARAH HANSEN
at Okay Creations
Cover Designer for Promise Me This

You can find Sarah on her website and Facebook

http://www.okaycreations.com

&

http://www.Facebook.com/okaycreationsSH

CHAD SPANN
Photographer for Promise Me This

You can find Chad Spann's work on Flickr

http://www.flickr.com/photos/chadspannphotography/

CHECK OUT THESE FABULOUS BOOKS

If you are looking for another book to quench your reading thirst, I suggest you check out these books by some very talented and wonderful people.

Never Let You Fall by Michele G Miller

The Daughters of the Sea Series by Kristen Day

Wolf Spell by M.R. Polish

Ageless Sea by M.R. Polish

The Premonition Series by Amy Bartol

The P.J. Stone Trilogy by D.T. Dyllin

The Exceptional Series by Jess Petosa

The White Aura Series by Felicia Tatum

Kaleidoscope by Mindy Hayes